Etched in
Tears

#4

Also by Cheryl Hollon

Webb's Glass Shop Mystery Series

Published by Kensington Publishing Corp.

Etched in Tears

Cheryl Hollon

KENSINGTON PUBLISHING CORP.
http://www.kensingtonbooks.com

KENSINGTON BOOKS are published by

Kensington Publishing Corp.
119 West 40th Street
New York, NY 10018

Copyright © 2017 by Cheryl Hollon

All Kensington Titles, Imprints, and Distributed Lines are available at special quantity discounts for bulk purchases for sales promotions, premiums, fund-raising, and educational or institutional use. Special book excerpts or customized printings can also be created to fit specific needs. For details, write or phone the office of the Kensington special sales manager: Kensington Publishing Corp., 119 West 40th Street, New York, NY 10018, attn: Special Sales Department, Phone: 1-800-221-2647.

Kensington and the K logo Reg. U.S. Pat & TM Off.

ISBN-13: 978-1-4967-1175-5
ISBN-10: 1-4967-1175-0
First Kensington Mass Market Edition: December 2017

eISBN-13: 978-1-4967-1176-2
eISBN-10: 1-4967-1176-9
First Kensington Electronic Edition: December 2017

10 9 8 7 6 5 4 3 2 1

Printed in the United States of America

For Beth Campbell
BookEnds Literary Agent Extraordinaire

Acknowledgments

This book exists because my publishing family believes in the Webb's Glass Shop Mystery Series. In these uncertain times, where a few publishers seem to ignore the loyalty and support of their readers, I'm delighted to be published by Kensington Books.

I've taken some artistic liberties with the timing of certain events in order to follow the general timeline of the series. The season is autumn, so I've moved the Orlando tragedy from June to September. I wanted to send David Parker to sort things out—he's a good man.

Eloyne and Bradley Erickson own Grand Central Stained Glass & Graphics, the business that continues to inspire this series. Thank you for kindly answering my complicated questions with helpful expertise and an unfailing enthusiasm for these stories.

Haslam's Book Store is a famous landmark in the Grand Central District of St. Petersburg, FL. The independent bookstore was started in 1933 during the depression by John and Mary Haslam. After World War II they were joined by the second generation, Charles and Elizabeth, and the business began to expand. In response to customers' requests, new technical books were added, then Bibles and religious books, and finally a complete line of trade books and a large section for children. The business has moved four times to accommodate the growing number of volumes and customers, and today it covers 30,000 square feet with over 300,000 books. In 1973, the third generation came into the business: daughter Suzanne and husband Ray Hinst. Ray has been incredibly helpful in launching each of my books. His son Raymond and my son Eric went to Boca Ciega High School together. When I first met the Haslams' Book Store staff, I was known to all as Eric's mother. Now, when my son visits the bookstore with his family, he is known as the author Cheryl's son. Life is good!

Mystery writers' organizations like the Sisters in Crime and Mystery Writers of America are continuing to support aspiring writers with the latest and most effective information on the ever-changing world of publishing. In particular, the Internet chapter of Sisters in Crime, named the Guppies (which stands for the Great Unpublished), was and is my primary source of information and support. So much so that when a new chapter launched in Sarasota this year, I quickly volunteered to be an officer. The Florida West Coast Sisters in Crime Chapter has now been officially chartered. I will serve as the vice president in the upcoming year.

Congratulations to Gina Wilkins, founder and CEO of the Kind Mouse Organization. She won a silent auction to name a character in this book. The mission of the Kind Mouse Organization is to assist families in transition and their chronically hungry children. No hardworking individual should ever feel despair due to economic hardships beyond their control. Everyone has a right to feel safe and secure in their own homes, and no one should ever go hungry. Check them out at www.TheKindMouse.org.

I am a mystery conference and reader convention addict. I wish to thank the organizers of the ones that I attended: Bouchercon, Killer Nashville, Left Coast Crime, Magna Cum Murder, Malice Domestic, New England Crime Bake, SleuthFest, and ThrillerFest. I learn something priceless each time I attend. I have also met the most amazing people that sponsor, organize, and promote these events under extreme pressure with unparalleled grace. It is not an easy task for all the volunteers involved. I'm thankful.

Thanks to feedback of my in-person critique group, I send better manuscripts to my agent and editor. They're not perfect, but better. As a group, we learn so much from each other. Giant thanks and gratitude go to Sam Falco, Amy Jordan, and Christa Rickard. As a Novel Pod, we're killer! I'm also grateful to my weekly goals partner, Cheryl Whitmore. For years, we have been exchanging an e-mail every week that lists our achievements for the week and our goals for next week. Talk about accountability—it works.

Thank you to the talents of Ramona DeFelice Long who guides my writing and inspires me to get my game face on each morning as part of her sprinting champions. We sign in to her early morning Facebook thread each day as a commitment to write without interruption for one hour. What a great way to start the day.

My agent, Beth Campbell at BookEnds Literary Agency, has been a champion of my writing career, not for just this book, not for just this series, but for my whole writing career. Query her. I feel lucky to have her as my advocate.

Many writers I've met do not have the support of their families in their desire to get published. Some struggle on alone even after achieving success. I can't imagine how difficult that would be. Thank you to my parents, Wendell and Marcella Hollon, for raising me in a family spirit that encouraged us all to try anything. Success was not the point. The joy of the experience was the point.

I am grateful for the full support of my family circle: Eric, Jennifer, Aaron, Beth, Ethan and Lena. They are proud of my successes and sympathize at the disappointments.

There are those unbelievers who scoff at the idea of a writer's muse. They are wrong. My muse has a name and it is Lujoye Barnes. She is a true believer in the power of good books, good writing, and several times a year she welcomes me to her woodland cottage to write in a bubble of rustic inspiration. I am deeply grateful.

My husband George inspires, prods, bribes, cajoles, and sometimes aggravates me into writing more than I expected in faster time and better quality. His motivation is simple—just so we can spend time walking together in our vibrant downtown to a small café and visit one of the many art galleries. Bribing me with food and art works every single time. We've been married so long that neither of us remembers being single. I love you a bushel and a peck.

Chapter 1

"They call it The Enigma," said Savannah Webb as she stared up at the dark blue glass structure ballooning out of the Dali Museum.

It stood proud against the warm evening light on the calm waters of Tampa Bay. The square concrete structure contrasted with the huge geodesic bulbous glass windows that oozed from the front of the building around to the other side. It fired the evening with an air of anticipation for a surrealistic experience.

"The building is as much an exhibit as anything inside." Savannah's balance wobbled and she quickly grabbed the arm of her boyfriend Edward Morris. She hadn't worn heels this high since, well, since high school. It was taking a little longer than she expected to find a comfortable stride.

Edward folded her hand securely into the crook of his arm. He lifted his chin as they approached the entrance. He wore the tux his parents had bought him when he'd graduated from University.

It had been a good investment. One of the many advantages of growing up British—elegance and frugality traveled comfortably hand in hand.

Savannah relaxed and her balance returned. "Thanks for the arm. Pitching onto the concrete in a face splat is not the way I want to be remembered at this reception."

Edward squeezed her hand. "I'm the lucky one. You look spectacular."

Savannah smiled. Her dress choices had been small. As the owner of the venerable family-owned Webb's Glass Shop, her wardrobe was basically logo shirts with comfortable slacks or jeans. Luckily, this little black dress fit like it was born to party. Using bits of red, orange, and cobalt blue, she had created a statement necklace of kiln-formed glass medallions with a matching pair of small button earrings. She had also created a barrette that she'd clipped into her black curly hair.

"The building opened on January 11th, 2011. It's apparently an auspicious date that adds up to a lucky number seven. I wouldn't know, but the museum has been incredibly successful. So, who can say whether that choice was lucky or predisposed to shower the museum with good fortune? Not me."

"It looks like a bunker," said Edward.

"Well, with such a valuable collection inside, eighteen-inch-thick hurricane-proof walls seem like the minimum precaution. I love it—perfectly Dali."

Edward handed the invitation to the uniformed security guard at the members-only reception desk. A name tag declared him to be Lucas Brown, Security Manager. "Thank you for attending the opening reception for our special exhibition." He looked at his display monitor and picked up a bright red Tyvek wristband. "Welcome, Miss Savannah Webb of Webb's Glass Shop." He peeled off the backing and circled it around her left wrist. He looked back at his monitor. "And Mr. Edward Morris, owner of Queen's Head Pub, guest of Ms. Webb." He fastened an orange band around Edward's wrist.

Lucas waved a hand to his left. "Refreshments are being served in the café. The exhibit is on the third floor and the celebrated artist is receiving invited guests in the Community Room. That's the large room behind and to the right of the Gala café." The monitor beeped a message, which he bent over to read. Then he leaned over to Savannah's ear. "You are most particularly requested to meet the artist." He straightened back up. "Make your way through the gift shop and you'll find the circular stairway to the right of the café. The elevators are just beyond the stairway. Please enjoy yourselves!" He smiled briefly and turned to the next guest.

They walked through the extensive gift shop to the café. Edward flagged down a server holding a tray of bubbly flutes. He grabbed two. "Here, luv." He handed her a flute. "I know you love champagne."

Savannah smiled. They clinked glasses and sipped. She licked her lips, then smiled. "Delicious. That's an excellent vintage. They're not stinting on the caliber of the refreshments." She looked at Edward's puzzled frown over the rim of her flute. "It's pretty common to get cheap eats at these exhibits. The artists usually have to buy everything."

They each took a skewer of grilled shrimp from another of the many servers.

"Scrumptious." She grabbed his hand. "Come around to the outside. There's something back there I think you'll appreciate."

They took a left at the café and exited the building through two sets of double doors onto an outdoor space populated by Dali-inspired sculptures. The most prominent was a giant up-curled black mustache with a space in the center for posing.

Savannah pulled on Edward's hand and stopped at an opening in the hedges at the far back of the property. "This is it."

"Is this a maze?" He looked at the entrance with his arms out wide as if to hug the world. "I love them."

"I know. I can't believe you didn't know this was here." She smiled and stepped into the graveled pathway on her tiptoes to prevent her heels from sinking into the sandy soil below the thin layer of gravel. "Come on. The party can wait a few minutes."

It took less than five minutes of curving loops and whirls to make their way to the central circle of the maze. Edward pulled her into his arms for a warm kiss. "Thank you. I enjoyed my surprise."

"I know these things are popular in Europe, but pretty rare here." She had given him a key to her house last month. Since her father's murder, she was finding it hard to commit to a permanent live-in relationship. "We need to get—" She screeched and began to fall. Edward caught her around the waist and lifted her up to extract her heels from the soft ground.

"Those delicious shoes are a hazard to your ankles in this footing. I'll have you back in a jiff."

"No need." Savannah wiggled herself out of his grasp and carefully onto the path. "I think I stepped on something. I'm fine now." She straightened her dress and looked down on the path. "There it is. That's what tripped me." She bent and picked up a cardboard hamburger container. "This is a strange place to eat fast food. Who would do something like this? I'll put it in the trash can inside."

"Speaking of inside, we need to get going," said Edward.

They returned to the building, and Savannah tossed the wrapper into the first waste can she saw. They replaced their empty flutes with fresh champagne then climbed the white spiral stairway to the third floor and entered the main exhibit hall reserved for visiting collections. A ten-foot-tall free-standing banner announced the exhibit with a picture of Dennis Lansing beside a tall, bloodred, heart-shaped vessel etched with scribbled writing and images of lilacs and daffodils.

Edward stood in front of the banner. "What an unusual combination. My mother is fascinated with the Victorian secret language of flowers. She would know what they mean."

"That's a thing?" asked Savannah. "Really? Explain."

He grimaced. "Ugh! Mum gave me this lecture frequently. She couldn't fathom that I might not be interested. You might as well have the short version. History relates that during the reign of

Queen Victoria, the language of flowers was as important to people as being well dressed. For example, the recognizable scent of a specific flower sent its own unique message. Flowers adorned almost everything . . . hair, clothing, jewelry, gowns, men's lapels, home décor and china, and stationery, to name a few. A young man could either please or displease a lady by his gift of flowers. They had a silent meaning of their very own, and could 'say' what was not dared to be spoken."

The exhibit space was filled with about thirty glass vessels, each resting on a tall white pillar standing about four feet high. Overhead track lighting illuminated the glass from several angles to show off the deep colors and highlight the intricate etchings. Savannah tucked her hand into Edward's arm as they walked slowly through the exhibit. It seemed a little intrusive to overhear the quiet crowd admiring and commenting on Dennis's skill and talent.

When they were approaching the last of the pieces, Savannah saw a familiar-looking fiftyish woman in a plain black cotton shirtwaist standing in front of the large red glass vessel. "Mrs. Lansing? Do you remember me? I'm Savannah Webb. I knew Dennis from St. Petersburg High School."

"My goodness. Yes, I remember you." The small lady's bright blue eyes lit up her warm smile. She grasped Savannah's hand with both of hers. "Savannah, it's wonderful to see you here. I do so wish that things had worked out differently between you and Dennis. It would have made such a difference." Her phone pinged from within a pearl evening bag. She slipped it out and her face stiffened. "Oh, excuse me. I should have been downstairs by now. I've dawdled among the display pieces for too long, again. Dennis's wife will be annoyed." She left and they watched her hurrying down the spiral staircase.

Edward tilted his head and raised his eyebrows. "I am beginning to suspect that you have a certain history with this artist. Am I right?

"Yes, but it was a long time ago. I was a freshman in high school. We dated for a few weeks."

"So, here in the States, as a freshman, you would have been about fourteen?"

"Yes, I was fourteen. It was at the very beginning of the school year. It will be nice to catch up with him and his career." She leaned in closer to look at the red vessel that was featured in all the promotional materials advertising the exhibit. It contained an etched image of a note in rounded loopy handwriting. Savannah straightened up quickly. That was her handwriting! Dennis had included one of her childish love notes in his featured artwork. She felt a warm flush grow from her throat to her ears.

"What's wrong?" Edward slipped an arm around her waist. "Has the champagne gone to your head already?"

She ran a hand through her curls and smiled weakly. "Yes, that must be it. I've only had two small glasses. We'd better do our meet and greet before I become insensible."

"That's not likely. You're too strong minded for that."

They left the gallery and made their way to the ground floor.

Savannah slipped her hand through Edward's arm. "I think we'd better get into the receiving line.

I want to tell Dennis how much I enjoyed his exhibit and how much I appreciate his support of my etching class."

Edward placed his hand over hers and they walked to the entrance of the community room. The chatter from inside was spilling out into the hallway. There were only a few people in line.

"Savannah! Savannah Webb, is that you?" said a trim man with a red cummerbund and matching red bowtie in an expertly fitted tux. "I haven't seen you since I graduated. You'd just finished freshman . . . maybe sophomore year. It's Charles." He shook her free hand like a pump handle. He stepped back and looked her up and down. "You've grown up. Definitely up." He smiled. "I'm still on the short side. You remember me. don't you? I'm Charles King."

Savannah scanned the craggy face and tried to age it back ten years. Nothing. "I don't seem to recall."

"I was a friend of our famous artist here. I used to see you at Webb's Glass Shop when your dad was running that apprentice program. Surely, you remember?"

Savannah smiled and shook her head. "I'm trying. I think I remember a Chuck, but he was . . . well, he was a big guy."

"Absolutely me. I was a big guy back then. Huge. Obese, even. Yeah. "He patted his slim waist with both hands. "I got that fixed when I decided to go into politics." He turned to Edward and pumped his hand while slapping him on the shoulder. "So, you're the lucky one who has captured our lovely Savannah's heart. I'm Charles King, your state representative up in Tallahassee. Yep, I'm a local boy done good. I hear good things about Queen's

Head Pub. Nice to meet you. Too bad you can't vote. I have an election coming up soon. Are you going to apply for citizenship?"

Savannah snapped her fingers. "I've got it! You were a couple years ahead of me. I remember now that you were a close friend of Dennis's." She turned to Edward. "Dad and I attended the commencement ceremony that year because of that apprentice program that Dad established."

"Good girl!" Charles looked behind them and nodded to another guest. "I'll come by the shop to see you this week. It'll be good to catch up. Excuse me, I must speak to a major party supporter over there." He disappeared in a half run to greet a man and wife in elegant evening wear.

Savannah shuddered. "Ugh. I remember now that he was exactly that overbearing when he was our student council president. It was a testament to his persuasive powers that we would elect the fat boy over the football star."

Edward frowned.

"I know. Politically incorrect," said Savannah. "But he was quite the organizer. Ugh! Will high school ever be over? I didn't like it at the time, and I have few fond memories."

"Wise girl." Edward immediately responded with, "Oops, sorry. I didn't mean to call you a girl. I know that makes you angry . . . but in my defense, everyone does it."

Savannah's voice tightened. "It doesn't make it right. I'm no one's girl. I'm a woman fully grown." She tapped a pointed finger into his chest. With her three-inch heels, she stood taller than their equal six-foot height and she was enjoying the temporary advantage. "Remember that."

"Sorry, sorry, sorry." Edward chuckled. "Remember, I'm still a work in progress. British girls—young women, I mean—are quite different. They seem to be on a suicide mission to be more like bad lads for rude behavior. I am sorry."

Savannah closed her eyes then opened them again. "You're forgiven. I'm sorry for being so prickly. I'm glad that you know that about me." She downed the rest of her champagne and Edward placed both flutes on the tray of the nearest server passing by.

"Let's get in line to meet Dennis. I think he'll recognize me. I haven't seen him since graduation either."

"Same year as State Congressman Hot Air?"

"Funny, funny. You know I've watched that television program, *MP Minutes* on BBC America. You Brits have some clowns, too. Both our countries appear to lack for any kind of qualified political leadership, let alone a true visionary. An absence of ethics and brains seems to be the perfect formula to be a successful politician. That certainly describes Chuck."

A tap on her arm caused Savannah to turn to see Betty Lansing standing at her elbow smiling up to her. "Savannah, I didn't mean to be so abrupt in the exhibit hall upstairs. I'm glad we can talk a bit more. You have bloomed into a beautiful woman. I remember your father fondly. In fact, we were good friends while Dennis was in the apprentice program, but after Dennis graduated, your dad and I drifted apart. He was so focused on you and his glass business, I didn't have a chance."

Savannah eyed Edward and mouthed *help*. She turned back and took the woman's hand in both of hers. "Of course, I remember your visits. You talked to my dad for hours about Dennis's progress. Dennis was one of the first students to turn his life around." She turned to Edward. "This is my friend, Edward Morris. He owns the restaurant pub next door to the glass shop. You remember that old gas station? It was converted about ten years ago into a bar. Edward added a commercial kitchen and a passel of talented chefs."

Betty's eyes narrowed. "Yes, I think I recall, but my memory isn't as good as it used to be and I don't really get about very much now. Anyway, I'll let you young folks be. It was nice to see you." She turned away back toward the Gala café.

"I remember her exactly like that—nice—and then she would disappear."

"So I'm a 'friend'?" Edward air quoted the word *friend*.

"Please, don't read anything into what I say. I've had the dreaded second glass of champagne. It whips my words into a swirling mess. Beer doesn't do that to me. I need to stick to beer."

"Fat chance," said Edward. "Relax. Enjoy this."

They joined the short reception line to greet the featured artist of the new glass exhibition. Dennis Lansing wasn't wearing a tuxedo. Instead, he wore a unique Dali-like navy silk suit with an outlandish tie and beside him stood a woman dressed as a perfect replica of Dali's wife Gala.

Gala was famous for wearing the latest avant-garde

couture designs to the eclectic performances that
Dali arranged for the display of his latest paintings.
It spoke of an incredibly confident persona to pull
off the Gala impression so well.

The line moved quickly. Most of the attendees
seemed to be sponsors and Dali Museum members
with no real connection to the artist.

As soon as Savannah and Edward reached the
front of the line, the artist smiled like a Cheshire
cat. "Savannah, Savannah. I'm so glad you could be
here." He held her upper arms and gave her a quick
peck on both cheeks, European style. He turned to
wrap an arm about the woman next to him and gave
her a side hug. "This is my long-suffering and inspirational wife, Harriet. She's my muse and my model
just as Gala was for Dali." He raised his wife's hand
to his lips as he continued to look at Savannah.

Harriet glanced at him wearing a much practiced
closed-mouth smile.

Savannah tucked her hand into Edward's arm.
"This is Edward Morris. He owns the Queen's Head
Pub right next to Webb's Glass Shop." *Why can't I
say* boyfriend*? Just because my last relationship ended in
disaster doesn't mean that this one will, too.* "It's a major
leader in St. Petersburg's new identity as a foodie
destination." Savannah could feel a deep flush
creep into her cheeks.

*Why? Probably because it sounds juvenile. But I'm not
bold enough to say partner or lover, either. Maybe I completely deserve to be called* a girl.

Dennis smiled kindly at Savannah. She flushed
even more.

She cleared her suddenly scratchy throat. "I'm
so pleased you'll be coming over to my new studio

to give a presentation to my etching students. Oh, and the personal tour of your exhibit is going to be the highlight of this week's workshop. I can't thank you enough."

Edward wrapped an arm around Savannah's shoulders and gave her a little side hug. "I'd be pleased to have you and your wife as our guests at Queen's Head Pub for a chef's table experience in the kitchen."

Harriet looked up at Edward. "Oh, that would be delicious! I've heard good things about the food and your online reviews are fabulous."

Dennis reached into the inside of his jacket pocket. "I have something for you that I think you would like to see."

Savannah had opened her mouth to respond when a woman in a royal blue, raw silk dress bustled up to Dennis and barged into the middle of the group of guests waiting to speak to him.

"Dennis, my darling, I must take you and Harriet away for a private tour with the governor of Florida, our senator, and naturally, of course, the mayor of St. Petersburg." She grabbed Dennis and Harriet by the elbow and literally dragged them away.

"But there are guests here who have been waiting." Savannah looked crossly at Harriet and Gina.

Gina looked back at the startled waiting line. "We can't keep the officials waiting, you know. We're dependent on city and state funding for some of our exhibits . . . this one included."

Edward frowned. "That was incredibly rude and the kind of treatment no one in this queue could possibly deserve. She should have apologized."

They both looked at the quickly retreating trio.

Savannah looked down at Edward. "She did say excuse me. Would you like more hors d'oeuvres or maybe another glass of champagne, I hope?"

"No." He wrapped an arm around her and pulled her close. "I'd rather spend the rest of the evening at home with you and your goofy dog Rooney. This crowd is giving me a chill."

"Good plan." She smiled and whispered over the mumbling in the line of guests behind them, "I guess we're definitely not A-listers."

Chapter 2

"Don't touch that!" Savannah Webb shouted at the pair of elderly twins over the high-pitched whine of the sandblasting equipment.

The loud warning did nothing to stop Rachel and Faith Rosenberg for a second. They were standing right next to the sandblasting cabinet on the outdoor patio of Webb's Studio. But like a cat who stares at you while knocking your coffee cup off the counter, one of them deliberately opened the access door on the side of the cabinet and sand whooshed out in a huge cloud.

All four class members tried to escape the powerful cloud of dust by ducking away, waving their hands, turning their backs, and covering their mouths. Everything was futile. The dust puffed out and covered everything within a ten-foot circle.

Savannah's shock delayed the release of her grip on the sand-etching nozzle and she dropped the dish she was etching into the bottom of the cabinet.

She quickly slipped her hands and arms out of the protective sleeves that extended into the sandblasting cabinet, reached around the side, and closed the access door.

After brushing the sand from her face and clothes, then spitting inelegantly onto the ground beyond the border of the small cement patio, Savannah turned to face the twins. They were both dancing a jig to slap the sand out of their newly treated lavender hair and the perfectly matched lavender capri pants, snug fitting camp shirts, and ballet flats. Their antics were surprisingly agile for the near-eighty-year-olds.

Savannah felt her scalp tingle as she heard her voice rise in both pitch and volume. "What were you thinking? I just talked everyone through all the safety steps."

Faith answered first. "But you didn't fully latch the door after the demonstration. It simply looked like it was latched."

"But it wasn't," continued Rachel. "Otherwise, the door wouldn't have opened."

Savannah looked at the access door and there was the safety latch swinging loose. She palmed her forehead and exhaled in a quick puff. "You're right. I forgot. Oh my goodness. I'm so sorry I shouted." She stopped for a moment, looked at the scene of dancing students, and began to laugh uncontrollably. One by one the students joined her.

"I'm glad you yelled," said Arthur Young, a middle-aged man who was a regular student of Webb's Studio.

The repurposed warehouse was Savannah's latest

business expansion. It provided work space to intermediate level glass artists.

"It gave me enough time to back away." He stopped laughing abruptly. Then he widened his eyes and stood stiff. "Uh, I need to go—now!" He bolted for the back door, opened it, and rushed inside.

"Too bad," said Faith. "He seemed to be getting better. You know, with the Crohn's incidents."

"This may set him back a few weeks." Rachel shook her head slowly from side to side. "How annoying, but at least the bathroom is just inside."

Crohn's disease is a condition that causes inflammation of the wall of the gut. That can lead to diarrhea, abdominal cramping, and weight loss.

"Did you tell him about avoiding dairy?" asked Faith.

"He said he was just starting a new vegan diet. That's why he's been doing a bit better."

"Okay let's settle down." Savannah caught her breath and wiped the laughter tears from her eyes. "Luckily, we all had our safety glasses on, so no eye issues. Also, the breeze out here took the dust away quickly. How are you?" she asked the last of her students.

"I'm completely unscathed," said Edith Maloney. "What a good thing I was standing behind Arthur, who was also standing behind Rachel and Faith. Will this delay your instruction? I have another appointment immediately after class."

"Not really." Savannah scrubbed her hands through her short curly black hair to release a miniature cloud of dust. "I was going to demonstrate the fine points of cleaning the equipment later in the workshop sequence, but this accident provides an excellent opportunity. We'll just move it up to today's lesson. Oh yes, Edith, we'll definitely end class on time."

"That's a relief," said Edith. "I was so happy to see such an early class time."

"It's an experiment I'm trying for our more advanced classes. Also, starting at seven a.m. for a two-hour class helps avoid the heat of the day as well as the afternoon thunderstorms—extremely important factors when working outside in Florida's steamy autumn heat."

Savannah led the students through the detailed steps for proper maintenance of the sandblasting equipment. She explained the setup and they all took turns checking the compressor, the sandblasting cabinet, and the dust collector. After the equipment had been thoroughly cleaned and readied for operation, she showed them how to break it down. Then they moved everything into the storage room inside Webb's Studio.

"As you witnessed this morning"—Savannah glowered in jest at the twins—"sand etching can be unexpectedly messy. Storing the equipment inside, then setting it up on the back patio for use, is a sensible precaution. Cleaning the entire studio of sand is a task I don't ever want to tackle ever. *Ever.*"

Arthur raised his hand. "What if it's raining?"

"Good question." She paused and pressed her lips together. "It hasn't come up yet, but I think if I accept a commission that requires a short turnaround and need to sand etch in the rain, I'll buy one of those easy-to-set-up exhibit tents to use as a shelter. Typically, it's not likely I would need to go to such an extreme. Our Florida rains are either torrential or a fine mist hardly worth calling rain. The downbursts usually give us about a ten-minute rumbling thunder as a warning so I can drag everything inside."

Edith glanced at her Rolex. "I'm sorry, but I've simply got to leave for my next appointment." She looked at each student in turn. "Please excuse me." She grabbed her large pale green Prada purse and quickly stepped out the front door.

Rachel and Faith turned to each other and raised their eyebrows. Then they each turned to Savannah.

"Who is she?" Rachel asked. "We haven't seen her before and your requirements for this class were quite clear. It is aimed at the intermediate level student . . . not at beginner level."

"Yes," said Faith. "We've been to every Webb's Glass Shop class for years now. We're definitely advanced students."

Not so much in skill level but an entertaining fixture in each class.

Savannah nodded agreement. "You're right. She came with class experience from a school down in Sarasota. She had a letter of reference and brought several finished pieces for me to evaluate. She'll be fine. Why do you want to know? Has she said something?"

The twins looked at each other and shrugged simultaneously. "It seems strange that she would be making things hard for herself," said Faith.

"Sarasota is at least an hour's drive, but she seems to have urgent business in St. Pete," said Rachel.

Savannah shook her head. "She's going to make

etched glass awards for one of the Sarasota charity events and it doubles as her class project. I think she only needs a few."

Faith patted Savannah on the shoulder. "If that makes you feel better, dear. Anyway, we'll see you tomorrow. I hope you forgive me for the kerfuffle."

"So, it was you." Savannah slowly shook her head and smiled. "I couldn't tell in the cloud. It wouldn't be a Webb's Glass Shop class without you two. Okay, everyone, I'll see you tomorrow at seven sharp."

The twins left through the front door and nearly bumped into Jacob Underwood, the apprentice that Savannah's dad had hired shortly before he died. She continued with his education as a tribute to John Webb's memory. Jacob was a little over eighteen, lanky and dark-haired. He was holding Suzy, his trusty brown, tan, and white Beagle service dog. Suzy was trained to assist Jacob to control the panic attacks that occasionally struck him when he was under stress. He walked up to Savannah and deliberately looked her in the eyes. "Good morning, Miss Savannah. How are you?"

"I am very well, Jacob. Thank you for asking."

A flash of relief played across his face and he looked down at the floor. "I'm practicing my social skills. Mom says I will need to be much better if I want to work with clients on glass commissions."

"What a good start, Jacob." Savannah's chest filled with pride. Jacob had what used to be known as Asperger's Syndrome and thrived in the routine—but creative—work of stained glass design and repair. "Good customer relations bring repeat business, along with referrals from satisfied customers. A little practice making eye contact every day will make it more comfortable for you. It may never be easy, but it will certainly be more comfortable." She scratched Suzy behind her ears. "Good morning to you as well."

Suzy licked her hand, then turned her gaze back to Jacob.

Jacob smiled slightly, and without another word walked quickly into his workroom to perform his first task of the day. He sat in his chair and slipped rubber booties on Suzy so she could run free in the studio without collecting stray shards of glass in her paws. Suzy looked up at him with her pleading big brown eyes, and performed an awkward goose stepping circle, but she relented to the shoes and settled into the routine of Jacob's day.

Savannah realized she was smiling. Jacob's efforts to socialize were strongly encouraged by his mother, Frances Underwood, a juvenile court judge. Only last week, they met for a long lunch at the swanky Vinoy Hotel at Frances's expense to discuss specific scenarios for Jacob to practice. This was his first attempt at making eye contact.

A tap on her shoulder interrupted Savannah's thoughts.

Arthur stood behind her, grinning like a possum. "I'm staying for a while to work on my new project. This early class is a great way to get me up and out of the house. I think it will help me create enough pieces for the next Second Saturday Art Walk. I want to thank you for encouraging me to participate." He laughed. "Although, *prodding* is probably more accurate in my case."

"A big part of my long-term plan is to inform the more advanced glass students about the mechanics of managing the financial side of this business. There's so much to learn about pricing, marketing, and promoting yourself, and I want to share the knowledge."

Arthur nodded. "It's overwhelming and then there's the fear that your work isn't good enough." He turned and walked back to his private studio space two doors down from Savannah's office along the back wall of the building.

Savannah had no sooner sat in her office chair when the front door opened. In walked Officer Joy Williams of the St. Petersburg Police Department, smartly dressed in a brand-new, freshly pressed dark blue uniform.

Savannah walked out into the exhibit space to greet her. "Joy, I haven't heard from you for a couple weeks. The new uniform looks great!"

The darker hue lent a natural authority. For Joy, a petite woman of color with neat braids coiled at the base of her slim neck, Savannah thought it would add a significant boost to her official presence.

"Was I happy to get rid of those white shirts trimmed in green over those horrible green trousers? Absolutely." She twirled a little spin. "I'm so lucky. I'm one of the trial squad members to give the new model a shakedown run. I love the pockets, the fit, and it's got a wicking thing going so it doesn't lose its shape. I was concerned about the dark color absorbing heat. We do live in hot, hotter, and hottest Florida, but this new fabric keeps me cool. The best thing is that the dark color doesn't shine up like a beacon at night. This will save lives."

"It looks professional. Didn't we say we would meet for lunch?"

Joy rubbed the back of her neck. "I'm sorry. It's completely my fault. I promised we'd get together for a beer and a good chat, but I've been preoccupied in trying to make a good impression with Detective Parker. I haven't gotten a lecture lately, but that doesn't mean one isn't about to happen."

Savannah laughed. She had worked with Officer Williams and Detective Parker on a murder case a few months ago. Officer Williams was the first woman of color to join the Homicide Division. She had a right to be worried about her perceived performance. Although she felt welcomed and a valuable part of the division, she was acutely aware she was the first and that meant all others would be judged by her example. The future of many young women to follow depended on her ability to achieve success. She appeared to be handling the pressure well.

"Yep, I've been on the receiving end of more than one of those lectures," said Savannah. "They're extremely uncomfortable in the heat of the moment, but I've always learned something vital. Every. Single. Time."

"I know the feeling. Anyway, I'm stopping by to invite you to participate as a consultant on a current case. The body of a young man was found early this morning at the Dali Museum. There is definitely an art community connection and Detective Parker wanted me to ask if you would be interested in helping out."

"Oh my goodness. What happened? I was at the museum last night for the grand opening of a new glass exhibit. Was it someone who attended the party?"

"Yes. It was the artist himself, Dennis Lansing," said Officer Williams.

Savannah's hands flew to cover her mouth, then she let her hands fall away. A deep sadness struck her into breathlessness. "Dennis? But . . . I was going to . . ." She looked down for a moment, tried to calm her breathing, and pressed her lips together. "We were going to— Never mind. I was in the receiving line speaking to him when he was pulled away for a VIP tour of his works. I didn't get a chance to say much to him. We left early to spend some quiet time at home."

"You knew him?" Joy took out her notebook and began to scribble. "Was he the one you met in Seattle who was involved with your scholarship?"

"No, my Seattle boyfriend—" Savannah pressed her lips together and choked back a curse. She paused and then tilted her head. "Dennis was my very first boyfriend right here in St. Petersburg High School. We had been corresponding by e-mail after I found out he was the featured exhibitor for the Dali Museum." She looked down at the floor. "I didn't get a chance to speak to him in person until yesterday."

"So, first thing. Where were you in the wee hours of this morning?"

Savannah looked up and she felt a professional mask steal across her face. "I was at home asleep with Rooney and my boyfriend, Edward Morris." She watched Joy note down those facts and saw Joy's shoulders relax.

"That's good, but it would help significantly if

I could confirm that with someone other than Edward."

"Of course." Savannah considered for a moment. "My neighbor across the street waved at me through the window when I took Rooney out for a walk."

"What time was that?"

"It was late, probably after midnight."

Joy nodded. "Good—not perfect, but I'll check that out. I still want to know if you can help as a consultant. It looks like your experience will be needed."

"The timing is disastrous. How do these things always happen when I'm starting a new class? Not only that, but I have a major commission due on Saturday, and this workshop is technically challenging. I think I may have to turn this down." She frowned and rubbed the center of her forehead. "Wait, what am I saying?" She pulled a hand from her forehead. "I can't believe this has happened to Dennis."

Savannah stood still for a few long moments trying to control the trembling of her bottom lip. "Working with you guys will give me a chance to help Dennis find justice. It hits me right in the heart. Of course, I'm interested, but since I knew him, you'd better get it cleared with Detective Parker. If he approves, trust me, I'll find a way to squeeze this in along with everything else."

Officer Williams opened her mouth to reply when her phone chirped. "One second. It's Detective Parker. I'll take this outside."

Savannah watched the trim young woman leave quickly and pull the front door closed. Savannah felt strongly connected to the police department due to her involvement in several murder cases. The most personal one was the investigation into the murder of her father and his trusted assistant about nine months ago. Since then, she had developed a reputation as an effective consultant who used wildly original thinking to help find justice for homicide victims. She felt connected to each victim's family. She understood their need for resolution and although it didn't make a dent in the loss, it somewhat answered questions for the families.

Detective Parker had hired her personally on the last murder investigation. It was a positive sign for him to extend an offer of assistance again. The consulting fee was always a welcome addition to her perennially depressed cash flow.

Officer Williams opened the door and walked up to Savannah with her dark eyebrows lowered. "Detective Parker wants to see you downtown at the crime scene as soon as possible."

"As soon as possible? Why?"

"The victim was propped upright on the green bench sculpture."

Savannah tilted her head, "Yes, I know the one. Edward and I strolled through the garden last night, but we didn't stay for the entire party. We left early. Why does he want me at the scene?"

"Detective Parker said a letter was found in the dead man's inside suit jacket pocket."

"So . . ." Savannah put her hands on her hips. "Oh, I remember. He was reaching into his jacket when the director pulled him away for a VIP tour.

Honestly, Joy, why are you making this so difficult? What's wrong?"

"The letter is dated ten years ago and appears to answer a request for a character reference for a permanent job. The letter recommended that the company not hire the applicant as he wasn't capable of honest, trustworthy behavior. It's signed by your father, John Webb."

Chapter 3

Detective Parker studied the body of the young man slumped in the corner of the green bench sculpture. The sculpture was at the beginning edge of the outdoor garden area of the Dali Museum. The body was carefully positioned with one elbow crooked over the armrest and his other hand stretched along the back rail touching the large melting clock form that drooped over the back of the bench. An open newspaper had been placed on his chest to mimic a typical homeless bench sleeper's need for warmth and privacy.

The forensic specialists were still processing the scene. He had watched them take the newspaper away as well as the contents of the man's pockets. The most interesting items had been a tattered letter from John Webb, late owner of Webb's Glass Shop, and a prescription strength inhaler.

He had sent Officer Williams to check in with Savannah Webb. He had authorized Williams to use her own judgment to determine if Savannah could be useful as a consultant on this case. He was impressed with Officer Williams. The probationary officer was a smart young woman who used her brains to full advantage. He was beginning to value her opinion. After the discovery of John Webb's letter, Savannah's participation was no longer optional.

"Good morning, David." Coroner Sandra Gray appeared at Detective Parker's elbow and looked down at the victim. "This is definitely too surrealistic not to get a big splashy article in the *Tampa Bay Times*. Did you know this is called the Avant-Garden?"

He stared at her with a quizzical look on his face.

"Okay, not a Dali fan then. Right." She was dressed in her coveralls and booties and holding her medical case. She leaned over and placed her gloved fingers on the throat of the body. "I am hereby officially pronouncing the death of the victim—time unknown." She looked at the face and moved his right arm. "It does appear that he died more than a few hours ago. Have forensics processed the area around the body?"

"They're done with everything associated with the body. It's all perimeter work now. Do you want to wait until they've completely finished?" asked Detective Parker.

"No, I can't wait. As long as the body is processed, I'm fine to take it away." Coroner Gray placed her medical case beside the green bench sculpture, opened it, and removed a large digital camera. She attached an external flash and adjusted the flash range to four feet. She took dozens of photographs of the scene to accurately orient the bench into its immediate area. Then she took shots of the body at every possible angle. As she looked through the viewfinder, she said, "Even these technical snaps look like a potential photography exhibit. Those huge glass protrusions on the museum are framing the body perfectly."

Detective Parker shook his head. "I know how much you enjoy the fine arts, but that's a bit too far."

"Of course you're right, but this setting is distracting." Coroner Gray continued to circle the bench taking snapshots. "Has anything been moved or taken away?"

"Yes, the contents of his pockets, which included a prescription strength inhaler. I have a sealed evidence bag containing a letter found in his inside jacket pocket. Also, his upper body was partially covered by a damp newspaper. The docent who discovered the body said it had covered the victim's face. He thought the victim was sleeping and poked him on the shoulder. When he didn't respond, the docent removed the paper. The forensic specialists have it and are going to try to extract fingerprints."

"From the newspaper?"

"Yes. It's not easy, but it is possible to lift prints from a newspaper. They're going to work on it back in the lab."

"Thanks." She removed the flash attachment from the camera and put the pieces in their designated slots in her crime scene satchel. Then she took out a large thermometer and rearranged Dennis's clothing enough to permit a reading.

Sandra pulled out her phone and opened an

app that copied her handwriting into a digital note. She recorded the temperature results. She stood and looked at Detective Parker. "So, what we have here is a healthy-looking male who looks to be in his late twenties or early thirties. I don't see any obvious signs of violence, but I'll know more when I get him on the autopsy table. Wait, I see a shadow."

She pulled out a flashlight and a magnifying glass and took a close look at Dennis's collarbone. "There's something here. A bruise doesn't really make sense in his current position." She stood up. "Do you have a list of what was in his pockets?"

"Certainly." Detective Parker flipped back a few pages of his notebook and handed it over for her to see.

She glanced at it, then took a picture of the page. "Not much."

"Young people these days don't carry around much. Their lives are all in their phones. Okay, except that he carried an inhaler containing a strong rescue medication. He must have had a serious respiratory condition to be carrying it around."

A short stocky man dressed in a brown and tan security uniform trudged up from the double doors of the Dali. He stopped to stand a few feet away and waited until Detective Parker acknowledged him with a nod.

"Sir, my name is Lucas Brown, head of security here at the Dali. May I interrupt for just a moment?"

Detective Parker smiled and shook his hand. "Thanks for coming forward. I'm going to need your help."

"Oh, yes sir!" Lucas bounced on his toes looking

like he wanted to salute. "I checked the video camera footage. The biggest problem is that the camera's focal point is on the gate, not near the bench at all. It shows some coming and going activity at about four a.m., then more activity at six a.m., and then nothing until John, he's one of the docents, arrived at about eight a.m. The tape also shows, well, everything that's happening now. Whoever was on camera at four a.m. was very careful to keep his face turned from the camera. The six a.m. activity looks like a person who kept very early hours and he stumbled on the scene and then left in a panic."

"His? You think the person is a man?"

"Well . . . oh. Of course, I get your point. The figure appears to be large and muscular. It looks male in dark clothes and a ball cap."

"Great, it's probably going to be useless for identification purposes." Detective Parker looked at the brass nametag pinned to the security manager's uniform shirt. "Mr. Brown, can you send us a copy?"

"Please call me Lucas. I'm so sorry. I don't have permission from Director Gina Wilkins. She has to approve everything associated with the museum." He lowered his voice to a whisper. "Absolutely everything."

"Contact her now and get permission, please."

"I've already tried. I've tried over a dozen times." Lucas removed his hat, smoothed his thinning auburn hair, and replaced the hat. "She isn't answering her cell phone, nor her home phone, and of course, she's not answering her office phone because she's not here." He shifted his weight to the other sturdy leg. "I'm sure she'll be here before the museum's normal ten o'clock opening time."

"Is she normally so late?" Detective Parker made a note.

Lucas shifted his weight again and his eyes grew wide. "Ten is not late for an executive person in her position. She works a ridiculous number of hours. She's here for every event and still gets here every morning except Sunday. Do we have to close the museum? I need to know."

"Yes. I would like to keep it closed until I speak to the director. Please put a sign on all the doors that the museum is closed until further notice due to an unforeseen circumstance."

"Yes, sir. I'll do it right away."

"If she wants the museum to open any time soon, she'd better find time to speak to me."

"Yes sir. That makes it doubly important. I understand."

Sandra tapped Detective Parker on the shoulder with her pen. "I'm scooting off now. I'm finished with my scene examination. You can order transport whenever you're ready. I'll start the autopsy as soon as he arrives at the morgue." She made sure no one was watching her, then winked. "I will see you later."

"Thanks for coming down. Yes, later." He smiled very wide, then turned back to the security guard. "We need that footage as quickly as possible." He paused for a moment. "Wait, did you know the victim?"

Lucas looked over to the body surrounded by the forensic specialists lifting fingerprints, adjusting their sketches, placing numbered plastic cones around the bench, and photographing everything from the gate to the bench. He glanced down at his worn but polished black shoes, then lifted his head. "Not personally. He was the featured artist at the reception last night, but I didn't get to meet him. There's a big poster in front of the ticket counter. His name is, I mean was, Dennis Lansing."

"What about access to this area? How did he get in back here?" Sandra sized up the space. The green bench sculpture was somewhat hidden behind the large, imposing museum, and a bit sheltered from the café entry door by a short patio. It wasn't visible from the street due to the height of the shrubbery and the bulk of the tall gingko wishing tree.

Lucas took out a handkerchief, lifted his hat, and passed it across his forehead and around his face in a practiced manner. "That's always been somewhat of a problem. It's not all that difficult if you are persistent and reasonably fit. I put in a budget re- quest for securing the fences to be more resistant to trespassing, but it was turned down."

"I'll bet approval is swift now." Detective Parker nodded to the activity surrounding the green bench. "Show me the ways to get in."

After ten minutes and at least that many ways to enter the garden, they returned to stand in front of the body. "I think the easiest access point that would permit carrying a body through to the green bench is straight through this gate." Detective Parker pointed to a waist high set of fiberglass panels that rolled back into the shrubbery to allow outdoor access to the garden. "But the problem with that is, you didn't see that on the video."

"No, I think it's more likely that the person came through the thinner shrubbery straight in off the street," said Lucas.

Detective Parker looked at Lucas. "So, the suspect could have been someone who is not familiar with this area."

Lucas nodded and mopped his handkerchief around his face again. "I agree, but another option is that Dennis walked in here himself."

Detective Parker nodded. "Okay, regardless of how he got here, I'll get the forensics specialists to cordon off a much wider area. Keep trying for permission to release the tape." He checked his watch. "As you say, your director should be here by ten. It will take me at least that long to get through the preliminary paperwork process." He tilted his head down. "Don't let anyone from the museum staff interfere with our ongoing case. I will hold you responsible."

Color drained from Lucas's face and he held his hands up and backed away. "I'm here to help you. Trust me, I want to help. I've always dreamed about helping with a murder investigation."

"Murder?" Detective Parker used his pistol-cold voice. "I haven't mentioned murder."

Chapter 4

Monday morning

A fresh autumn breeze fluttered the yellow crime scene tape. The sound contrasted harshly with the intermittent calls of squabbling seagulls in the waters of Tampa Bay only a few yards from the Dali Museum. The tape was stretched tight in a huge makeshift circle tied to various trees, door knobs, signs, and around the green bench sculpture. The area extended to include the sliding gate at the entrance to the garden.

The bench represented a tongue-in-cheek homage to both Dali's famous melting clock paintings and the historic images of St. Petersburg's downtown streets crowded with tourists seated on hundreds of green benches. Half of the sculpture was a normal green bench and the other half was a large clock drooped over the green back, and then the rest of the bench seemed to melt into a pool of cement on the sidewalk.

Savannah walked up to the broad-shouldered

man standing just inside the yellow crime tape and holding a small black notebook. A badge hung on a lanyard around his neck. Tall and official in a navy suit, with a white shirt and plain maroon tie, he slipped the notebook into his pocket, then ducked under the tape to join her outside the crime scene perimeter.

"Good morning, Detective Parker." They shook hands. "Joy—er, Officer Williams said you might need me. What's this about a letter from my dad in the victim's pocket?"

"Good morning, Savannah." Parker smiled and reached into his inside suit pocket. He handed her a piece of paper encased in a small plastic evidence bag. "What do you make of this?"

She took the bag and could clearly read that it was a letter from her father. It was written on Webb's Glass Shop letterhead and dated ten years ago. "The handwriting is definitely Dad's." She tilted the evidence bag to catch the sun so she could get a better view.

August 15, 2007

Webb's Glass Shop
2401 Central Avenue
St. Petersburg, FL 33713

Dear Sir,
*   I deeply regret that I cannot in good conscience recommend {smudged name} for a permanent position with your company. Although he has achieved impressive improvement in demonstrating responsible behavior during the past year, it is abundantly clear that he is still adjusting to the*

*ethical demands of a corporate employee. The fact
that he asked you to write to me indicates that he is
not ready to accept the consequences of his lack
{smudged words}.*

  *Due to the ongoing status of his court hearings,
I am unable to share the details of Chase's current
difficulties and I would have preferred that he
disclosed {smudged words} voluntarily.*

  *I am confident that you will find another
applicant from our program that would suit your
needs and provide an opportunity for that
apprentice. Please let me know if I can assist in
your search.*

  *Respectfully yours,
John Webb, Owner
Webb's Glass Shop*

*cc: File Copy
cc: Social Services*

"Dad regrets not being able to recommend someone for a job. It's too creased to read easily and the
full name of the apprentice is too smudged to make
out. I don't know which apprentice this might be.
It looks like it has been folded and unfolded a million times. It says here in the last paragraph that his
first name was Chase, but why did Dennis have
this?"

"That's what we were hoping you could explain.
I can't figure out why he would bring this to the
exhibit opening. Because your dad sent the letter,
I thought you might know more about both of
them."

"I absolutely knew Dennis in high school. If I

could make out a few letters under the smudge, I could confirm that Chase was an apprentice. It looks like the last name starts with an *R*, but . . ." She held up the handwritten reference letter and tried several angles in the light to read the name in the crease. "From the date, I would have been a freshman at St. Petersburg High School when Dad wrote this. I would like to make sure the victim is Dennis. Do you have a picture?"

"I thought you might want a photo." Parker pulled out his phone. "I had the morgue send me an upper body photograph. Don't worry, it's not graphic." He handed the phone to Savannah.

She looked at the image of a young man whose body was pale gray with his eyes closed and a sheet drawn up to his waist. In the center of his chest was a colorful and beautifully rendered image of Buddha sitting in lotus position. Savannah felt a chill snake down her spine.

Oh, no. This is Dennis. He was my first date, first dance, and first kiss. What happened?

Savannah covered her mouth against a rising sourness at the back of her throat. "Yes, I know him." She bowed her head until the feeling subsided. She spoke quietly. "This is Dennis Lansing. He was the guest of honor right here for the opening of his exhibit last night. I dated him for a short time in high school."

"Did you see him last night?"

"Yes, I did. Edward and I stopped in for a few minutes for the exhibit opening. We only got a glimpse of him. He was taken away by Director Wilkins before I had a chance to say more than a few words." She sighed deeply and pressed her lips together. "He was in my art class at St. Petersburg High School. He was three years older and seemed so sophisticated and worldly." She handed the phone back to Detective Parker. "What happened?"

"We're not entirely sure. The most likely scenario is either natural causes or, more probably, a drug overdose."

"I wouldn't have expected that. When I knew him, he wasn't a drug user at all."

"People change. You say you were in the same art class, but that he was older?"

"Yes, I was an experienced artist already because of the work I did in my dad's shop, so they allowed me to skip ahead to the advanced class in media studies. I was the only freshman in with the upper-class students."

"How well did you know him?"

"He was a great friend despite everything, actually. Those three years were a big age gap back in high school, but he was also a bit of a bad boy and had been in some sort of trouble. My dad was not pleased when we started dating." She looked up at Detective Parker. "Dennis and I were supposed to meet for lunch this week while he was here for the exhibit. He was going to conduct a private viewing along with a sand etching demonstration for the students in my workshop. We've been communicating through my website."

Detective Parker softened his voice. "I'm sorry. It didn't occur to me that you two would have a history. I would have notified you personally before Officer Williams gave you the bad news."

Savannah sniffed and pinched her nose. "I'm

fine, really, just a little shocked. It didn't seem real to me until I saw his picture. He was a fantastic glass artist. He integrated hand cutting and sand etching using computer scanned documents as embedded images. It was a style that paid homage to Andy Warhol." She paused and lowered her voice. "He was a big fan of Andy Warhol." She shook her head and said in a strong voice, "How can I help?"

"Given that this letter is from your father, is it possible Dennis and this unknown subject were both your father's apprentices?"

"Oh, yes. Dennis was one of many. Dad mentored lots of kids. Jacob was the last one and he wasn't part of a formal program. He was personally selected. I haven't been brave enough to start my own program. Maybe next year. Have you notified Harriet—Dennis's wife?"

"Do you know where she is? We are, of course, trying to notify her and determine any existing medical conditions."

"No, I don't know where they are staying. She was with him at the exhibit opening. The museum director will most certainly know. I think this exhibit was fully funded by the Dali, so she would have authorized and even arranged local accommodation for him and his wife."

"The staff here are having difficulty locating the director." Parker frowned and looked back at the museum. "So far, we're investigating widely and almost blindly. I think it would be helpful if you could search through John Webb's apprentice files and see what additional information he may have regarding Lansing. If you don't have time, could Officer Williams spend some time pouring through them?"

"I'll do it. It's not a problem. I can save her from that tedious task at least." She pointed to the twisted green bench sculpture. "Is this where he was found?"

"Yes. Do you know if there might be a prior connection between Lansing and the Dali Museum?"

"Well, certainly not back at the time of the letter. This Dali Museum building is only a few years old . . . since 2011. Before that, the museum was housed in a waterfront building near the Bayboro Campus of the University of South Florida. That dark cramped space was never the right place for such a magnificent body of work. They really couldn't display more than five percent of the collection at a time." *I'm rambling all over the place. This is an information dump. Not useful.*

"So, no connection?"

"I'm sorry. I'm blathering. We lost touch after he left school. He might have been a student docent. That was—and still is—a way of integrating youth into the art community. Can I see that picture again?"

"Sure." Detective Parker touched a few icons, then handed the phone back to Savannah. "Something ring a bell?"

Savannah scrunched her brow, then rubbed her left temple. "This is right about the time Dad started an outreach program with boys who were at certain risk for dropping out of high school. He worked with the board of education and social services to create an apprentice program so they could work in the shop. He paid them a fair wage and they were let out of school early each day to participate. Dennis was one of the apprentices."

"Where would your dad have kept the records? I am assuming that he did keep records on his apprentices."

"Yes, he needed to establish the effectiveness of the program for the board of education, so he would have kept meticulous records. The problem is going to be finding them."

"Wouldn't they be at Webb's Glass Shop?"

"Probably. There's a seriously old file cabinet in the corner of the office at Webb's Glass Shop. I haven't looked into it other than to open all the drawers to look for cash."

"Cash?"

"Don't look so shocked. Dad left a few emergency stashes in the name of hurricane preparation. I found several envelopes filled with cash in the house, too. He figured that the ATMs wouldn't function without power or signal, nor would the cash registers at stores.

"Cash?" Detective Parker's voice raised an octave.

"Don't worry. I got them all. I don't believe in having that much cash around. It's not that I don't think it's a convenient idea, but my cash is tied up right now. Dad also had some very old files stored up in the attic of the house. I haven't been up there, yet. Too many memories. But it's certainly worth looking through them. I feel like I can handle it now."

"Well, take a look and let me know what you find. Did Officer Williams ask to sign you on as a consultant for this case?. Would that be possible?"

"Absolutely possible. So, you're investigating this as a murder?"

"The definitive decision will be after I get the autopsy results, but my gut tells me he didn't die of an overdose posed on this bench with his inhaler still in his pocket."

"Right. I want to help with Dennis's case." *Of course, I can also use a little extra income. I recently invested a nice little chunk of money in sand etching equipment that has so far attracted a grand total of four students.* "By the way, how was he—his body, that is—how was it found?"

"One of the docents arrived early to open up the community room for a class."

"A class on Surrealism?"

"No, it was a class in Tai Chi." He pulled out his notebook and flipped back a few pages. "The docent is John Zeflin, who is also an instructor with the local Tai Chi organization. He volunteered to conduct a beginner's class. He was given a time slot early Monday mornings, before the museum opened, to ensure the students didn't interfere with museum operations. He was out here checking the space for the outdoor portion of the practice."

"So, Dennis was discovered over there on the melting bench?"

"Yes. The docent thought he was one of the homeless veterans who was late making his escape after spending the night on the bench. He said it happens a few times a month. He discovered his mistake when he tapped Lansing's shoulder."

Savannah shivered. "What a horrible way to start the week."

"It was a lot worse for Lansing."

Chapter 5

After Savannah left the museum, Detective Parker returned to stand in front of the green bench sculpture. It was an unusual place to find a body. He sat on the bench and mimicked the pose that Dennis had been in when discovered. It was uncomfortable. The bench was sturdy enough, but not the right proportions for sitting any longer than it took to have a snapshot taken to post to social media.

Ping!

Detective David Parker stood and took out his phone. He opened an e-mail from Coroner Sandra Gray. He smiled at the thought of their deepening friendship. She was the top-rated coroner in the state of Florida. They worked extremely well together and he was close to asking her out on a date. They were meeting for a beer after work. He'd ask her out then. The Miami Dade County Police's coroner's office had been aggressively courting her for months. He hoped they wouldn't lure her away with promises of a higher salary and—even more enticing—a better lab.

The attachment to the e-mail was her preliminary report. He quickly scrolled down to the detail he wanted first—the time of death.

The report estimated death to be early Monday morning within a range of two to three hours before the body was discovered at seven o'clock. Further into the report, she noted that the body had been moved shortly after death because there were signs of blood lividity pooled in areas inconsistent with Dennis's position on the bench. At the end of the e-mail, Sandra had written, No cause of death— yet! Be patient.

That was a little disappointing. She was famous for determining cause of death literally within minutes of getting a body onto her table. He frowned. It must be complicated.

Nearby, Lucas had been making another series of phone calls to the museum's director. He hitched up his uniform pants, took his security cap off, and wiped the sweat from his forehead. Then he walked over to the detective. By the hound-dog look on his face, Detective Parker concluded that the calls had been fruitless.

"I'm sorry, sir. I have not been able to reach Director Wilkins. Would you like to wait inside?" Lucas looked at his watch. "It won't be long now. Probably less than fifteen minutes."

After Detective Parker nodded, Lucas unlocked the back doors of the Dali Museum and led him through the garden access entry that opened into

a small-bites café and coffee shop. It was adjacent
to the gift shop that was almost a museum itself.
There were large artwork installations tucked throughout the cups, T-shirts, and posters of the museum's
famous paintings.

Lucas waved a hand to a table. "You'll be comfortable here, I'm sure. Can I get you a coffee?"

Detective Parker nodded yes. "Black, please."

Lucas left as quickly as his bulk would permit and
headed to place the order with the newly arrived
café staff.

Detective Parker sat in one of the white metal
chairs in the café of the Dali Museum. He noted
that it had been named Cafe Gala after Dali's wife.
He angled his chair so he had sight of the front
door. He had finished interviewing the custodian,
only to learn that no one had been in the building
after the cleaning crew left at 11:30 p.m. He still
needed to interview the museum's director, Ms.
Gina Wilkins, and she was expected to arrive any
minute. That would be the last interview at the
museum and he could return to the station.

A thin dark-haired twenty-something woman
walked up to him. "Hello. I'm Peggy, Director
Wilkins's assistant." She wore a black pencil skirt
and classic white shirt with a large Dali mustache-
printed scarf looped around her neck. "I know
you're trying to reach her, but I haven't been able
to contact Director Wilkins by home phone or cell
phone. I'm so sorry, but I'll direct her your way
as soon as she arrives." She spoke in a rapid-fire
burst, then left him before he could speak and
paced in front of the entrance to the museum in

anticipation of a highly irritated director. Although young and probably inexperienced, she obviously knew that annoyed directors tend to take out their irritation on their assistants. She intended to divert the director to Detective Parker right away and would probably make a quick escape after the director arrived.

Detective Parker heard the automatic doors open and the proactive assistant pounced upon Director Wilkins with the alarming news that a body had been found on the green bench sculpture and a police detective was waiting to speak to her. The director's reaction was visible; she stiffened and squeezed her eyes shut.

The assistant took advantage of the director's distraction and literally ran through the entry and up the spiral staircase to the offices on the second floor.

Gina opened her eyes, rolled her shoulders, then tucked an artfully curled lock of her strawberry blond hair behind her ear. Frowning at the stairway where her assistant escaped, she then looked toward the café. She nodded an acknowledgment to Detective Parker, walked to the counter, then rattled about fifteen orders to the café server in rapid-fire succession. The server handed her a waiting cappuccino, then scribbled madly on an order pad. Director Wilkins took a long drink of her coffee, then approached Detective Parker.

Gina displayed a practiced and photogenic smile as she extended her hand. "Good morning, Detective Parker. I'm so very, very distressed to learn that Dennis was the unfortunate young man found on our green bench sculpture this morning. He was such a talented artist and a lovely, warm young man. The museum's opening reception was an astonishing success. It's sad beyond words that we have lost him so early in his career. I'm simply devastated. Was it a drug overdose?"

Detective Parker stood to shake her hand and motioned for her to sit at the café table. He noticed that her eyes were red and swollen under what seemed to be heavy makeup for daytime. "We're still investigating the cause of death. My most pressing issue is that I need the address where Lansing and his wife were staying. We need to contact his wife and apparently they weren't staying at any of the nearby hotels we checked. I also would like to ask you a few questions about access to the museum and the outdoor spaces."

"Of course. Security Manager Brown should have given you the address right away." She reached into her large designer purse and pulled out a business card and a pen. She scribbled on the back of the card. "Here's where Dennis and his wife Harriet are staying. They're guests of Mrs. Granger. She's a dear widowed friend of mine who happened to have a few spare rooms. Artists need to be supported by their adoring patrons whenever possible. I managed to secure complimentary lodging and they were grateful. Their income stream is erratic at best." Glancing at his empty cup, she said, "Would you like another cup of coffee?"

"Thanks, that would be great. Black, please."

"Good. I'm a caffeine addict." She waved a hand to the server behind the café counter who scurried over to their table. Gina continued to look at Detective Parker and not to the server. "Another of my usual and add a few biscotti."

Detective Parker brought out his notebook and flipped it open to a blank page. He placed it on the surface of the table. "Ms. Wilkins, where were you in the early hours of this morning?"

Gina's jaw dropped and her eyes widened. "You're asking me a very provocative question. I'm an ordinary person, Detective Parker. I was at home."

"Can anyone substantiate that?"

"I was home alone." Gina folded her hands in front of her and straightened up to look directly into Detective Parker's eyes.

He scribbled in his notebook. "Did you know Dennis Lansing well?"

"Of course. I got to know him through our negotiations for bringing his exhibit to the museum. There were many phone calls, video chats, and I even flew out to one of his exhibits to ensure the quality of the works." She pressed a finger to the corner of her left eye. "This is such a shock." She reached into her handbag for a tissue which she pressed to the outside corner of each eye.

Detective Parker nodded. "Were there any problems with the exhibition?"

"Nothing out of the ordinary. There were the usual issues of lighting the space, shipping the art works, accommodations, and negotiating the fees. We had those all worked out before the installation began."

Detective Parker looked up from his notebook. "The outdoor space is only accessible through a locked barrier gate and this rear café door. The victim died at another location and was transported here. How do you suppose he was placed on the green bench?"

"Obviously, it was either someone strong who has access to the museum or there is a way to get into the garden that hasn't yet been discovered by the security officer." She looked vaguely in the direction of the green bench. "Also it could have been more than one person."

The server returned with a cup of black coffee, a cappuccino, and a plate of biscotti.

Gina nodded curtly to the server, grabbed her cup, and drank deeply. "I can get you a copy of the alarm system code times, if that will help."

"Yes, that will be helpful, but you do have video cameras that might have recorded any entries, correct?"

"Yes, I'll put you in touch with our security manager. I'm sure he's here already. I have a ton of text and voice messages from him. We don't open until ten." She waved the hand with the pen in it to the server and made a pantomime of writing a note. The server provided a small pad of paper. "What's wrong with me? I have notepaper." Gina pressed her lips together and waved the server away. She dived back into her purse, then scribbled a number on a pink sticky note shaped like lips and handed it to Detective Parker. "Here's his Dali extension and his cell phone number."

"I've already spoken to Lucas." Detective Parker emphasized his use of the security officer's first name. "In fact, he was most cooperative except for the areas where he said he needed permission from you. He wouldn't budge on providing me access to your video files until you gave the word. Do I have that permission?"

Gina tilted her head and squinted as though trying to read a tiny menu in the dark. "I don't know why on earth he would need to ask me for permission. You may, of course, have anything from our records you need. I'll let him know that he can send them to you. This unfortunate event needs to be cleared up as soon as possible."

"I'm glad you feel that way."

"Well, this will change everything for the exhibit." Her eyes began to widen and she flushed from her collarbone to her chin. "His work will be the newest buzz of excitement from New York to Paris." Her eyes darted up to the second-floor offices. "Social media is going to go viral with this. That could enhance our efforts to put sleepy little St. Petersburg on the map." She rose from the chair, gathered up her purse and the coffee.

Detective Parker stood up quickly and spoke sharply. "I hope you don't mean that you're glad a young man has been found dead in suspicious circumstances just to add spice to your publicity campaign?"

Gina gasped and pressed her hand to her throat. "My goodness, of course not. Nothing could be further from my mind. What a dreadful accusation, Mr. Parker." She looked up and blinked her false eyelashes rapidly. They glistened with moisture. "You don't seriously mean that?" She folded the tissue to a clean surface and carefully dabbed the corners of her eyes.

"It's Detective Parker, ma'am. I do mean that. Those tapes had better not end up in the hands of the media. I will be taking legal action if there's even a minute's delay in sending the video tapes to my forensic department."

"Oh wait. There's more than one camera. Which tape do you need?"

"Your head of security knows. If there's any question, send them all." He tipped his head. "I'll be in touch." He left, walking as briskly as he could toward the continuing activity outside.

Chapter 6

Monday afternoon

Savannah completed her remaining administrative tasks and then walked the few blocks from Webb's Studio to Webb's Glass Shop. Her recent expansion from her family's small retail stained glass business to include the secondary studio space was turning out to be a great decision. Webb's Glass Shop on Central Avenue had been in the family from the time the building was constructed in the 1920s. Her grandfather had operated a motorcycle business before her dad opened the glass shop.

She pulled open the front door and the bell over the door jingled her entrance. "Hi, Amanda. Are you ready for your class this afternoon?"

Amanda Blake poked her head through the door of the classroom located directly off the back wall of the display room. "Hi, yourself. I'm getting set up now." She motioned for Savannah to step into a classroom that was outfitted with six work benches laid out in three rows with an instructor podium and whiteboard in the front of the room. A narrow aisle ran from the entry to the shop's office in the far rear of the old building.

Amanda was wearing one of her more original looks, which meant that her hair was dyed in a patchy calico cat palette, perfectly coordinated with a tan linen shirt over cheetah print leggings and tall Converse shoes in a chocolate brown. As a woman of size, she rocked her looks and that confidence always made Savannah smile.

"How's your mother? Has her breathing gotten better?"

"She's a bit better now and only needs oxygen at night. It's a relief to the caregivers at the nursing home. She keeps pulling it away from her face during the day, anyway. The fact is she's so much calmer without it. I've been saying that for ages and they finally agree with me."

Savannah patted Amanda on the shoulder. "That does sound better for her. I'm going to do some searching around in Dad's old file cabinets in the office. Don't mind me."

She sat down in the creaky oak spindle office chair in front of the antique desk. It sat in the same spot that it had when her grandfather used it and then her father, and now she sat there to pay bills and place orders. At first, she thought that the vintage furniture might have felt uncomfortable. It was familiar yet heavy with so many comforting memories attached to them. Now that she had fully taken charge, she felt secure in the belief that they were looking over her and guiding her decisions.

She pulled open one of the tiny drawers and sorted through the keys she kept there. The old file cabinet was kept locked. Now that she thought about it, it was likely that her dad would have been mindful of security protocols when it came to the personal records. She found the keys and opened the top drawer of the first file cabinet.

Although she knew the files were at least ten years old, they were neatly organized with each green hanging folder containing a manila file. The labels were precisely written out in her father's handwriting with a nonsense string of numbers and letters and symbols. "Of course," she sighed. "You would have created a code for the records."

Savannah's dad had been a cryptographer for the US government during the cold war. He had helped her solve the mystery of his death by leaving her encoded messages. This was completely in character for a paranoid code enthusiast—frustrating, but completely expected.

Savannah pulled the manila file from the first folder in the drawer and took it over to the desk. She spread the contents out. There was a record of that student's history. In addition to the file tab, every instance in the record where you would ordinarily find a name, address, or date, her father had used a coded identifier. She had no clue who this file might belong to. That would make finding Dennis Lansing's records a bit more difficult. First, the code needed to be broken.

Maybe these files are for another project. I also need to check on the ones in the attic.

She opened the remaining three drawers and they all contained a similar type of file—encoded names both on the filing label and within the records.

"What are you searching for?"

Savannah jumped. "Goodness, Amanda! You startled me. Somehow skulking through Dad's records make me feel like I'm spying. I forgot you were here. No, in fact, I forgot everything. I'm looking for the records that he would have kept for his apprentices."

"Why?" Amanda leaned against the door of the office. "Jacob is doing fine, isn't he?"

"He is. I'm looking at these older records for a consulting job for Detective Parker."

"You have a consulting job and didn't tell me?" Amanda stretched tall and folded her arms across her ample chest. "I thought we were best friends."

Savannah bent her head into her chest. "Of course, we are. I'm sorry. I guess I'm more upset than I thought." She waved for Amanda to come over to the desk, stood, and gave her a giant hug. "We are forever friends and you can call me out on that anytime." Savannah showed her the contents of the records. "I'm not sure I'm going to be much help to Detective Parker and Officer Williams this time. All the records have encoded entries for the names and personnel information. Dad was playing tricks to hide the data."

"Well, of course he would." Amanda said. "He was obsessive about hiding information."

"I think this is a bit too obsessive—even for Dad. I wonder why he felt it was necessary to encode the personal information. The locked cabinet should have been more than enough."

"Why do you need to know?"

Savannah propped her chin in her hand. "It's

sad, really. The police found a body on the green bench sculpture at the Dali Museum this morning."

"What?" asked Amanda.

The front door bell jangled. "That's probably your students. Go ahead and get the class going. I'll tell you afterwards. In fact, let's have a meeting at the studio at about three. I want to tell you, Edward, and Jacob all at the same time. I'm going to need some help with this. The victim was my first ever boyfriend, Dennis Lansing."

Amanda put a hand to her throat. "Really? This is major. Your first boyfriend is like, well, that's something special. I'm so sorry." She enveloped Savannah into a long giant hug and looked up into her eyes. "If you think I can wander away quietly with a million questions in my head, think again." She raised her eyebrows and folded her arms across her ample chest. "I'm waiting. Don't make me tap my foot."

"Honestly, Amanda, my thoughts are swirling around in such a mess right now, I don't think I could string two sensible thoughts together. I promise I'll be a good deal more coherent this afternoon." Savannah shooed her away like a pesky child. "I need a little time to come to grips with how I feel. You know that's hard for me. I'll tell all later at Webb's Studio. Go on. Go teach your students."

Savannah settled back into her task and opened the top drawer. She took out the first coded folder again and placed it on the desk. She took out a fresh pad of ruled paper from the lowest desk drawer and then grabbed a pencil to begin working on solving the encryption code.

She first tried the simplest substitution code:

1=A, 2=B, 3=C, etc., without success. Then she tried several more complicated substitution codes with no luck. Then she made a few more attempts based on the limited set of complex codes that her dad had taught her. She threw the pencil down in frustration, leaned back in the squeaky chair, and folded her arms across her chest.

I've only got one more code to try and then I'm lost.

She started with a fresh sheet of paper and started decoding with the transposition cipher, which was the most complicated one that her Dad had taught her, but that one yielded no clarity either. She sighed. *I give up.*

She glanced at the clock, surprised to see it was approaching three o'clock.

Savannah walked the few short blocks over to Webb's Studio.

The conference room at the studio was large and contained a long table with a colorful assortment of second-hand office chairs. Since antique and collectible shops surrounded both Webb's Glass Shop and Webb's Studio, Savannah supported both the Reuse and Buy Local campaigns. It also supported her goal of staying in business by not spending money where she didn't need to.

She stood inside the conference room door with her hands on her hips. Jacob walked in with Suzy in his arms and placed her in a seat before settling into the one next to her.

"Thanks for showing up, Jacob. I think I'm going to need you."

Jacob lifted his head and looked at Savannah, "Good. I'm excellent at your puzzles." He quickly looked back at Suzy and petted her in one long stroke from head to tail.

Savannah heard a key in the front door and both Edward and Amanda made their way through the bright studio. Edward was balancing a large tray with a large traditional brown betty teapot with floral cups and saucers while Amanda held a large serving platter covered with a kitchen towel.

"We're here. Even better, we're here with treats," she said as she placed the platter in the center of the table. She whipped off the towel. "It's Edward's famous cranberry scones with clotted cream and strawberry jam."

"Finally," said Savannah, eyeing the heaping stack of scones. "You haven't made them in a long time."

"I also brought afternoon tea." Edward doled out cups and saucers to each of them and placed a small dish of cut lemons on the table.

Jacob reached for his and lined up the flowers on the cup with the matching flowers on the saucer. "The tea is Earl Gray, correct? It is afternoon and it is also my favorite."

Edward smiled and then he high-fived with Jacob. "Spot on. I know very well that you like it." He picked up the squat brown teapot and poured all around.

Everyone ate at least one scone. Jacob had already gone through two, but at eighteen, his appetite flipped erratically between voracious or non-existent. He liked some foods obsessively and others he avoided. He was the only one who knew the ever-changing rules.

Savannah cleared her throat and waited until the

other three looked at her. "I have a situation and I need your help."

Jacob talked through a mouthful of scone. "Is there a puzzle for me?"

"I think so, Jacob. But I am worried about our order for the Vinoy Hotel. They need those three hundred glass charger plates on Saturday. I'm not sure we can spare you from the process of loading and unloading the kilns."

Jacob picked up Suzy and hugged her close. "We can share the task of unloading. I'm the best at loading. That's what you said."

Savannah nodded slightly and smiled. "Good thinking. Your ability to load the kiln is incredible, but any of us can unload. Well done!"

"He's right," said Amanda. "I can take over the unloading and that will free up Jacob to help you with—"

"Just one more thing." Savannah looked directly at Edward. "I also need some help with my paperwork. I don't see how I can take on an investigation and still manage the payroll, social security deposits, retail taxes, employee insurance, workman's comp, and everything else that has to be done this week."

"You lookin' at me?" Edward smirked. "You lookin' at me?" He reared back his head and pointed to the middle of his chest.

Savannah laughed. "Yes, I know this is a busy time for you, but I'm hoping you will volunteer to take on some of them at least during this week so I can assist Detective Parker."

Edward paused. "Nicole is the best bartender cum manager I've ever met. She's got everything running so well that she's politely pretending that I'm sometimes needed. Except for the paperwork of course. She feels the same way that you do on that front."

"What if I make a few more of these Vinoy Hotel chargers for your tables at the pub? Would that be a good trade? We can do them right after we deliver our order."

Edward nodded. "I'm good with that. Our basic paperwork processes are similar. It also helps that we use the same horrible cash register application. The only thing I need is to meet your accountant to catch me up on your business categories. It shouldn't be too difficult."

"I am so grateful. You actually enjoy that part. I sincerely don't."

"And my other secret super power is that I have Nicole the wonder bartender. She really runs Queen's Head Pub. I only have to show up now and again for her to tell me what she needs me to do."

"Enough already." Amanda clipped her words. "What's the job?"

Savannah waited until each of them was looking at her. "Let me explain." She propped her elbows on the table and wrapped her hands around the hot cup of tea. "I was called to the Dali Museum this morning by Detective Parker to help gather information on a young man they found dead in the museum's garden. His name was Dennis Lansing."

"Isn't he the chap with the exhibit opening we attended last evening?" Edward asked.

"Yes." Savannah felt her cheeks get warm. She looked at Amanda. "Although it was great to be invited, it was such a madhouse and he was so popular, we didn't get to speak to him for more than an introduction when the museum director pulled him away. Dennis and I had been exchanging e-mails over the past few weeks. He had agreed to narrate a tour through his exhibit for my etching students and hold a demonstration here at the studio. He was a generous artist." She turned her cup around to hold another spot. "Anyway, Detective Parker found a decade-old letter from my dad in Dennis's jacket pocket and wanted to know what I knew about him and the letter."

"You told him everything, right?" Amanda sat up straight.

"Yes, of course." Savannah stood up and added more tea to her cup and Edward's as well.

"So why are we here?" asked Amanda. "What's wrong?"

"I'm not sure anything is wrong, but I knew Dennis pretty well." She looked at Edward. "He was my first ever boyfriend when I was a freshman at St. Petersburg High School."

"First serious boyfriend? As in, you know, first kiss?" Amanda's voice stumbled over the word *kiss*, then she gulped behind her hand. She looked directly at Edward.

"Yes, he was," said Savannah, also looking at Edward "We were quite close for a few months during his senior year, which was my freshman year."

"This is tragic." Amanda rose, walked around the table, and gave Savannah a giant hug that lasted for at least ten seconds. "You must feel awful." She returned to her seat and grabbed another scone.

"Thanks, but I'm not really sure how I feel about

it. Yet, anyway. I mean, it was a long time ago and we hadn't kept in touch after he dumped me, but I do remember him as a charmer. I was looking forward to catching up with his successes."

"How much of a charmer was he?" asked Edward in a gentle low voice.

"Like a very close funny friend. Nothing more." She grinned. "When we went to the opening launch last night, I got a chance to see him and his wife. He did the right thing by breaking up with me. He seemed to be happy with his wife."

"He broke up with you?" Amanda put her hands on her hips. "No way."

"Way," said Savannah. "He was sensitive about my age and thought he was a bad influence. Turns out he was right."

"How was he a bad influence?" asked Jacob.

"He was in quite a bit of trouble as a member of a neighborhood gang. In fact, he was one of my dad's first apprentices. Dad started a program with a social worker to rescue high-risk students. The dropout rate at school was rising quickly so he met with a social worker to create a work-school program that assigned them to work in art-related businesses as apprentices."

Edward poured himself more tea and snagged an extra lemon. "So why do you need our help? Wouldn't the information all be in your dad's files? I don't see what the problem is."

"There are at least two," said Savannah. "First, Detective Parker wants me to research Dad's old records and see what I can find out about Dennis's past, based on the letter that was found in his pocket. The problem with that is that Dad's record identifiers are all encrypted and I'll need Jacob to help to decipher the filing system. There are also some old files in the attic."

"I can help with that when I come over tonight." Edward raised his eyebrows.

"Absolutely. Second, Detective Parker doesn't have a cause of death yet. But he thought it was possible that Dennis might have died of an overdose and is basically thinking it was a result of the very successful opening of his exhibit at the Dali."

"Is that unreasonable?" asked Edward.

"Well, the body was moved after his death. That needs explaining. It's not the behavior of the Dennis that I knew. He was not a drug user. He was seriously opposed to drug use."

"He could have changed his tune."

"That's entirely possible. One of the stressors back in high school was that Dennis was casually selling drugs, but not actually taking them. He was doing it for spending cash. It seemed so innocent and harmless at the time."

Jacob looked at Savannah. "What happened?"

"His older brother died of an overdose and Dennis had sold him the drugs. Dennis was there when it happened."

Chapter 7

Monday afternoon

Detective Parker knocked on the door of a large multistory house in the elite neighborhood called the Historic Old Northeast neighborhood. He glanced over at Officer Williams who accompanied him. This was her first experience with a death notification. She stood stiffly with her eyes wide and a hint of paleness around her full lips. This was a part of the job that he found uncomfortable, but he wouldn't let anyone else on the team take over. Giving a family member the bad news about a loved one took an emotional toll on everyone associated with the investigation.

Officer Williams needed to learn about this part of the job.

The door was answered by a stout woman of mature age and wearing a flowing caftan printed with birds-of-paradise along with matching orange sandals. Her voice was hesitant. "Hello?"

"Hello, Mrs. Granger. My name is Detective David

Parker and this is Officer Joy Williams. May we speak to Mrs. Harriet Lansing? I understand she is your guest. Is that correct?"

"Yes, that's right, Officers. Dennis and Harriet are staying here for the next few weeks. Is there some sort of trouble at the museum? I haven't seen either Dennis or Harriet yet this morning, but they have the run of the cottage, so that's not a big deal. It has a private entrance along with a dedicated parking place. Parking is such a problem here."

Detective Parker interrupted her obviously rehearsed speech about the problems of parking in their neighborhood. "It is urgent that we speak to Mrs. Lansing immediately. May we come in?"

Mrs. Granger appeared to grasp that she had two police officers standing in front of the door for all her neighbors to see. "Certainly. Pardon me. Of course, please come in."

They were led through a formal entry into a palatial living room with at least six separate sitting areas and into a sunroom. The floors were tiled with twelve-by-twelve-inch rustic red tiles. The sunroom looked out onto the red brick street. It was furnished in classic white wicker with over-stuffed floral printed cushions and vases of tropical flowers on every flat surface. Mrs. Granger waved them into the room. "I'll just pop out back to get Harriet, but first may I offer you some iced tea or coffee?"

Detective Parker glanced at Officer Williams. "We're good, thank you, but if you know what Mrs. Lansing drinks, having something for her would be appreciated. After you tell her we need to see her, of course."

"Is something wrong?" asked Mrs. Granger. She looked from Detective Parker to Officer Williams and back again. "It's something terrible, isn't it?"

"Please, if you could, ma'am, tell Mrs. Lansing that we're here to talk with her."

In a few minutes, Harriet Lansing entered the sunroom dressed in black yoga pants and a multi-colored crop top. She wore a white hand towel draped around her neck. Her hair was held in a ponytail and a slight sheen of perspiration glistened on her forehead. "What's this all about? Why have you come to see me?"

Detective Parker stood and glanced over to be sure that Officer Williams stood as well. "Please sit down, Mrs. Lansing. I have some very bad news."

Harriet stiffened and pulled the towel from around her neck. "Are my parents okay? Have they been in an accident?" Her face tightened along her jaw and she wiped her forehead with the towel. "I just spoke to them last night."

"Please sit down, Mrs. Lansing."

"No, I'll stand. Would you just tell me straight out?"

Detective Parker cleared his throat. "I'm sorry to tell you that your husband died early this morning."

Harriet stiffened, then released a fast bark of laughter. "Dennis? Are you sure?"

Officer Williams stepped forward and extended her hand a few inches under Harriet's arm and stood ready with a hand behind her back. When Harriet didn't appear ready to collapse, Joy took her by the arm and gently led her to the chair next to the sofa. They all sat without a word.

"I didn't expect that you would be telling me

about Dennis. You see, my father has been in and out of the hospital with a heart condition, but he still insists on driving. That's what I thought. I thought you were here to tell me that Dad had been killed in a car accident." A row of furrows appeared on her forehead and she pulled the elastic band out of her hair. "I didn't think about Dennis."

"Is there anyone I can call to be with you now, Mrs. Lansing?" asked Joy.

"We have some friends here, but no, I don't want anyone." She looked at the floor while pulling a hand through her long hair. "No one."

Mrs. Granger entered the sunroom with a tray crowded with a carafe of coffee, four china mugs, along with a pitcher of cream and a container of sugar packets. She placed the tray on the coffee table. She poured coffee in one of the cups and added three yellow packets of sweetener. "Harriet, take this." She took Harriet's hand and wrapped it around the mug. "Drink it."

Harriet looked down, put her other hand around the mug, and took a sip. She looked up at Mrs. Granger. "Thank you."

Mrs. Granger smiled and poured coffee for Detective Parker, Officer Williams, and herself. "Please help yourselves to cream and sugar," she said in a loud whisper, then sat down next to Harriet.

Detective Parker leaned forward. "Mrs. Lansing, do you feel up to talking about what happened last night?"

Harriet took a deep breath and looked directly at Detective Parker. "How did he die? Was it an asthma attack?"

"Our investigation has just begun, Mrs. Lansing. Could you tell me when you last saw your husband?"

"He was terrible about keeping up with his medication and treatments. He had three different types of inhalers and prescriptions, too."

"When did you last see your husband?" Detective Parker used a slightly louder voice.

She looked down into the coffee. "He didn't come to our cottage last night after the exhibit opening." She pressed her lips into a thin line. "That wasn't unusual. He was always very keyed up after an opening. He probably went for late night drinks with some of his fans."

"So, the last time you saw him was at the museum."

Harriet stood up so quickly that her coffee sloshed out onto the tile floor. "I'm upset. I'm going to my room." She placed the cup on the coffee table, turned, and left.

Silence filled the sunroom until Detective Parker cleared his throat. He stood and pulled out his billfold. "Thank you for your hospitality, Mrs. Granger. Here is my card. Please give it to Mrs. Lansing as soon as you can. Tell her to call me as soon as possible."

Mrs. Granger took the business card and looked at the details. "Homicide? You're from the Homicide Division?"

"Yes, ma'am. We suspect Dennis was murdered."

Chapter 8

Savannah answered the doorbell wearing a floral cotton dress of peach and tan with a pair of tan kitten heels. "Hi." She led Edward into her living room and gave him a deep kiss. Savannah's one-year-old Weimaraner puppy woofed, wiggled, and wedged his way between them. At over seventy-five pounds, he was innocently effective in cutting their greeting much shorter than either one of them wanted.

"Rooney! Stop that." Savannah pulled her way out of Edward's strong embrace before everyone lost their balance.

"Mmmm. You taste good." Edward looked down. "Hey, Rooney." He bent and scratched Rooney behind the ear. "You know I wouldn't forget you, boy" Reaching into a pocket of his worn black motorcycle jacket, he pulled out a small resealable pouch and shook the contents at eye level over Rooney. "Look here. I brought the organic snacks you like." He went into the kitchen and placed the bag on the kitchen counter, slipped his jacket off, and hung it on a hook by the back door, then opened the dog treat package. He took one and held it up. "Now, do your stuff. Sit!"

Rooney hustled around in front of Edward and performed a textbook sit with his eyes on the snack.

"Good boy," said Edward as he gave Rooney his reward.

"You're spoiling him." Savannah crossed her arms. "He expects a treat every time you arrive, now. Rooney is loyal once he makes up his mind. He reminds me of my dad—tough to get to know, but a forever friend when you managed. I'm pretty much like that, too."

Edward raised his eyebrows, but said nothing.

"I know, I know," said Savannah. "I know very well that I'm having a tough time making room for someone in my life." She looked at the floor. "I'm struggling, but I don't even know why I'm dragging my feet."

"I'm having trouble understanding. You cleared out your dad's bedroom and bought new furniture when you moved in there. You've replaced his recliner that was in the living room. You've painted the kitchen and reorganized the cupboards. What's left?"

"His office."

"What about his office?" Edward's voice rose ever so slightly. "Have you sorted through that?"

"No. Every time I open the door, I get overwhelmed and close it again."

Edward frowned. "We're going to have to address this sooner rather than later." He stood there looking at her for a full minute. When Savannah didn't respond, he turned around. "I'll start cooking. You have about thirty minutes to feed Rooney and take him for a walk."

Savannah stood scratching Rooney behind his ears as she watched Edward start making their dinner. *Will this ever work? He's a good man. I'm the one who has to change, but how do I start?*

Savannah busied herself by feeding Rooney, then stood by his bowl. As usual, his dinner disappeared in a few minutes. She got Rooney's leash, but before she could clip it to him, the doorbell rang.

"Are you expecting anyone?" said Edward over Rooney's barking.

"No." She commanded Rooney to be quiet and looked through the peephole. A small woman with dark hair stood there shifting her weight from foot to foot. Dennis's mom was wearing a light blue shirtwaist with tan pumps and a straw handbag. Everything well-worn but clean. Savannah opened the door. "Mrs. Lansing, what a—"

"I'm so sorry to bother you at home, Savannah. I'm sure you've heard the news about Dennis's death. I remembered that I spoke to you at the reception and thought of you a little while ago. I need to ask you a question."

"Yes, yes, of course. Please come in." She led Mrs. Lansing into the living room. "I remember you from when Dennis was an apprentice and you came to the shop to talk with Dad about his progress. Would you like a glass of iced tea or water?"

"No thank you. I'll only be here a minute." Mrs. Lansing stopped and looked around the living room. "This is such a lovely house. It's so cozy."

Edward appeared at the kitchen door for a moment. He opened his mouth to speak but quickly ducked back into the kitchen.

Savannah motioned Mrs. Lansing to the couch. "Thank you. It's one of the first houses built in the neighborhood."

After they sat down, a silence grew and Savannah felt uncomfortable. "I'm so sorry for your loss, Mrs. Lansing. I can't imagine how you feel."

"Please call me Betty. Everyone does." She reached into her straw handbag for a tissue and crumpled it in her hand. "He never stopped being a good son. Never. He called every week. He sent me cards and flowers. I'm going to be so lonely without him." She stared beyond Savannah's eyes. "It was just the two of us, you see, after his brother died. My idiot husband took off the moment I told him I was expecting Dennis. In truth, I expected that. He wasn't interested in family life." Her head lowered to look at her lap.

"Mrs. Lansing . . . I mean, Betty . . . why are you here?"

Betty startled. "Oh, I'm sorry. I'm not thinking straight." She sat up tall. "I heard about your involvement in solving your dad's murder and the other cases you've worked on with the police. I need you to use your skills to find out why my dearest Dennis was murdered."

"Murdered? Why do you think that? The police think it was a suspicious death. Something to do with an overdose."

"The police are wrong."

"The police don't have the autopsy results back yet, but I'm sure they're doing everything in their power to help you get closure. They have been in contact with you, haven't they?"

"Yes, but I'm convinced they think he was just a typical wacky artist with a drug problem. I think you're the only one who can find out what happened and who killed Dennis. I heard about your successful investigations from my friends. It was in the newspaper about how you are helping the police as an art consultant."

"Yes, I have been doing a little consulting work. But there is the fact that Dennis was in trouble when he was young. He might have turned back to drugs."

"That's not possible. Dennis hadn't used any drugs since he went into the apprentice program for your father. In fact, after his brother's death, he would never touch anything or talk to anyone involved with drugs. I know that. He adored working with glass and wouldn't risk being suspended from the program." She looked down and a tear slipped down her cheek unchecked and fell onto the front of her dress.

Savannah reached over to hold her hand. "I know he was troubled as a teen, but I don't understand how I can help."

"He was in some trouble when he was young, but he turned his life around completely. I want you to find his killer. It has to be something connected with the time when he was running with that horrible gang."

"But you say he wasn't involved with drugs."

"I'm sure of that, but he still had plenty of money to support his art. I think that originated from the drug source." She opened her purse and pulled out a checkbook. "I can pay."

Savannah shook her head. "No, I can't do that. I'm already working with the police as an expert consultant, not as a private investigator. You need to find a professional."

"But they won't care like you do." Betty replaced the checkbook and pulled out a tissue. "He was your first boyfriend. He really loved you."

Savannah frowned. "But he broke up with me." *I was heartbroken for months. I sulked like only a teenager can. I forgave him barely in time to attend his graduation.*

"That's how much he cared. He knew that he was the wrong type for John Webb's precious daughter." Betty used the tissue to wipe her eyes and blow her nose. "He never stopped talking about you over the years. He followed your career and was determined to make you and your dad proud of him. This exhibit accomplished that dream for him."

"I didn't know that. He seemed genuinely happy at the reception last night."

"The success of that exhibit represented his art—he was elated. Having his work in the Dali Museum put him in the prestigious company of Walt Disney, M. C. Escher, and Picasso. He was honored to be invited to exhibit."

"So, what do you think went so wrong that the police can't investigate?"

"Savannah, you know his character, you know the art community, and you can look for connections in his young life that they are certain to miss. You can also look behind his public face. As far as his personal life, that was a well-practiced piece of fiction. He was unhappy in his marriage."

"He was?" Savannah felt a tinge of satisfaction.

"I overheard them fighting about their finances. He needed money to promote his work. She didn't want him to spend any money on his art . . . only sell it for high prices." Betty looked down at her worn hands. "He married too quickly, you know. That needs looking into as well. He told me she was probably going to file for a divorce very soon because she didn't want to share her trust fund with him. What a petty thing to do. I never liked her."

"Seriously, Betty, I can't promise anything, but I am working with Detective Parker by taking a look into Dennis's records while he was in the apprentice program. You have been questioned by Detective Parker, haven't you?"

"Yes, he came over right away on Monday. He was clever about trying to make sure I had an alibi, which I didn't have, of course. I needed to meet a client early on Monday, so I left the reception early to go to bed. I live alone. Realizing that I was a suspect was a bit of a shock, but then he also gave me information about support programs for parents of murdered children."

"That sounds like him." Savannah held both of Betty's hands in hers again and looked her in the eyes. "I give you my promise that I'll do everything I can to make sure the police have all the information I can provide. They're good people, but I will help."

Betty stood, straightened her dress. "Thank you. That's exactly what I would expect from John's daughter." She wiped her eyes again, then put the tissue back in her purse and snapped it shut. "Oh, wait." She opened her purse again and pulled out a business card listing her occupation as a local real estate agent. "Call me at this number when you find out who killed Dennis." She walked out the front door without a backward glance.

Edward appeared and leaned against the kitchen doorway. "What was that all about?"

"That was Dennis's mother. She wants me to prove that Dennis was murdered."

"I gather that she confirmed that Dennis carried a torch for you all these years."

Savannah nodded. "I didn't have a clue, but I have thought of something we know about that the police don't know."

Edward waved his hand in a "gimme" motion. "And it is . . ."

"That hamburger wrapper that I tripped on that night at the museum. What if it was evidence? I threw the wrapper away."

"Evidence of what?"

"That someone could have been a witness to what happened to Dennis. I'm going to get Jacob to look at the outside spaces behind the museum."

She reached for Rooney's leash, clipped it to his collar, and slipped out the front door. Edward was right to feel uncomfortable with her inability to move forward. In fact, she was surprised that he wasn't complaining more. Investigating her first boyfriend's death would be another complication. What on earth was she waiting for? Edward was a wonderful partner, loyal friend, and inventive lover. Her dad would have been overjoyed to learn that the two of them were in a relationship.

I need to overcome my fear of losing him. First, I lost my dad, now I've lost my first boyfriend. I need to get over this or risk losing Edward altogether. He's the marrying kind, but even he won't wait for me forever. Get on with it, girl.

Rooney enjoyed his routine sniff and trot around the oak lined streets of the Historic Kenwood area. She had grown up on the redbrick-lined streets and knew most of the residents in the traditional Craftsman bungalows. It was good to see younger families beginning to move in. She waved to her neighbor, Barbara Taylor, across the street.

Barbara was out watering the plants in her front yard. "Hi, Savannah. That's a lovely dress. Are you having company? Is it Edward?"

Savannah smiled, then started across the street for a quick chat. Then she stopped in her tracks. *I'm not ready to talk about our relationship with her. Not ready at all. But that's not Mrs. Taylor's fault. It's my fault. I need to leave the past behind me.* She plastered a big smile on her face and led Rooney across so he could greet his favorite pet sitter.

Barbara dropped the hose, stooped down, and gave Rooney a big hug. She stood and tilted her head. "Is that pretty dress for your young man? I've been seeing that motorcycle parked in your driveway quite frequently. Do you have anything to share?" Barbara's eyes twinkled.

Savannah smiled in return and received a generous hug as well. "No, no, Miss Taylor. Nothing yet. You know I would tell you first." Barbara had been Savannah's honorary auntie while growing up. Her late mother had asked Barbara to keep an eye on the ten-year-old Savannah and Barbara had more than kept that promise. "I'm probably being too cautious, but I have a lot going just now."

Barbara smiled, "You always do. Bye."

She and Rooney crossed the street, then stepped back into the house.

After a quiet dinner and clearing up, Savannah leaned against the kitchen sink and turned to catch Edward sneaking another treat. "Stop trying to convince Rooney that he's going to get a treat every time you walk over to the counter. You're making him anxious."

"Agreed." He sighed and refilled Rooney's water bowl, then stood in front of Savannah. "Where is that attic that you want me to climb into?"

"It's in an access panel in Dad's office. You can only get up there with a ladder. That's in the shed out back."

"No worries." He slipped out the back door and returned with a giant aluminum extensible and reconfigurable ladder. "Where on earth did you get this monster? Can you even use it?"

"Certainly. It's lightweight, so I can carry it, but you know how I feel about heights. I'm still terrified stiff. This is the most stable ladder on the planet. That's the best I can do . . . other than talk you into using it." She smiled a saccharine grin and batted her eyelashes.

He laughed. "Well played. Let's get this done."

Savannah led Edward toward her dad's office, then stopped abruptly, not quite ready to enter. Edward bumped her in the back with the ladder.

"Ouch."

"Oh. Sorry, luv. I didn't expect you to stop there."

"No, I'm sorry." Savannah stepped into the office. As Edward set up the ladder, she looked down at the worn surface of the gray metal desk that he had salvaged from a used-office-furniture consignment shop. When he'd quit his government job, he'd said he missed having a sturdy surface so he bought the desk, a black rolling office chair, and some lockable file cabinets for filing paperwork. She moved beside the desk and looked at the ceiling.

She stepped out into the hallway, let Edward into the room, then returned.

Edward placed the ladder under the wooden hatch in the ceiling, climbed up a step, and opened the hinged door. He looked down at Savannah. "If you haven't been in here since John died, how do you know what's up here?"

"I don't. Dad said he had the oldest papers from the shop up here. I've never looked." She wrung her hands unconsciously, then noticed it and stopped.

He climbed up a couple of steps so that he was standing on the next to the top step.

"Blimey, this is a large attic. Did you know there are about fifty office storage boxes up here?" He ducked down to look at Savannah, who had moved to the ladder and held a death grip on the sides. Her pale face was lifted a little and her eyes fixated on his shoes.

She cleared her throat. "Rats. This is going to take a long time. How are they labeled?"

"It's some sort of weird numbering system. I'll climb up and take snapshots with my phone so you can see what's up here."

His feet disappeared and his footsteps echoed

down through the ceiling as he stepped and stopped and stepped and stopped.

The silence lengthened to Savannah's breaking point. She yelled up into the access opening, "What's wrong? Are you okay?"

"Yes," he yelled back. "I've found something curious. I'm going to bring it down. Ugh, it's heavy!" He walked back to the opening, placed something near the entry opening, then his foot landed on the top of the ladder.

"I want you to be careful!" said Savannah as she held tighter to the legs of the ladder.

"I'm fine. I'm fine." He came down two steps and paused to lift something from the attic floor. "Oufff." His foot searched for the next step and missed. Edward slipped off the side of the ladder and crashed into Savannah, pitching them both into a heap on the wooden floor.

"Are you hurt?" His voice was high in tension. He placed the box on the floor without pinching his fingers beneath the dusty box. When he let it down, it plunked on the floor with a bump that puffed up a little gray cloud of dust. Then he turned and pulled Savannah out from in between the legs of the ladder. "Tell me where it hurts?"

Savannah gave her head a quick shake and rubbed the back of her head. "I'm fine. It's just a little knock against the floor."

He folded her into his arms and kissed the top of her hand. He helped her up, then held her at arm's length. "Let me see your eyes. You could be concussed."

Savannah backed up a step and stared at Edward.

"No, I'm fine. I had mostly caught my balance so it was a light tap."

"Woo, that was tricky. I'm sorry. I know that stresses you out. I think you might have left finger impressions in the sides of the ladder." He took each hand and kissed her palms until the blood returned.

"Thanks," Savannah whispered. "Yes, it still freaks me out even when you're doing the climbing." She pointed to the wooden box about the size of a color printer. "What on earth is that?"

They stood over the wooden box. "I brought this down because it was stacked right on top of the last pile of boxes. I thought it might be important. Here's what it looks like upstairs." He pulled his phone out of his front pocket and flipped to the current pictures. "Look at all the file boxes. They're stacked three high and two deep, so that makes . . . thirty-six boxes."

Savannah took the phone and swiped through all the photographs. "The boxes are dated in sequence back to my Granddad's time. Okay, I see the wooden box. Yep, I agree that he thought it was important. Let's clean it up and see what's in there."

Edward carried the box back into the kitchen and placed it on the counter. Savannah took a soft dish towel from one of the small drawers and grabbed a bottle of wood polish from underneath the sink. "It looks like this is oak. I think I know what it is."

"What? What? Tell me."

"Patience, Grasshopper." She smiled. "It's not going anywhere and it might be fragile."

She sprayed the cloth lightly and cleared the dust from the entire outer box. "Look at the craftsmanship. This is beautifully miter joined. You don't see that much these days."

The front of the box had a leather handle attached with brackets. Below that was a small serial number plate. Savannah opened the lid. "Oh, for heaven's sake. This is incredible. How did Dad get hold of one of these? It's an—"

"You don't have to tell me. I know my country's history. This is an actual Enigma machine from World War II, isn't it?"

Savannah looked at Edward and nodded slowly. "Yes, and I'm sure this machine isn't for looks. Dad wouldn't have saved this without using the code generating capability. The amount of work for decoding the files has taken a huge jump in difficulty."

Chapter 9

Tuesday morning

Savannah yawned for the sixth time. "I'm so sorry," she said to her etching students. "I'm not used to getting up at four—five is not unheard of, but four, not yet. Rooney isn't keen on such an early morning run, either. Luckily, it's only for this week."

In unconscious unison, Rachel and Faith said, "We get up at five—"

"—every morning to read our papers," Faith finished.

"Mostly to make sure we get our papers." Rachel pursed her lips tightly. "We're having a lot of trouble with the deliveries. Combining the *Tampa Tribune* with the *St. Petersburg Times* is making problems."

"It's not called the *St. Petersburg Times* anymore," said Faith. "It's been the *Tampa Bay Times* for years, now."

"That's not the problem. It's this business of two

separate delivery people. It is not working right. Why don't they use a single delivery person instead of two?"

"They haven't got that figured out yet. It's complicated. Don't you think they would if they could?"

"Ladies, ladies." Savannah held up her hand. "Attention, please. I'm going to cover the steps for the artwork you need for etching your piece of glass." They were seated around the large table in the conference room. "We're going to start with one of these basic designs that I printed onto ordinary paper with the printer settings adjusted to give a dark image."

"This isn't going to work for us," said Rachel. "Faith and I have the same design. We won't be able to tell them apart."

Faith nodded. "I'm pretty sure mine will be more beautiful, but it would make it easier if they were completely different."

"Not to worry, ladies." Savannah took back Faith's artwork of a star and handed her a sheet of paper with a heart in the center. "Is that better?"

Faith looked over to Rachel. "Definitely."

"Does anyone else want a different practice design?"

No one responded.

"Great. Now, tape your artwork to the square piece of wood in front of you. Also tape this piece of stencil paper over your design." Savannah handed them out. "You need to cut out the design with your X-ACTO knives. Make sure there are no jagged edges or errors. Those will be replicated exactly on your etched sample. A smooth image is what we're trying to make. That will create the best etching."

"Miss Savannah!" Jacob walked into Webb's Studio through the front door. His voice sounded strained and he was holding Suzy high and tight in his arms. "Miss Savannah, there's something terribly wrong with the kiln."

A cold knot formed in the pit of her stomach. "What do you mean? What happened?"

Jacob opened his mouth and froze. Suzy wiggled violently in his arms and Jacob managed to let her down carefully to the floor and open a little pocket in her service vest. He pulled out an inhaler, sat down on the floor, and quickly breathed in a dose of medicine.

Faith pushed her way around Savannah. "Jacob, dear, do you need us to call your mom?"

Rachel squeezed in beside Faith. "We know her number." She pulled out a flip phone from her pocket. "It's on speed dial."

Jacob shook his head.

Savannah sat down on the floor and put a hand on Jacob's shoulder. "Are you okay?" She looked at Suzy who stood still and looked intently at Jacob's face for a few seconds. Then her tail wagged and she licked Jacob on the face.

Jacob nodded yes and replaced the inhaler back into Suzy's vest. "I'm fine, now." He took a few calming breaths and picked up Suzy. His voice sounded calm and strong. "I was upset." He looked at Rachel and then looked at Faith. "I'm okay now. There is no need to call my mother."

Savannah stood and took the twins by their arms.

"Go back to the class. He says he's fine and he's never been wrong about that."

They reluctantly returned to the conference room and sat at the worktable to finish their etching artwork.

"What did you want to tell me?" Savannah asked Jacob.

"When I stopped by Webb's Glass Shop to unload the kiln, I noticed that the fused charger plates weren't alike. Some were perfect and some were not fused completely. Something must have happened during the overnight programmed heating cycle."

"Hmmm." Savannah scratched Suzy behind her ear. "Uneven fusing wouldn't be associated with the programming. There must be something wrong with the actual heating elements. I'll go over and look after class." She placed a hand on Jacob's shoulder. "Try not to worry so much. Things do happen in our business, but it's not worth getting sick about. The world won't collapse because of a few plates." *So says the person whose reputation hinges on this high-profile delivery.*

Jacob nodded, but looked unconvinced.

"We'll go over together." She bent down, turned her back to the class, and whispered into his ear. "Then I can show you what the file identifier codes look like. If you can't load the kiln today, you might as well work on the encryption puzzle. Oh, there's one other thing. I want you to stop by with me after class to search the area behind the museum for clues. I found a hamburger wrapper in the maze the night of the exhibit reception. There might be more information for us back there."

She resumed her normal voice. "This will give you a chance to make some progress with that restoration panel. Our client has been patient, but we need to show where we are next week."

Jacob straightened his shoulders, kissed Suzy on top of her head, and headed toward his workroom. "I'll be ready."

A large panel from a local church was awaiting restoration. As a direct result of his highly publicized work on The Last Supper panels at the United Methodist Church downtown, Jacob was known as the best stained glass refurbishment expert in town.

Savannah turned back to her students and caught the twins placing their artwork on the light table ready to expose the film. "Wait!"

They looked up in all innocence.

"We're ready for this," said Rachel.

"This is the next step, isn't it?" said Faith.

"Yes, but I haven't gone over the timing of the exposure. Let me set it and we'll let it burn."

Savannah continued with the lesson and soon each student had artwork ready for sand etching. "We'll get these images etched tomorrow and gear up for a final piece on Friday. I'll see you tomorrow."

As she was cleaning up, her phone pinged. She answered, "Webb's Studio, this is Savannah."

"Good morning, this is Matthew Nicholas. I'm the Events Manager at the Vinoy Hotel. My colleague was the one who ordered the glass chargers for the banquet on Saturday."

"Hi, how can I help you?"

"We've had a last-minute increase in the number of invited guests, so I would like to also increase the number of plates. I sincerely hope it isn't too late, yes?"

"Well, it depends. How many extras would you need?"

"Another twenty-five would be the absolute minimum."

"Wow. That's a significant increase. Can I confirm that for you tomorrow? I need to check about ordering more glass and account for the extra kiln time."

"Sure, sure. If you can't manage the extras, we'll probably need to redesign the table décor to eliminate your chargers. That might be a reason to cancel the order. The contract does say that we can adjust the final quantity by plus or minus ten percent."

Savannah pinched the bridge of her nose. "I really hope that won't be necessary, Mr. Nicholas. I'll call back tomorrow as soon as I know about the availability of that color of glass." *I need to pay more attention to small print in the paperwork.*

Chapter 10

Detective Parker looked up from the opened autopsy report that had just hit his email inbox. He didn't think he would get far into it before the coroner, Sandra Gray, dropped into his office.

"Knock, knock," said Sandra as she tapped on the doorjamb to his office. "Want to discuss the details?"

He smiled and nodded to one of the guest chairs facing his desk. "I believe this is a record. You've arrived almost before the electronic report."

She moved the chair closer to the desk so that she could cross her arms and lean forward. "I'd tell you how I do that, but it would destroy the illusion."

"Speaking of magic, what was our victim's cause of death?"

"He died of suffocation."

"But there were no marks around his throat."

"Agreed." Sandra leaned back in the chair. "Nevertheless, that was the cause. Somehow, he was convinced to stop breathing."

Detective Parker shook his head. "You're not helping."

Sandra stood and walked around Detective Parker to use his computer. "First, he had a large knee sized bruising at the collarbone that we saw yesterday morning. When you scroll down here to this section, you can see that our victim had advanced interstitial lung disease. It was in his medical records. He was evidently a sufferer for many years, probably as a child. His type was an autoimmune-associated lung disease that was either caused or aggravated by cigarette smoking or living in a house of smokers and breathing their second-hand smoke."

"How bad was it?"

"His lungs were compromised and I'm sure the toxicology report will indicate that he was taking significant doses of corticosteroid medications to reduce the inflammation. The report will come in sometime next week if the lab isn't too busy. I didn't mark it as a priority. Bottom line, he was not in great health. If someone held him down and prevented him from getting a dose from his rescue inhaler, he would panic. That panic would lead to a breathing crisis which appears to have been fatal."

Detective Parker tilted his head up to look at Sandra. "Does this change your time of death estimate?"

She straightened up. "I've narrowed the window a little, but not by much. He died sometime between four and seven in the morning. Work with that timeline. I don't think I'll get a better estimate." She placed her hand over his. "Will you have time for another coffee later?"

He nodded, then smiled. "Yes, I'll be there. Have you decided where we'll have dinner?"

She walked to the door. "Not yet. Let me know if you have further questions . . . on the autopsy report, of course. Later." She left. Her light fragrance lingered for a few minutes.

He smiled again, then picked up the phone and dialed. "Officer Williams, would you mind meeting me in the Murder Room, please?" He walked across the hallway to one of the special conference rooms used to centralize the information and facilitate the discussions necessary to support a murder investigation.

Officer Williams was already in the room with a thin manila folder cradled in her arm. "What's new?"

Looking around, Parker noticed that the room was missing much of the expected information. The white board at the head of the room had a picture of the body of Dennis Lansing slumped on the green bench sculpture. A list of his effects was pinned to the strip of corkboard that ran across the top of the whiteboard. Other than that, a copy of the Webb's Glass Shop reference letter was all that was posted.

"Is this all we've managed to gather since yesterday morning?" He frowned at Officer Williams.

"Sir, I have this whole stack of information to post. I've only been here for a few minutes. I had some difficulty getting the Murder Room scheduled and reserved for our use. I have learned that sometimes there is quite a bit of competition for these rooms. It won't happen again. I've met the administrative assistant that schedules the room so I know how to get that done quicker."

"Good initiative. An organization runs on the backs of many clerks, administrators, and assistants. The quicker you learn to work with them, the more effective you'll be. Let's review what you have ready to post."

Office Williams nodded and put the folder on the conference table that ran the length of the room. "First, this is the advertising material the museum used for promotion of Dennis Lansing's exhibit." She spread out two of the tri-folded brochures and pinned both sides to the corkboard. "His artist's biography mentions that he grew up here in St. Petersburg, but now he was living in Corning, New York with his wife's parents." She tacked up a photo of Dennis, Harriet, and an older couple, along with a chocolate Lab. "Dennis worked in a converted barn behind their period Colonial house."

"That's a lead. What do you have on the wife and her family?"

Officer Williams pulled out another sheet of paper and read it aloud. "Dennis Lansing was married about six years ago to the former Harriet T. Adams. She was born in Panama City and then grew up in St. Petersburg, Florida. A preliminary background search shows nothing about her except that she has a job as an online travel agent, more as a way of getting discounts than serving customers. Her parents are in the travel business as well, but sold their agency right before the Internet killed most of the small agencies. Apparently, she has been the principal financial support of the marriage from the beginning."

"That could certainly cause tension . . . given that

Dennis was not only an artist, but an artist in poor health. We need to check out the terms of his will."

Officer Williams pulled a notebook and pen out of her pocket. "I'll see if he had one. Not likely for someone that young.

"Next, I have a picture of the museum docent who discovered the body, John Zeflin." She placed it on the whiteboard and put a magnetic pin in the center of his forehead. "We've started a background check, but he lives here only part of the year. He left for two months in France late yesterday."

"What! How did we let him leave?"

"That would be my fault. I didn't think we had any reason to hold him or even question him further than the statement he already gave us. I have the address for his Paris apartment. He lives with his sister while he's over there. I also have his cell phone number." She put up a picture of a bright red door surrounded by summer flowers facing out to a cobblestone street.

"Lucky man. Paris for two months, then St. Petersburg for two months."

Officer Williams smiled ruefully. "Yes, extraordinarily lucky. Next is the security guard Lucas Brown who was questioned extensively at the scene and he also voluntarily came by the station yesterday to provide more information. He's being extremely cooperative—almost too cooperative."

"Meaning, what?"

"He seems almost delighted with the circumstances. I mean, most citizens are horrified by the violence involved in a murder case, but Lucas is tripping over himself sharing information. For example, again, without being asked, he dropped off a set of engineering drawings for the Dali Museum. Not just the artist's renditions, which he also included, but he gave us a copy of the builder's entire package in a rolled-up bundle. I laid it over there on that separate table." She pointed to a portable table with a three-inch stack of large architectural drawings piled onto it.

Detective Parker walked over to the table and flipped through the top few pages. "This is helpful. I won't have to beg, plead, or threaten the museum director to get them." He turned to look back at Officer Williams' folder. "That reminds me. Have we received the surveillance videos from the museum?"

"I haven't seen them." She frowned and jotted down a note. "I'll give the director another call."

"Another call?"

"Yes, I called late yesterday to remind her that you had requested them. But she wasn't in. I left a stern message with her assistant."

"What else?"

She pulled another picture out of the folder and held it out. "This is Gina Wilkins, director of the Dali Museum and responsible for inviting artists to exhibit. The main reason I'm putting her up here is because she's being uncooperative. No tapes. No validation of an alibi. We have no evidence that she and Dennis were anything but professional, but she has not been helpful. It's been more than twenty-four hours. Those tapes should have been delivered by now." She placed the photo on the board and put the pin in the center of Gina's nose. "I'm betting she hasn't given Lucas permission to send them."

"Let's bring her in for questioning. Use a squad car and pick her up from the museum. That may give her a clearer understanding of our need for urgency."

"I'll take along a couple new recruits. They'll be glad to get some in-the-field experience."

"Have we heard anything from Savannah? She may have something by now."

"No, I would have expected something by now. I'll give her a call. Knowing more about Dennis's past may give us a better view of his life."

Detective Parker stood in front of the pictures. "Pretty thin. We need more." He looked at Officer Williams. "A lot more."

Chapter 11

Savannah drove her gray Mini Cooper over to Webb's Glass Shop and parked in the remaining spot behind the store adjacent to a vintage pink Cadillac. It belonged to Amanda's mother who now lived in a nursing home. Used only for a weekly hair appointment, a trip to the Publix Super Market, and church on Sundays, it was still in pristine condition. Her declining health meant that her driving days were done. The land yacht was a dinosaur of a car, but with extremely low miles and meticulously maintained, it suited Amanda perfectly.

Savannah unlocked the back door and held it open for Jacob and Suzy. They walked through the office and classroom to the front of the shop.

Amanda was standing behind the small glass display and sales counter staring at the blank screen of a cash register system. "I think it's dead this time."

"No, please, no, not now. It needs to last until January. Burkart says that I can purchase a new system in January. For a young accountant, he has old-fashioned financial advice—don't replace something that still works." Savannah looked at the dark screen. It was an old PC-based cash register system that had been causing trouble since before she'd arrived to take over the shop. She stooped down to look at the base unit tucked into the display counter. "What have you done so far?"

"It first came up with the dreaded blue screen of death, so I powered it off, waited for a count of twenty, and turned it on again. Now it seems to be stuck on a black screen."

Savannah smiled. "Right. Okay, I call that the black screen of confusion. Sometimes, that means that the monitor isn't playing nice with the computer. Cross your fingers." She turned off the power to the monitor, checked its connection to the PC, slowly counted to twenty, then switched the power back on. Savannah crossed her fingers on both hands. The monitor flickered and displayed the log-in screen for the cash register.

Clapping her hands, Amanda laughed. "Super. That's perfect. I am now an expert in the black screen of confusion." She entered the shop's username and password and the system finished its initialization routine. "I can't wait until you get this replaced. Do you really want to wait?"

"Well, I've been following Burkart's advice since I inherited Webb's and he has certainly been right in helping me to establish Webb's Studio. I think I'll go over tomorrow and discuss the risks of such a problematic cash register. He doesn't know how much trouble we've been having with it lately."

"Good idea. I'll call him for an appointment . . . say, two p.m.?"

"You really are anxious," said Savannah. "Okay, I'll be there. Anyway, Jacob and I are here to look at the kiln. Any equipment problems take priority over the PC."

Jacob spoke, looking down at the top of Suzy's head. "When I started to unload, that's when I noticed that some of the plates were strange looking."

Amanda frowned. "I haven't even looked in there in days. My stained-glass students keep me hopping. Don't get me wrong. That's a good thing. This is one of the smartest classes I've had in here. They're getting twice as much glass work done, which means that our profit in class materials is great."

"A good problem to have, but you'd better get ready. They'll be here in"—Savannah looked at her watch—"about ten minutes. Okay, Jacob, let's figure out what's wrong with this firing. We don't have much spare time. We don't want to miss our big delivery to the Vinoy Hotel this Saturday."

Savannah walked into the adjacent room followed by Jacob, who still held Suzy. This was where Savannah kept the large kiln she used for creating the glass chargers from cut squares of glass. She lifted the large kiln lid with the assistance of a pulley and counterweight system. The interior was filled to maximum capacity thanks to Jacob's clever loading skills. He had created a multi-tiered stacking method that tripled the number of chargers that could be fused each night.

The chargers on the left side of the kiln looked perfectly formed and were ready to wash and wrap for delivery. On the right side of the kiln, the chargers were untouched by the heat of the kiln and looked as perfectly flat as when they were loaded. The row in the center was the strangest sight. Each plate was partially slumped on the right-hand side and then appeared to be floating above the ceramic mold on the left.

"I see what you mean, Jacob. There's definitely something wrong."

Jacob nodded and kissed Suzy on the top of her head.

"Okay, first things first. Let's empty it out and clean everything up."

It took them almost half an hour to unload the kiln of plates, the molds, and all the spacer blocks, stack the good pieces ready for cleanup, then place the bad pieces aside.

"It's not so bad for the glass, really. These are simple mold forms and we should be able to load them into the kiln again for another firing." Savannah looked at the open kiln. "The problem has to be with the heat." She looked at the lid of the kiln and noticed that the heating coils were split into two separate channels. "Jacob, I need to test the theory that there's a problem with the heating so we don't try to fix the wrong problem."

She programmed the kiln to heat to 1500 degrees at a rate of 999 degrees per hour. That number signaled the kiln to heat at its maximum rate. By the time they had washed the perfectly fused chargers and wrapped them in corrugated paper ready for packing, she looked at the kiln's internal temperature gauge. It registered 600 degrees.

Using the pulley system, Savannah lifted the lid and her fears were confirmed. The left-side coils in the lid were cherry red-hot. The right-side coils were still black, meaning that they were cold. The right-side coils were defective. Lowering the lid, she frowned, then powered off the kiln.

"What's wrong?" Amanda stood in the doorway. "Have you figured it out?"

"Yep. Bad news. One of the heating coils in the lid is broken. I've got to get it fixed right now or we'll miss our delivery."

"What are you going to do?"

"I'm going to call the manufacturer. With any luck they'll have replacement coils in stock."

Her cell phone rang. The caller ID screen displayed a picture of Joy Williams.

"Hi, Joy!"

"Savannah, Detective Parker just asked me if you had made any progress with your dad's files. He sounded a little irritated. It is Tuesday, you know."

"Joy, I'm so sorry I haven't reported back to you. It's been a particularly frenzied morning. My large kiln has broken and I'm in danger of missing an important delivery."

"I know this sounds harsh, but that's not our problem." Joy paused a moment. "Oh, wait a minute. This is my problem. If you can't sort through your dad's files, then I will have to do it. Please, please, please tell me you've found something."

Savannah laughed. "That was a quick about-face. You must really despise paperwork."

"You've caught me out. Paperwork is my biggest weakness." Joy also chuckled. "Seriously, what's the status?"

"Some progress. I have been able to find files that

look like they relate to the student records you need, but there's a huge problem."

"What's that?"

"The identifying information about each file is encrypted." The phone went silent. "Joy? Are you still there?"

"Um, sure. I don't know what you mean by that. How are the files encrypted?"

"My dad was a US government cryptographer during the Cold War. He not only decoded Russian messages but also created codes for our government to use. He was a talented master at his job."

"And so . . ."

"Well, it carried over into his personal life. He used to teach me codes and leave messages all over the place for me to find. It was part of his paranoia."

"So how long will this take?"

"Sorry, Joy, this situation is not easy to predict. I'm going to have Jacob help me. He's got a real talent for intuitive code breaking, but there's another serious complication."

"Which I don't want to know about, do I?"

"No. You. Don't." Savannah shook her head slowly. "But I'm going to tell you anyway. While Edward and I were looking at some older files in my attic, he came across a small wooden box."

"And . . ."

"It turns out that wooden box contains an authentic German Enigma machine from World War II. In short—a rotary electromechanical enciphering device, which kinda resembles a typewriter. There were a lot of variants of the Enigma machine, but the most common version, and the version my dad has, is the standard Army and Luftwaffe machine.

Its main components are a keyboard, a lampboard, a plugboard, and a set of three rotors."

Joy let the silence grow between them. She finally said, "So . . ."

"I got that from the Internet."

"It sounds like it. And so . . ."

"I believe the codes that my dad used for all these files were generated by this machine. This complicates the identification of the correct files by a factor of a million. I don't know how long this will take. It took the British months and months to crack the first codes and they had a large staff. Sorry to be so bleak, but that's how I see things right now."

"Okay, I understand," Joy said in a low voice. "I sincerely wish you were here to tell Detective Parker instead of me."

As soon as Savannah ended the call, the front door bell jangled. "Hi, luv. I'll bet you would like some iced tea."

Savannah smiled. "Does it come with a side of scone?"

"All righty, then!"

"I hate it when you try to use slang. It doesn't sound right in a British accent."

"I'll try to restrain myself."

"Good." She punched him in the arm. "Jacob, you might as well go back to the studio. This is going to be a long day. Do you want a scone?"

Jacob shook his head. "No, thank you. I will wait in the back office. Suzy needs water." He turned and left.

Savannah shrugged her shoulders, then she and Edward followed Jacob back to the tiny office in the rear of the shop. She explained to Edward, "I've got to call the kiln manufacturer immediately. I have a broken coil in the lid."

Edward frowned, then set the small serving tray down on one of the pullout leaves in the oak roll-top desk.

She searched the Internet for the name of the manufacturer who, it turned out, was located near Lakeland, Florida, a mere sixty miles away. She dialed the number.

Her call was answered. "Jen-Ken Kilns, this is Laura Cumby. How can I help you?"

"Hi, I'm Savannah Webb, owner of Webb's Glass Shop in St. Petersburg, Florida. Do you have replacement coils? I have a broken coil and naturally, I have an important order due on Saturday. Can you help?"

Laura chuckled. "That's the only time coils ever break, sweetie. They seem to know when you need them the most. Can you give me the model number of your kiln? I'll see if we have some on hand."

"Just a second." Savannah walked through the shop and leaned over the control panel and read the numbers off to Laura.

"That's definitely one of ours and pretty new as well. It should be covered by warranty. Hang on." In short order, Laura came back on the line. "You're in luck, sweetie. We have the coils in stock."

Savannah looked at her watch. "How long are you open? I need to get this fixed tonight."

"I can tell you're in a pickle, sweetie. Have you replaced coils before?"

"Nope. Never."

"Replacing a coil isn't rocket science, but there are a million ways of doing it wrong. I can't take a break now, but I can stay after hours until you get here so I can show you how. I can teach you everything you need to know after five."

"I'll be there right on the dot. Thanks," said Savannah. She ended the call, grabbed the cool glass of iced tea, and chugged more than half of it down. "I've got to get to Lakeland to pick up a replacement coil. They're staying open to give me instructions on how to do it. Meanwhile, Jacob and I can check out the maze for clues."

"You need to go right now?" asked Edward. "I thought we could look over some of the paperwork you want me to wrangle."

Savannah pointed to a four-inch stack of neatly piled papers. "All the paperwork is right there. Untouched for at least a month."

"A month? Savannah, that's terrible. You could be in deep trouble by now. What on earth is your issue with—" He looked at her huge eyes and the down-turned corners of her lips. "Sorry, I know you asked for my help. I can see why. I'll dig in and see what needs to happen today. Okay, pet?"

She stood and lightly held his face in her hands to give him a long and hearty kiss. "That's something I truly admire about you. You just dive in and help." Savannah grabbed her backpack and keys to the Mini. "Tell Amanda that I've gone and she can—what am I saying? She can do everything that needs doing. It is absolutely vital to get those coils replaced tonight. I won't be back until late. Good luck with the paperwork. Come on, Jacob. Let's go down to the Dali and do some skulking." She kissed Edward again and left.

* * *

Jacob stood in front of the low gate to the Dali Museum garden. He held Suzy in his arms and peered slowly from the bottom to the top of the plastic barrier. "People who have dirty hands have been touching this gate." He pointed to faint smudges on the top of the half-height gate. "Someone has been cleaning it with Windex so frequently that the paint is becoming thin, but it is still dirty."

"Hi, miss." Lucas was behind them with his thumbs in his waistband. He smiled so wide, Savannah thought it must make his cheeks ache. "Have you lost something? No, wait. You were at the exhibit reception on Sunday night. Miss Webb, right?"

"Yes, I'm Savannah Webb. You have a good memory. I was a guest on Sunday. I haven't lost anything, but I am searching the area. I'm assisting Detective Parker with the investigation." She looked at Jacob. "This is Jacob Underwood. He's good at noticing details that the rest of us ordinary humans would overlook. So, I thought he should look at the site of the incident and also take a look at the garden area."

"That's a great idea. I'll unlock this gate for you and give you a tour. Anything to help Officer Williams." He paused. "Oh, and Detective Parker as well, but Officer Williams is very nice." Lucas looked at Suzy, still cuddled in Jacob's arms, big brown eyes calm yet alert. "Is that a service dog?"

"Yes," said Jacob. "It says so on her pack. Her name is Suzy. She warns me if I'm going to have an anxiety attack. I need her with me at all times." He adjusted her position in his arms and stared directly at Lucas.

Lucas dropped his gaze.

"Very well. We support all service animals." He pulled a large key ring from his pocket and used a small key to unlock the gate. He opened it and let them through, then locked the gate again. "Normal access to the garden is through the café inside the museum."

"Yes, I've been here many times." Savannah wished he would go away, but that was probably not going to happen. Officer Williams was right to feel a little creeped out by this guy. Savannah was also concerned that the looming presence might bother Jacob, but he didn't seem to take any notice. "Jacob, see what you can see. I'll wait over there at the café tables."

Still holding Suzy, Jacob nodded and stood silent for some long minutes. He scanned the garden methodically from the extreme left to the extreme right side of the outdoor space. It was as if time didn't exist and he was recording a 3-D scan of the landscape.

Lucas looked at Jacob and at the receding back of Savannah. He followed Savannah and after she sat in one of the white wire chairs, he leaned over to whisper, "What's he doing?"

She got a whiff of his cologne and wondered why on earth he felt the need to douse himself in the stuff. She put her finger in front of her lips. "I don't know exactly," she whispered, "but I have learned to give him all the time and quiet he needs. I'm going to sit here while he works." She pulled an e-reader from her small black backpack.

Lucas stood looking from Savannah to Jacob.

"He's going to be quite a long time," said Savannah.

Jacob walked over to the left side of the garden and scanned the hedge and the large, stacked, volcanic boulders that bordered that side of the garden. It appeared that he was boring holes into the boulders with his gaze.

Lucas watched Jacob minutely examine the grass in front of the first boulder for a long five minutes.

The growing heat and lack of drama finally got to Lucas. "Check in with me before you go." He appeared on the verge of melting into a puddle. "Please?"

Savannah turned to look at Lucas. "Just one thing. Could you find a bowl of water for Suzy? She will be thirsty when Jacob finishes."

"Yes, ma'am." Lucas ducked into the café and returned in a few minutes with a dish and three bottles of water. He silently placed two bottles on the table, poured half of the last bottle into the bowl, and set the bottle next to Savannah. He gave her a broad smile.

Savannah nodded her thanks and returned to her e-reader. As a Florida native, she knew that as long as she stayed under the shade of the umbrella, a cool breeze would find her.

Lucas stood for a few moments, looking at her, then looking at Jacob, then returning to the relief of the air-conditioned museum.

Savannah envied his comfort, but she knew that the only way to escape him was to stay in the heat.

It worked. Not the kindest approach to avoidance, but certainly effective.

It was nearly an hour later when Jacob returned. He was still carrying a panting Suzy who wiggled to be let down and slurped up the water in the dish on the ground beside Savannah. When she finished that, Jacob took the remaining half bottle and poured it into the dish.

After Suzy drank a little more, Jacob took his bottle of water and downed most of it. "It's hot," he said.

Savannah smiled. "Understatement of the year." She stowed her e-reader and looked at Jacob. "Did you find anything?"

"Yes. Lots of information. Some of it could help our investigation."

"Do you want to tell me about what you've found in the cool of the café or do you want to go back to Webb's Glass Shop?"

"Let's go back to Webb's Studio."

"Good plan, but I don't think we'll be able to get out the locked gate. Let's walk through the café and out the front as quickly as we can. I don't want to talk to Lucas."

"Me neither. He is very curious."

They got into her Mini and while waiting for the air conditioner to overcome the stifling heat, she texted Edward and Amanda that she was on her way back to Webb's Studio with Jacob.

After settling down in their preferred seats, Savannah spoke. "Jacob has spent the last hour scouring the garden area of the Dali Museum. Tell us what you found, please."

Jacob scratched the top of Suzy's head and looked at the center of the conference table. "I found traces of many kinds. The museum visitors stand to take pictures of the giant mustache sculpture and the melting green bench installation, and finally, they tie their plastic wristbands to one of the strands of the wishing tree. Then they leave."

He paused for a minute, then pulled Suzy into his lap. "Then I found traces of people who are regularly sleeping in the garden. Most of these overnight visitors are using the part of the garden called the maze. It's easy to get into the maze from the street side and it's far away from the cameras."

Edward frowned. "What do you mean by *regularly*?"

"I mean, every night there are at least two or three overnight sleepers in the garden. Most of them have little areas back in the maze or near one of the big boulders. One of them regularly uses the green bench. That appears to be the favorite, of course. It's off the ground and the most comfortable. Whoever uses it puts a backpack in the same spot every night and that has made an indention in the gravel in the shape of the bottom of a pack."

Amanda jumped in. "But that couldn't be happening without someone knowing that they're staying there all the time."

Savannah snapped her fingers. "That's why Lucas was so nervous about us searching the area. He must be letting them stay."

"I'll bet that the museum's director doesn't know anything about it." Edward steepled his fingers in front of him. "I would think that Lucas would be vulnerable to a bit of blackmail should anyone find out about it."

"Maybe that's what has happened," said Amanda. "Maybe Dennis found out about the overnight visitors and threatened Lucas that he was about to tell the director."

"There might be some social media evidence about that." Savannah looked at Amanda. "Could you look into her online presence and get what information you can out of that."

"Of course. Even the homeless have social media access through basic pay-as-you-go phones. They also have access to public PCs at the Mirror Lake Library. That's about a twenty-minute walk from here."

"Thanks." Savannah rose from her seat. "I've got to get over to Lakeland to see the kiln manufacturer for coil parts. Fingers crossed that I can fix it."

In a little more than an hour, Savannah pulled into a packed dirt parking lot of a low concrete building that looked like it had sprouted additions like a cactus. When she entered the doorway, she was convinced that no planning went into determining what each room should be used for. Mostly everything was scattered randomly in powder-covered piles throughout the large warehouse.

A dark-haired woman in a droopy T-shirt over dusty ripped jeans waved a hand from the far end of the open space. "Hi, sweetie. Are you Savannah Webb?" she called as she walked over to the entrance door.

"Yes, ma'am. I called earlier about replacing a heating coil for one of your kilns."

"I've been expecting you." The woman walked over to a steel rack and grabbed a small Amazon box that had seen quite a bit of reuse. "Here are the coils you need. You said you've never replaced one?"

"No. Do you have some instructions?"

"No written instructions. It's easier to show you the tricks rather than having you try to make sense out of the installation directions." She took Savannah back to another part of the warehouse and proceeded to give her a wealth of tricks and tips for quickly removing and replacing a defective coil.

Savannah had scribbled everything into a small notebook. She stowed it in her backpack. "I'm very grateful for all this help. You've gone way beyond what anyone could expect for customer support."

"Small businesses have to support each other. It's the only way we'll survive. Here's my private cell number if you run into trouble. Good luck, sweetie."

Chapter 12

While Savannah and Jacob were at the Dali, Detective Parker had called Officer Williams and said he needed to talk to her right away. As soon as she hung up the phone, a familiar worry spun through her thoughts. *Am I being called in to be reprimanded?* No matter how much success she achieved, that was always her first thought when being summoned.

As soon as she appeared at his door, he asked, "Did you pick up Director Wilkins?"

"Yes, I have her waiting in the interview room. She's steaming."

"Very good. Let's let her steam for just a few more minutes. She may get careless." He waved Joy into his office.

After she sat in the guest chair in front of his desk, he handed her a copy of the final autopsy report. "I would like your opinion on the state of this case, based on the information that the coroner documented. You've read the report, right?"

"Yes, sir. What is your concern?"

"Concern?"

"Well, if there was nothing to interpret from the file, you wouldn't be asking for an interpretation."

"Good logic," Parker said, then grinned. "Perceptive even, but how can this information be interpreted differently?"

She paused and pressed her lips together.

He lifted his hands up to show the palms. "I won't hold this first assessment against you. Let's treat this as a learning experience in exploring every available avenue in a suspicious death investigation."

"Okay. I was thinking as I read the report that perhaps this might not be a murder."

Detective Parker smiled and steepled his hands on the desk. "Go on."

"If his breathing condition was out of control . . . say, he forgot to take his evening medication because of the excitement of the event. Then what if he had too much to drink and leaning over the bench compressed his chest too much?"

"How would that present in the report?"

"It could be worked to fit the results. There would be bruising around the midsection from the arm or the back of the bench . . . if that's how he got into breathing difficulties."

"How would that account for the body being moved to the bench sculpture?"

"Oh, that's a complication," she said slowly and pulled at a braid in her hair. "Then, possibly, he had his breathing episode somewhere else close by and someone who didn't want to call for help placed the body on the bench." She finished with a rising voice of satisfaction.

Detective Parked nodded. "Good thinking. I've been running a similar scenario in my head. It could very well have been an accidental death. What would you recommend as the next steps? Tell me what you would do if you were investigating on your own?"

Officer Williams's eyes widened and she swallowed before speaking. "That's a good question, sir."

"Excellent stalling technique, but there's something I need to get straight with you." He tilted his head slightly and looked her straight in the eye. "Unless you blatantly screw up, you are safe in this job. The last officer I had to work with was so bad, you look like Sherlock Holmes himself in comparison. I'm impressed with your work so you can relax and start polishing your investigating skills."

Officer Williams leaned back in the guest chair. "Thank you, sir. I'll try to do that."

"I'm not asking for *try*. I'm asking for you *to start*."

"Sir?"

"This is not a question of you trying to do your job. This is a situation where you absolutely perform this job without reservations. There is no 'try.'" He finger-quoted the word *try*.

"Yes, sir. I understand." Officer Joy smiled with confidence.

"Great, now let's hear your first idea about this case."

"Well, the first thought would be to find the location of the actual death. We should widen our search of the museum grounds."

"Good." He paused. "As far as it goes."

"We should expand our search even farther to include short distances from the Dali Museum. Maybe even ask the public for information about Dennis's whereabouts in those few hours between the end of his event and the time his body was discovered."

"Excellent. Those are right in line with what I was considering." He stood. "Make them happen, Officer Williams, but do your interview first. Well done. We'll review the video afterwards."

She left his office with a pleased look on her face and walked straight into the small plain interview room.

Gina Wilkins sat on the industrial gray steel chair with her arms folded and her legs crossed. Her right foot bounced a staccato. The look on her face reminded Joy of an angry cat ready to strike out at the next thing that moved. Gina held a crumpled tissue in her right hand.

"Thank you for coming down to talk with us, Ms. Wilkins." Joy sat in the chair across the sturdy stainless table. "Would you care for some coffee from our break room? It would only take a minute."

"Absolutely not. I'm particular about my coffee. I don't understand why I'm here. I told that detective everything I knew yesterday morning. This is extremely inconvenient. I have a museum to run."

"We're wondering why the tapes that Detective Parker requested by the end of the day yesterday haven't been delivered."

"Humph! Is that all? You could have called." She dabbed her eye with the tissue. "We're having some trouble with the computer. They tell me that there's something wrong with the application that makes CVs, or DCDs, or whatever it is."

"Ms. Wilkins, you could have called us about that. Do you know when the problem will be fixed?"

"We've called our service. They're arriving today. For all I know it could be fixed by now."

"Good idea. Make that call."

Gina unfolded and dived into her large purse sitting on the floor. She rumbled around in its depths and came up empty. "Where's my phone? I had it just—"

"We can use mine. Joy handed over her cell and watched calmly as Gina glared at her.

She dialed. "Lucas. What's the status of the server?" Gina listened and her lips thinned into a slim streak of scarlet. "That's not good enough. I'm here at the police station simply because we can't get those tapes delivered. Find another service, immediately." She handed the phone back to Joy.

"That sounds bad."

"You heard that we're doing everything we can. Can I go now?"

"I would like to know more about Dennis. How did he seem during the installation? Was he nervous or anxious about anything in particular?"

"If you don't let me leave now, I'm calling my lawyer."

"Very well. I'm disappointed that we can't discuss his behavior during the time you were with him, but yes, you may go."

In her stilettos, Gina made tracks that could be heard around the entire floor.

* * *

Back at her desk, Joy picked up the phone and
called the public relations office. They gave her the
number of the form she needed to fill out in order
to make a public appeal on both radio and television news programs. She wasn't surprised that the
bulk of the announcement text needed to be written by herself.

She pulled up the correct form and filled out
information blanks and began to type into the
announcement block.

> *The St. Petersburg Police Department is requesting
> the assistance of the community in determining the
> movements of Dennis Lansing, featured artist at the
> Dali Museum, from the hours of midnight to seven
> a.m. on Monday morning of this week.*
>
> *Anyone with information pertaining to his where-
> abouts or who can identify the male in the attached
> photograph is asked to contact the St. Petersburg Police
> Department at 727-555-4321 or the St. Petersburg
> Police Department's Crime Tip Line at 727-555-1234.
> Information can be left anonymously.*

Officer Williams filled out the remaining blanks
in the form, printed it out for her records, and
pressed the SEND button at the bottom of the form.
She waited for the confirmation e-mail.

Nothing.

She refreshed her inbox.

Nothing.

Another refresh of her inbox.

Nothing.

Joy sighed and let her head fall to her chest. *I'll have to start all over again.*

Her e-mail pinged the notification receipt from the public relations office. She smiled, then decided her next best action would be to meet the search team at the Dali Museum while the light was still good. She was in Detective Parker's good graces right now and was determined to shine.

Chapter 13

Savannah felt groggy after the long drive from Lakeland and across the Howard Franklin Bridge after the peak Tampa commuter rush. She parked behind Webb's Glass Shop. Instead of going into the shop, she walked over to Queen's Head Pub.

As soon as she perched on one of the barstools, Nicole Barowski, longtime manager of the pub, smiled hello, and started up the espresso machine. "Hi, Savannah. Give me a minute here." With a few deft movements with the commercial grade espresso machine behind the bar, she placed a large glass of iced café mocha in front of Savannah.

"How are earth did you know that's what I needed?"

"That's why I'm the best bartender in the Grand Central District. Long drive. Lots of traffic. Still a lot to do at the shop. You need a tall cool glass of ambition. Chocolate is almost always the answer to any question."

Savannah took a long sip and could feel her energy respond to the taste. "Thanks, you're right on target. That's perfect."

"Did you get the part you needed?" Edward came out from the kitchen.

"Even better, they taught me how to repair the kiln and I even bought a spare coil." She took another long sip of her mocha coffee. "I love having spares. I need to set aside a bit of space and money to stockpile critical parts before we risk a delivery again."

"Can you still make the deadline for the Vinoy Hotel order?" He grabbed a glass and pulled the tap handle for a lager.

"If I can get this new coil installed and I can borrow the use of a kiln, we'll be good. However, if anything goes wrong . . ." Savannah shook her head from side to side. "Remind me to stop taking last-minute commissions."

Edward looked down at her through the black eyelashes that framed his green eyes. He held that look until he finished drawing his beer. "Honestly, luv, if you think I'm going to step one toe in your approach to making money at Webb's? No way, pilgrim."

Savannah laughed. "Don't say that! You are not a cowboy, no matter how worn your western boots are."

He looked sheepish. "Well spotted."

"That kiln isn't going to fix itself. It's a good thing I built an extra day into the delivery schedule. Now that I've got an extra twenty-five charger plates to deliver, I'm going to have to call Frank Lattimer and arrange to use his industrial kiln as an emergency backup."

Nicole wrinkled up her nose. "He owns that glass shop downtown, doesn't he?"

Savannah drained the last of her coffee "Yes. He's a sleaze bag and wants me out of business, but at this point, he's a sleaze bag with a large kiln. All I have to do is flatter him. Works every single time." She batted her eyelashes like a Disney princess. Using a princess wave, she left by the front door and entered through the street side door of Webb's Glass Shop. Waving another queenly hand to Amanda, she immediately went into the supply room and started work.

After an hour, more than a few scraped knuckles, and a half dozen curses, Savannah stood and stretched her aching back. The coil was replaced. She punched the test firing numbers into the control panel and went out into the display room. Everything was shut down and in overnight mode. Amanda knew well enough not to interrupt her during a delicate job.

Savannah trudged back to the office and plopped down in the oak office chair. She sat for a few minutes until the ache in her back dissolved, then glanced over at the ancient file cabinet. She imagined that it looked at her with irritated sulkiness. That old file cabinet mocked her.

Maybe there's an easy pattern I can figure out for the encrypted file names. She opened the drawers and gazed down at the labels. They were handwritten, placed in two rows, and the first row was consistently just eight characters. She grabbed a pen and pad, and copied down about twenty labels and returned to the desk.

She started by writing down all the things she could represent in eight characters. She finally determined that the most sensible would be a form of a calendar date. She started with the most common format: MMDDYYYY.

She started plugging in numbers in substitution for the letters, but she couldn't crack a single letter. Her feeling was that the codes were based on the results of using the Enigma machine. She tried again to match the letters with individual Arabic digits, but again, no luck.

When the office phone rang, she started and lifted her head from the desk. *How long have I been asleep?* Her watch said eight p.m. Clearing her dry throat, she said, "Webb's Glass Shop. This is Savannah."

"Are you ever going home? Snowy and I miss you." She could hear the kitten mewling in the background. Snowy must have heard her voice.

"Hi. I miss you both, too."

"Did you get the kiln fixed?"

"I think so. I need to check that both coils are heating properly. I'm walking back into the supply room now to check."

She looked at the control panel. It was normal. She used her left hand to lift the kiln lid a few inches and peeked in to find that both lid coils were a beautiful cherry-red. "Fantastic! The coils are fixed. Jacob can load this up tomorrow and with Frank's help, we're right on track to deliver to the Vinoy Hotel on time."

"That's brilliant," said Edward. "In celebration,

I'll come over and cook tonight. I know you're tired. But did you remember to get dog food? I think you fed Rooney the last bit this morning."

Savannah palmed her forehead, then grabbed her keys. *So much for the glamorous life of the small business owner.*

Chapter 14

Savannah arrived home with a bag of Rooney's favorite dry food and met Edward with a huge kiss on the front porch.

He held one hand behind his back and smiled. "I'm liking this Tuesday night routine. It is a slow night at Queen's Head Pub. Tonight, however, I've brought another guest." He pulled his hand out and little Snowy meowed her welcome. Her little white paws reached out for Savannah and began kneading dough in anticipation of Savannah's cuddles.

"What?" Savannah grabbed Snowy and tucked her into the curve of her elbow. "This is supposed to be our night . . . just the two of us. Really, Edward."

He smiled wide and took the bag of dog food from her other hand. "This is bonding. We need to bond as an entire family. I've brought Snowy with me for tonight. I thought it was time to see if our fur babies get along."

"Now? Why didn't you warn me? I haven't prepared the house for a kitten."

"Relax. Your place is a palace compared to my condo. You, Rooney, and Snowy can make friends while I cook dinner."

"But—"

"I'll go and get her stuff from the car."

"Car? You don't have a car," said Savannah. "Please tell me you haven't sold the antique Indian. I adore that motorcycle."

"Absolutely not. I borrowed Nicole's car so that I could bring all the bits and pieces. She's working tonight, so I left her the Indian and the spare helmet. We'll switch back again tomorrow."

"You know that Rooney has never seen a kitten. We don't go anywhere that has even the sniff of a cat. There are a few on our block, but they all stay indoors one hundred percent of the time, so he might not even know what they smell like."

"Snowy is a completely indoors cat. It's the only responsible way to make sure they stay healthy."

Savannah raised her eyebrows. "You really should have let me know first." She put her free hand on her hip. "This could be a complete disaster. I'm not really a cat person." She shook her head.

Why am I so afraid of every step that strengthens our relationship? Maybe it's because Dad died so quickly. Maybe I don't want to lose Edward. Actually, I don't want to lose Edward.

Savannah shook off her fear. "Okay, now that she's here, let's at least put Rooney in his crate. He's comfortable in there and that way Snowy can explore without being stalked by a curious giant." She took the dog food back and kissed Snowy on the top of the head before she handed her over to Edward.

Edward nodded and went to the car and came back with Snowy in her transport carrier stacked with a litter box, a bag of litter, and a small bag of food and toys. "This should do it," he said as he placed his burdens down on the living room floor. "At least you don't have carpet. That's good."

"No, I don't have carpet, just century-old heart-of-pine wooden original flooring. To be fair, Rooney is more dangerous to the floor than a kitten." She stood in the doorway between the kitchen and the living room with her hands on her hips. "Go ahead, let her go. Rooney is in his crate here in the kitchen."

"First things first." Edward picked up the litter box and the bag of litter. "Do you think the guest bedroom will do?"

Savannah sighed. "No, that bedroom is too small and it somehow feels a little icky. How about putting it in the bathroom at the end of the hall? There's plenty of room in there. Let me get an old rug to put underneath to catch debris." She ducked down the hall, opened a linen closet, and came back with a faded rag rug that looked worn to shreds. She put down the rug in the bathroom and they set up the litter box. "This is perfect."

Edward opened the remaining carrier bag and pulled out two aluminum bowls. "Should I put these by Rooney's feeding dishes?"

Savannah frowned. "Although I've never had a kitten before, I do know that dogs can get territorial about their food. Let's do the safe thing and feed them at opposite ends of the kitchen." She watched as he put down a small floral bone china saucer, then filled the matching tea cup with water from a bottle of spring water.

"Really? She gets bottled water?"

He looked up with confusion in his eyes. "Of course. She's only a kitten. I don't want to risk her getting kidney problems. That's the biggest concern with cats."

Savannah spread her hands wide and backed away from the kitten's feeding station. "Where on earth do you keep her when you're at work?"

"I have a neighbor who takes her in while I'm gone."

"Fine." Savannah nodded her head.

"It's hello time for Snowy," he cooed to the travel box that was beginning to mew in that pitiable scratchy kitten voice. Edward unlatched the crate and scooped the tiny, pure-white puffball that howled mournfully, crawled up his arm, and tried to curl up into his ear.

"See, isn't that adorable?" He extracted her tiny sharp claws from the top of his shirt and took her over to the center of the kitchen. "I think we should let her discover Rooney on her own."

"I'm not sure about this," Savannah cautioned.

They both stood back and watched. Rooney had curled himself up in his crate, but his head lifted when Snowy was placed on the floor. He barked a high-pitched greeting and stood up in his crate with his head lowered as close to the floor as possible.

Snowy launched into full Halloween cat pose, hissed like a vampire, then shot straight up off the floor and ran up Edward's pant leg, tiny claws embedding themselves in his flesh as she ran up to his shoulder.

"Ouch, ouch, ouch!" He tried to remove her from his neck, but she squalled and held on even tighter.

Rooney barked happily again as if he was opening birthday presents. He bounced up and down and nearly tipped over his sleeping crate.

"Rooney! Stay! Stay, Rooney." Savannah put her hand out in front of him so he could see her command. She looked from Rooney to Snowy and back again. "Yep, it's bonding night all right."

Savannah took the trembling kitten from Edward's shoulder and held her at arm's length. The tiny kitten tried to turn inside out to escape, but Savannah kept a firm hold. "Get the carryall. I'll put her back in it."

"But we need to start getting them acquainted." Edward's voice rose in timbre.

"Is that what you think?" Savannah took Snowy over to the carryall and placed the kitten inside without a protest from Snowy. "She seems to be quite happy in her crate, as well. This needs to be taken in careful steps."

"Right, but you don't appear to want to take any steps at all! I don't think you're ready for the next steps."

"I'm ready, but I need to have this planned out a lot better."

Edward grabbed the reusable grocery bag and picked up the food and water, spilling a little of both as he dumped their contents in the sink. He pressed his lips together in furious silence as he packed up the litter box, food, and dishes. "I am appalled at the amount of planning you require and I am also disappointed in the amount of planning you refuse to do in order for us to live together as . . . as a committed couple."

Then he snatched up Snowy's carryall and started toward the door.

"I'm trying to make changes. Just not at the pace that you want."

"Your pace right now makes it look like you don't care."

"That's not true!" Savannah could feel her throat tighten. "I am trying."

Edward wedged the door open with his foot. "Try harder." Then he walked down the porch steps, put Snowy and the carryall in the backseat, and drove away.

Savannah stood in the doorway. "Yes," she whispered. "I will. I'll try harder."

Chapter 15

Wednesday morning

Savannah started the third day of class right by arriving ahead of time at 6:30 a.m. She was not feeling overly chipper, but the espresso coffee machine in the studio kitchen had provided her morning addiction with a large strong cappuccino. By the time her four students were in the building, she had sorted out the handout materials and brewed each student the caffeine drink of their choice.

Worst case, if the glass business goes bust, I'll make my living as a barista.

Their project for the day was to use a chemical method for etching a wineglass with holiday images or monograms. She supplied everything needed, including the wineglasses, all laid out on the large conference table. That way everyone had materials that were properly suited for etching.

As usual, the most difficult part was preparing the artwork image for etching. In this case, the designs were simple, but still it involved cutting the artwork with an X-ACTO knife. Knowing her students, she had placed the first aid kit at the head of the conference room table in anticipation of cuts. She also checked the rinse time for washing out the chemical if someone flicked a drop in an eye, or in his or her mouth, or . . . anyway, she was prepared as much as possible.

At the end of the class, each student stood before their finished wineglasses. She had lined them up for a photo. Amanda would post it on social media for her.

Savannah was amazed that it only took three bandages and one dash to the rinsing sink to accomplish the lesson. Each student had four personalized wineglasses. Well, except for Arthur. He had broken one of his glasses against the faucet in the rinsing sink and he dropped another one after applying the etching solution. He'd said it was not a problem, of course, since he and his wife never had company.

"Can we try this again?" Rachel asked. She was admiring her set of four wineglasses all etched with a monogram of the letter *R*.

"We want to do this to our martini glasses," said Faith, who had etched her wineglasses with the letter *F*.

"I'm not the least bit surprised." Savannah chuckled and started clearing away the scraps of paper, disposable brushes, and newspapers that had protected the conference room table. "You can schedule a time with me after this workshop is over. I'd be happy to help you."

After wiping the studio conference table spotless, Savannah walked over to Jacob's workroom and knocked lightly on the doorjamb. "Jacob, I have a challenge for you that I think you will enjoy."

He looked up from a large stained glass panel nailed to his worktable and his eyes focused level with her collarbone.

Reminding herself that he would only respond to direct questions, Savannah rephrased. "Would you like to work on a difficult cypher?"

Jacob's eyes lit up. He looked her in the eye. "Yes."

"Good. First the good news. In the conference room, I left a pad of paper with a list of twenty coded labels from the file cabinet in my dad's office. That should be a large enough sample for you to try a decryption solution."

He nodded slowly and stood waiting for more information.

"Now for the not-so-good news. I also placed a machine in the conference room that was probably used to generate the cipher. It's called—"

"It is an Enigma machine. I saw it when I arrived. I know the history about them."

"You do?"

"Yes. Mr. Webb told me about them when I first started to work for him. He liked using it for fun. He brought it into Webb's Glass Shop several times for me to learn how to use it, too. He knew how much I liked ciphers."

"Oh, that's wonderful. I was wondering how we were going to figure out how to use it. The information I've found on the Internet looks helpful, but this is fantastic: that you already know how to use it." She lifted her eyebrows. "Did Mr. Webb say anything about why he had the machine?"

Jacob was silent for a long minute before he spoke. "Not exactly. He didn't say how he got it. He mentioned that he was using it to keep some important records private. He didn't tell me why."

"That's too bad. So, can you guess what I want you to do then?"

Jacob grinned with his eyes bright. "Yes. You want me to solve the label identifiers so we can find Dennis Lansing's file among all the other files in the old cabinet. Correct?"

Savannah smiled. "Yes, that's correct."

"There's a problem." Jacob frowned. "Mr. Webb taught me how to create coded messages on the machine. He didn't teach me how to decode them."

"But you can figure that out, can't you?" Savannah held her breath. *Maybe this was a dead end after all. No information. No consulting fee.*

Jacob stared at his worktable for more long moments. "I need to know the year that Dennis Lansing was in the apprentice program."

"Of course. Let's see, it was probably 2004, but could have been as late as 2005. I knew him from dad's apprentice program while I was still in grade school. Does that help?"

Jacob grinned like the Cheshire cat. "I'll let you know if it works." He headed to the conference room, sat down at the conference room table, then put Suzy down in the chair beside him. He carefully tore off the top sheet of paper with the labels listed and placed the single sheet to his left.

The Enigma machine consisted of an entry keyboard with the keys arranged like a QWERTY keyboard like a typewriter. Above that was a lampboard of lights with a letter on each lamp in the exact same QWERTY configuration. Where a manual typewriter would have the keys and a ribbon, the Enigma machine had rotary dials. It was designed so that when the operator pressed the letter *T* on the keyboard it created an electrical signal that began the journey through the Enigma machine wiring that ended with a lamp flashing on the lampboard.

Jacob bent over the machine and pressed a key and wrote the illuminated key onto the paper next to the notation of the key he pressed. Then he pressed another key and did the same, picking up and putting down the pencil for each key.

Savannah stood for a second watching him tackle each key one by one. She took a deep breath. *This might take years, but he has the patience of a saint. I hope he gets lucky.* "I'll check back as soon as I make a call."

He nodded and continued pressing the keys.

Savannah went to her office and looked up the number for Frank, owner of Lattimer's Glass Shop downtown. He was her nearest competition and they had had some nasty confrontations over the past several months. Their last few meetings were at least civil. She dialed.

"Hi Frank, it's Savannah."

"Hey, Vanna!"

She clenched her teeth and ignored the fact that she had told him a thousand times not to call her that. It was the pet name her mother called her before she'd died when Savannah was ten. No one else was to call her that without her permission.

"Frank, I need your help."

"You do? Do you want to sell Webb's? I'm always ready to make you a fair offer. I knew you would come around. Running a business is no business for a pretty little girl like you. When do you want to go back to Seattle?"

"Frank, stop. I don't need that kind of help. I need to rent some kiln time over the next few days. I have a big order to deliver on Saturday and my kiln broke yesterday."

"Oh, I heard about that order. I bid on it—cheaper, in fact—but they wanted you for some reason."

"I have already repaired the heating coil, but I lost almost an entire kiln load when it failed. I need to make up the firing time to complete the order. Will you rent me an overnight firing on your large kiln?"

"Well, that puts me in an awkward position. I have classes that keep my kilns running pretty much non-stop. I'm not a charity, you know."

Savannah propped her head on her hand then controlled the impulse to hang up. "Please, Frank. Do it in the spirit of your friendship with my dad. He would have advised you to help out a local business. Wouldn't he?"

Frank was silent. Not his natural state.

"Frank, are you there?"

"Yeah, yeah. Just thinking. I can let you have one overnight run, but only one."

"Thanks. This means a lot to me. I appreciate it very much. When can Jacob and I come over to load the kiln? How much will you charge? My profit margin is pretty small, you know."

"Yeah, I know, I know. Let me check the class schedule for a minute." He rustled some papers and called out, "Hey, are we teaching a fusing class right now?" There was an answer in the distance that Savannah couldn't understand. "You're in luck. We're between classes. You and Jacob can come over anytime this afternoon. Does he know how to program the kiln?"

"No, but he's the best at loading a kiln I've ever seen. I'll be with him to program the kiln. I'm so glad we have the exact same model."

"Well, Vanna. My offer still stands. I want to buy Webb's."

Savannah hung up and put her forehead on the surface of the desk. *Business does indeed make for strange bedfellows.*

Chapter 16

Wednesday noon

Savannah pulled into an open parking spot in front of a new restaurant she was excited to try. She was finally meeting Officer Joy Williams for their long-delayed lunch. There had been a recent surge of new eateries in the area. A flurry of activity by a group of local business owners and volunteers had renamed the formerly blighted historical area the Edge District. The organization began following an ambitious revitalization and preservation plan, and achieved Florida Main Street and National Main Street accreditation.

Hawker's Asian Street Fare was right next door to the St. Petersburg Police Department headquarters building so it was easy for Joy to pop out to meet her.

Joy rushed out onto the sidewalk and arrived a little breathless. "Sorry, I almost didn't make it. I had to go down the back stairs so I wouldn't get waylaid at the last second."

Savannah laughed. "Surely, they know you need to have a lunch break now and then?"

"It's not them. It's me." Joy lifted an eyebrow. "I'm afraid I'll miss something so they're used to seeing me all the time." They were seated at the non-smoking patio outdoors with a view of the police station. Before they could start a conversation, their server introduced himself and asked for their order. They each asked for water and then agreed on a shared family style order of satay chicken, basil fried rice, wok fired green beans, coconut curry shrimp, and roast duck steamed buns.

Savannah sipped her water then spoke first. "I'm glad you could get away for a little bit. You must feel pressured to perform over and above expectations. Let me assure you that by merely showing up each day, you far outstrip your predecessor."

"You knew Officer Boulli? I didn't know that."

"I sure did. He was working with Detective Parker when we collaborated on our first case. Although, I think *interfered* would be Boulli's description of my involvement. It was during the investigation of the murder of my dad and his assistant. Officer Boulli is essentially the reason I got involved. He was a miserable waste of space. I think Detective Parker has forgiven me by now . . . well, he mostly tolerates me and my friends. I do appreciate the occasional consulting jobs almost as much as my bank account does."

Joy removed the paper wrapper on her straw and put it in her water. She smoothed and folded the wrapper until it was shaped like an accordion stack and continued to fiddle with it. "I'm counting on you to save me a massive amount of work by finding those records for Dennis Lansing's high school years. Things are pretty much stalled until we get some more information about his past. I think the motive for Dennis's murder is tied to his past here in St. Pete."

Savannah paused until their server had delivered the green beans and the satay chicken.

"I believe that, too." Savannah smiled. "Anyway, Jacob is working on breaking the Enigma machine code, but it may take some time. The good news is that you can't possibly sort through the files until the labels make sense and once Jacob decodes the labels, I'll know which file it is."

"How long did you say?" asked Joy around a mouthful of satay chicken.

"It shouldn't be more than a couple days. Dad had given Jacob some lessons on the machine, so we've got a huge familiarization advantage. Plus, Jacob is brilliant with code."

"That's good because the museum director is giving us fits. She has delayed handing over the video camera records and been difficult to contact by phone. She is, in general, being a pain in the neck. I'm frustrated."

"Is she a suspect?"

"I'm not sure at this point if we have any suspects at all other than the wife. We always suspect the spouse. Oh, also the mother, but only because she told us she doesn't have an alibi. But what normal person plans for an alibi? I don't have one for early Monday morning, do you?"

"Yes, I do," Savannah mumbled through a huge

bite of one of the roast duck steamed buns. She covered her full mouth. "Edward stayed over."

"Detective Parker is still categorizing it as a suspicious death, mostly because of the location. We're now trying to find Lansing's phone. He didn't have it on him. There is evidence that he was moved after he died so I'm working on trying to find the location where he was killed." Joy shook her head from side to side. "I'm hoping I can find it. That would be a feather in my cap."

Savannah frowned. "I'm not sure where I would start, but you know that Jacob has an amazing eye for detail, right? Well, last night I took him over to the Dali Museum to scan the whole garden area. I've known him to find a pattern or clue that hundreds have overlooked."

"I wish I had thought of that. I mean, I'm glad you did because that kind of evidence disappears quickly after the site is released back to the public.

"The idea was triggered by a discovery I made during the exhibit reception. I literally stumbled and tripped on a hamburger wrapper in the maze. I didn't think two cents about it at the time, of course, so I picked up the wrapper and threw it away. That's why I wanted Jacob to look."

"Did the security manager help you? His name is Lucas Brown. He's been helpful despite the reluctance of the director. In fact, he's beginning to creep me out. He calls every few hours to see if we need his help. It seems fishy to me, but Detective Parker doesn't appear concerned."

"I understand what you mean. He hovered over me and Jacob the entire time we were there." Savannah took a knife and split the last duck bun in two and transferred half of it to her plate. "Anyway, in the outside space, Jacob found evidence of night visitors that sleep in the maze every night. Whoever they are, someone might have seen something. I think it's worth following up, don't you?

"Yes. That's great. I'll put it up on the board in the Murder Room."

The rest of their order arrived and Savannah dived into the basil fried rice.

They ate in silence for a few minutes. "How are things going at Webb's?" asked Joy.

Savannah scowled and put her chopsticks down. "My kiln broke yesterday so even though I fixed it last night, I'm renting time with Frank Lattimer. He owns the only glass shop near me and is gloating in his beer that I need his help. Jacob and I will be downtown to load up his largest kiln and program it for an overnight firing."

"And with the new place, Webb's Studio? You were concerned that it might stretch you too much financially and take too long to earn its keep."

"Well, it's not setting any earnings records, but I think I'm holding on. As soon as the Canadian and British visitors make their appearance in a few weeks, the number of students that want private studio space will increase and that will make all the difference. St. Petersburg is still a city subject to the fluctuation of the tourist industry. I'm going to see my accountant this afternoon so we can make things work better on such a weird pattern of feast and famine."

Joy sipped her iced tea. "I also want to know more about this gang that Dennis was associated with when he was a teen. What happened?"

"I never heard anything, but his mom might know. She seems to think something from the past raised its ugly head and caused Dennis's death."

"What do you think?"

Savannah shrugged her shoulders. "It sounds right to me. Everyone has past secrets."

After splitting the bill and getting a firm promise from Joy to meet for lunch at least once a month, Savannah drove west down Central Avenue for her meeting with Kevin Burkart. His firm was thriving among the many new businesses in the area. The growth was entirely due to word-of-mouth recommendation—the best way to grow. She pulled into the newly bricked parking lot to the side of the 1924 two-story Craftsman style house that he bought for his financial consulting business. It had recently been refreshed with a new coat of smoky gray paint accented by white trim. The preparation process of pressure washing and scraping off the old paint had, as in any old building, revealed a few extensive repair issues.

Savannah climbed the front stairs and entered through the large double doors directly into a formal living room that featured a large brick fireplace. To the right side of the fireplace, a pair of glass French doors led to Kevin Burkart's office. The doors were not completely shut so they did very little to dampen the heated conversation he was having with an upset woman. Savannah sat in the settee by the fireplace and concentrated on trying to make out what Kevin and his client were talking about.

"I come of age next month. My trust fund will be totally under my control after that. Totally mine."

This was followed by Kevin coming to the French doors and clicking them completely closed. He saw Savannah and mouthed *Sorry*, then returned to his client.

After about fifteen minutes, Kevin, tanned and frowning, opened the doors to his office and guided out a petite young woman who appeared upset. Her cheeks were flushed and she alternated holding a tissue to the corner of each eye to keep from spoiling her eye makeup.

Kevin looked up. "Savannah, I knew you would be right on time. Let me introduce you to Harriet Lansing. You two may know each other. Her late husband attended St. Petersburg High School at about the same time you were a student there."

Savannah stepped forward. "Yes, we spoke very briefly at the exhibit opening on Sunday."

Harriet looked puzzled but said nothing.

Savannah continued. "I knew Dennis in high school so he invited me to the exhibit's opening reception. You two were taken away by the museum director just as we reached the front of the reception line. I'm so sorry. May I offer my sincere condolences? This must be a difficult time." Savannah extended her hand.

Harriet transferred the tissue to her left hand and shook Savannah's hand using a slack grip. "Dennis was a fine artist, but not at all good with accounting. We were considering moving here permanently, but now I'm not so sure what I'm going to do. The city is a great place and I still love it." The tissue went to her eyes again. "I am grateful for one thing." She looked directly at Burkart. "He won't be able to spend me into the poor house, now. That bit of nonsense is done forever."

Kevin stepped back a half step and a shocked look swept his face, then disappeared as he recovered. "You have my number, so if you decide to use my services, make an appointment with my administrator, Stephanie, and I'll be happy to help you manage your affairs."

Harriet looked over to Savannah. "I come of age next month," she explained. "My trust fund will be totally under my control after that. Totally mine." She dabbed her eyes once again and then left through the front door, leaving Kevin and Savannah staring at her rapidly disappearing back.

Through the large living room windows, they watched her drive down Central Avenue toward downtown in a car that looked like it had been on its last legs for a long time.

Kevin spread his hands wide. "I'm sorry about that. Our meeting went way over the scheduled time. I hope this doesn't wreck your day. I know you have a lot on your plate right now."

"She seemed upset for an initial consultation." Savannah walked with Kevin into his corner office. It was full of windows and had obviously been a sun porch or more likely a summer sleeping room before the days of air conditioning. "She certainly shared a large chunk of personal information with me. Why would she do that?'

"I think she's obsessive about controlling everything around her. If I agree to take her on, she's going to be a high-maintenance client."

"How on earth did she find you? I didn't think you were accepting new clients."

"I'm not, but she was incredibly persuasive. She said unless she could find someone she liked to manage her trust fund, she wouldn't be moving here at all. I don't like emotional blackmail."

"But after Dennis's death, I wonder why she is still considering St. Petersburg at all." Savannah sat in one of the guest chairs in front of Kevin's desk. "I'm consulting with Detective Parker again so I'm going to have to tell him about this chance meeting."

Kevin's eyes grew large and he cocked his head to one side. "But you overheard all that by accident. Do you have to report it?"

"Yes, I'm afraid so."

"Did I say anything that would jeopardize the reputation of my business? I was shocked into revealing more than I should after she blurted out such private information to a total stranger."

Savannah smiled. "No, you were trying to stop her. She didn't even seem to recognize my name or consider who I was."

"Well, that's a relief. My business is my reputation and my reputation is how I got the businesses that I have in my portfolio." Kevin huffed, then pulled up Webb's Glass Shop on his computer.

"I'm not relieved at all," said Savannah. "She blabbed the perfect motive for wanting Dennis out of the picture. Acute negative cash flow is usually the best way to describe a starving artist's financial status."

Chapter 17

Detective Parker walked out into the open seating area of the Homicide Department and stood in front of Officer Williams's desk. "Have you got a minute?"

"Yes, sir." Officer Williams grabbed a pen and her notepad and stood up from her seat.

"Let's talk about the Lansing case for a few minutes." He turned and walked into the conference room that held the information about Dennis's investigation.

Detective Parker pointed to a picture of a young woman that was enlarged from a driver's license. The image had pixilated and was blurry. Underneath was written "Harriet Lansing, Wife" with a magic marker. "I got a call from Savannah Webb. She said that she ran into Dennis's wife as she was arriving for an appointment with her accountant. Savannah overheard that Mrs. Lansing is about to come into control of a large trust fund and she was apparently relieved that Dennis wouldn't be able to waste it to support his artistic endeavors."

Officer Williams frowned. "That doesn't seem appropriate for a grieving widow."

"No, it doesn't. She and Dennis were staying in a private home on a side street off Beach Drive. When we spoke to her about Dennis's death, she seemed stunned into silence. She hasn't called me back to even ask about the progress of our investigation. That's not the normal reaction. What do we have on her?"

"Not much." Officer Williams flipped a few pages backwards in her notebook. "They have been living with her parents in Corning, New York. They got married immediately after she graduated with a master's degree in marketing. They apparently lived in an old RV while he traveled the country visiting craft shows, art exhibitions, and building up a reputation. It was where he taught himself the skills he needed for producing those large etched vases and mixed media glass pieces. Apparently, she oversaw publicity, marketing, and the promotion for his events."

"Interview her and let's see if there's any chance that she doesn't have an alibi for the time of Dennis's death. Find out why she didn't wonder where he was. Also, make double sure we didn't get a missing person's report."

"Yes, sir." Joy was making notes. "I'll follow up with Savannah as well."

"Good. On the other hand, take her with you. She'll understand the art festival component of their traveling. I'm beginning to think that we're looking at something more than merely shock at her husband's death."

Joy left the Murder Room and dialed Savannah's cell. "Detective Parker wants me to conduct a follow-up interview with Harriet Lansing based on the information you provided. Are you available to go along?"

There was a long pause. "Let me see how I can squeeze that in. I'm on my way to Frank Lattimer's shop to load up his kiln. His place is right downtown. Can you wait until I'm on my way back from there?"

"Sure, I'll meet you where she's staying. How about 4:30 p.m.?"

"That works out great. Let me have the address of her hotel."

"She's not staying at a hotel," said Officer Williams. "She and Dennis were staying with an arts patron. I didn't know, but that's how some of the higher profile artists manage to travel without spending tons of money at fancy hotels. Anyway, here's the address." She read off the number and street.

"That's in an exclusive part of town. It looks like Dennis really was a rising star." Savannah's voice sounded heavy. "That makes it even more sad."

Chapter 18

Savannah drove the heavily loaded Mini downtown. The back was stacked with sheets of glass, charger plate molds, kiln spacer blocks, kiln paper, and release spray. Although she was grateful for the one-time use of Frank's kiln, she didn't want to borrow any materials from him. She knew that he cut corners when teaching his classes by stocking second- and even third-rate supplies. She wasn't willing to risk scrapping a single charger plate due to substandard materials.

Jacob was sitting in the backseat with Suzy buckled into the seat behind Savannah. Driving smoothly turned out to be impossible. Even the painted stripes on the road seemed to give her cargo of glass a nerve-wracking jiggle. She was also doing everything she could to provide a calming environment for Jacob. She'd let him stack all the supplies, not only to make him feel a part of the process, but honestly, no one could pack more into a limited space than Jacob. His natural skill with spatial challenges was astounding.

"How is the decoding coming along? Have you had a chance to make some progress?"

Jacob reached over to give Suzy a scratch behind the ears. Savannah knew the answer was troubling him, but she also knew to give him all the time he needed to answer an uncomfortable question. Perversely, it was the fastest way to get an answer. It did require patience, though. Not her strong suit now.

She drove another cautious couple minutes and avoided a large double pothole on Beach Drive. That maneuver prompted a toot of the horn from the driver behind her. She made an apology wave into the rearview mirror and shrugged her shoulders.

Jacob cleared his throat. "I haven't started the decoding process, yet. There is still much I need to learn about how the machine functions. There are three rotary cogs that give the machine a unique code, so I first tried to use the combination that the machine was set on just in case Mr. Webb left the rotary cogs in place after he created the cipher."

"And . . ."

"That wasn't the setting. I was certain he wouldn't leave the machine in the coded configuration, but it was an easy setting to eliminate. I am now familiar with how the machine works and I am working on an approach for eliminating most of the combinations."

"If you need help with the code elimination algorithms, make sure you let me know. The rest of us can set up trials with the actual machine while you are generating more combinations."

Jacob scratched Suzy's ears again followed by another long silence. "Thanks, that's a good idea."

She continued to avoid bumps in the road and turned in a block off Beach Drive. She parked in front of Frank Lattimer's Glass Shop. The mid-century, flat-topped single story building looked like it was in sore need of some attention. The paint was faded and peeling and one of the downspouts wasn't even connected to the gutter. It was an eyesore.

Savannah thought it was possible that Frank could be having some financial difficulties. It would be typical of him to hide the real state of his business under the guise of continually offering to buy Webb's Glass Shop. *No wonder he was annoyed with me when he lost the banquet order from the Vinoy Hotel.*

She carefully backed the Mini into one of the five parking spots out front. She recognized Lattimer's red BMW as the only car there. Each parking spot had a large sign in front threatening towing if anyone other than a student used one of the parking spaces.

Where on earth do his students park? His classes are large.

"Let me get the door propped open first," said Savannah

She knocked on the front door and Frank immediately opened it and stood in the doorway blocking it completely. His comb-over was still plastered with who knows what kind of hair glue and he was wearing lifts in his shoes to augment his height. It didn't help much.

"Hi, Frank."

"Hey, Vanna. You're right on time." He stood

back and held the door while he propped it open with a small red brick. "I don't think you've been in my shop, though not from lack of invitations. Let me show you where the kiln is." He led her through an open classroom into a small room that had three large kilns crammed side by side with barely a hand-breadth between them. Frank opened the lid on the rightmost kiln. The other two kilns were already programmed and firing. "You can use this one, but only tonight."

"Thanks, I really appreciate this." She looked at the compact kiln room and then out to the class-room. "Can I use one of the student worktables to stage the load?"

"Sure, sure." He checked his watch. "Just don't take too long. I have an appointment with the mayor."

"No problem. We won't be long. Your kiln is the same as mine."

She went back to the Mini and told Jacob he could use one of the worktables if he needed it, but he shook his head in the negative. He stationed Suzy inside by the front door with a firm "stay" com-mand and proceeded to unload the car straight into the kiln.

Savannah watched him load the kiln, using every available millimeter, and then looked at Frank whose faced showed his utter amazement. "Yeah, I don't know how he does it," she said. "Even after I've seen what he does, I can't do it."

When the last piece was loaded, Savannah pro-grammed the kiln and started the fusing cycle. Jacob walked over to Suzy, picked her up, and kissed the top of her head. He looked straight at Frank. "Thank you for letting us use your kiln."

Savannah smiled. *Jacob at his customer-relations best.*

She dropped Jacob and Suzy off at home and made her way back to the historical Old Northeast neighborhood, an exclusive section of town, to interview Harriet with Officer Williams. After enduring a cloying welcome by the owner, accepting a glass of iced tea, and getting settled at a poolside table under an umbrella, the owner left to summon Harriet.

Savannah turned to Joy. "Why am I here?"

"I think you know her. She grew up here and graduated from St. Petersburg High School."

"I didn't recognize her when I met her at the reception or even when I bumped into her at my financial advisor's office. But even back then, I wasn't exactly in the cool group."

Joy leaned over close and whispered, "I need to find out why she didn't file a missing person report."

"Why are you here?" Harriet stood in front of them with her arms folded over her chest and a scowl aging her face a decade. She was fully primped and wearing white capri slacks with a watercolor printed gauzy top and bright red wedge heels. "I'm busy. My realtor is arriving shortly and he has a series of appointments that were difficult to set up. I'm not missing them."

Joy stood and extended a hand to Harriet. "I'm Officer Williams. We met on Monday, and you may know Savannah Webb. She was a classmate of yours while you attended St. Petersburg High School. I have a few questions relating to the death of your husband."

Savannah also stood. "Hi, Harriet. I spoke to you earlier at Kevin Burkart's office. I also ran into you at your husband's opening reception. Nice to see you again."

Harriet shook hands with them both, then pursed her lips and looked at her watch. "I can give you exactly seven minutes and then I'm leaving. I'm buying a condo as an investment."

Savannah raised her eyebrows at Harriet's abruptness.

"I would appreciate your full cooperation, Mrs. Lansing," said Joy. "This is a murder investigation and you are a key resource for information about your husband. Although this may take a little more than seven minutes, I think you can agree that the seriousness of this matter deserves your full attention." Joy waved her hand at a chair.

Harriet hesitated, then plopped down after noisily pulling the chair a bit away from the table. She deliberately checked the display on her cell phone, then placed it on the table, screen side up.

Joy and Savannah sat back down and Joy pulled out her notebook. "I need to follow up on some details about the morning of Dennis's death."

Harriet huffed. "I already told everything I know to you and that Detective Parker of yours on Monday. Don't you share your information? This is wasting my time."

"I'm sorry you feel that way, but it's part of our

investigation process. I would really appreciate it if we could cover the main details again."

Harriet glanced at her phone screen, then nodded yes.

"First, can you tell me where you were during the hours of four and seven a.m. on this past Monday?"

"I was asleep right here in our bedroom. I felt exhausted after that tedious exhibit opening and could feel a headache coming. There were so many people to talk with in order to keep Dennis front and center as a 'fresh new talent.'" She fingered air quotes with a sad smile. "He was a special darling with the event manager. He had that effect on most of his sponsors. I was irritated with the way she fawned all over him. Anyway, I gave her assistant the excuse that I had a migraine and then left Dennis at the museum. I walked up Beach Drive and let myself in."

"The museum is quite a distance from here. Were you feeling well enough to walk?" said Savannah.

"Walking usually fends off my migraines, which it did in this case. I arrived after about thirty minutes and didn't go out after that."

Savannah continued questioning. "What time did you start to walk home?"

"Oh, it must have been sometime after eleven-thirty. As I said, the last person I spoke to was the museum director's assistant to thank her for the reception. It was particularly well organized."

"Did you meet anyone on your walk?"

"Not anyone I knew. It was quiet, but even for a Sunday night, there were enough people out and about to make the walk safe. I think there was a soccer game letting out. There were a lot of noisy people along that stretch close to the museum."

"When did you notice that Dennis hadn't returned?"

"I didn't notice at all. I had taken a strong sleeping pill after my walk. I didn't wake up until you and your Detective Parker arrived to tell me about finding Dennis's body on the green bench sculpture. I was still woozy from the after effects when I talked to him."

"Did Dennis have a will?" asked Officer Williams.

"Him? Planning for a future? Don't make me laugh." Harriet looked at her small watch again. "He lived only for his 'art.'" She finger quoted again with the same sour look. "He was literally spending me out of my income allowance. I have credit card bills that are all at their limits. He was obsessed with making a big splash and it's not cheap nor is it easy. I spent a lot of time and effort making sure he was accepted into the best fairs and festivals. He used all of his money as well." Harriet's phone beeped. "Excuse me, but that's my realtor. I've got to go." She stood quickly and stepped away but returned to look down at them both. "Do you know when they're going to release Dennis's body? I want to dump him in the bay on Saturday."

Chapter 19

Savannah struggled through the fourth day of the workshop. Everyone, including the Rosenberg twins, had managed to create artwork that would be used in Friday's final class. The capstone project was to create etched pendants with small designs sandblasted in the glass. All of them had learned techniques that would be incorporated into the pendants.

It again caught the students by surprise that the real skill in etching was not the actual sand etching. The real skill was paying attention to the quality and precision of the artwork. It was a difficult lesson not made easier with Edith Maloney constantly reminding everyone of the extreme urgency of her next appointment.

Savannah simply couldn't understand the logic behind scheduling two appointments so close together. Edith was stressed to distraction during the workshop. It was a problem that could have easily been avoided. On the other hand, if you were constantly on the go, maybe you didn't have to face your real problems.

Is that what I'm doing? Avoiding facing commitment to Edward? Probably. He deserves more attention from me. Just because my last boyfriend was an absolute disaster, Edward shouldn't suffer for it.

After they left, Savannah walked over to her office and signed into her e-mail server to start the administrative part of her day. She filed, replied, archived, and deleted her routine e-mails. Then she opened a newsletter from the Dali Museum.

It was an announcement that the Dali Museum would be sponsoring a candlelight memorial ceremony on Friday evening to celebrate the life of glass artist Dennis Lansing. She felt a small knot in her chest grow into sadness. It had been a short life and she had been only a tiny part of his time on earth. Had he known from the first that they were wrong for each other? Could his rejection be the root cause of her commitment issues?

She pulled a tissue from the box on her desk and blew her nose. She wadded it up, then threw the tissue in the wastebasket and read the rest of the announcement. Participants were to wear white clothing and candles would be supplied by the sponsors of the memorial. Savannah could hear Gina's voice in the parking information, location of the museum, and the time of the ceremony.

She would be going. She pulled another tissue from the box, folded it into a small square, and stuffed it into her pocket. *I didn't expect to be so sad.*

Savannah shut down her computer, then walked into the conference room. There was Jacob still fiddling with the Enigma machine and trying new rotary combinations. She was about to say hello when he put his pencil down, grabbed Suzy, stood up, and hopped a little jig.

"Jacob! What is it?"

He froze in midhop. A rusty flush spread from his throat over his cheeks and he didn't seem to know where to look.

"Jacob, I didn't mean to startle you, but have you found the key machine setting?"

A broad smile lit his face. "Yes!"

"How?" Savannah looked at the conference room table, which was covered with sheets of paper with coded numbers. "There must be a hundred sheets of paper here. How many combinations did you try?"

"Using the three rotary dials, there were an impossible number of combinations that could have been the solution to the cipher. But one of my assumptions was that the eight-digit labels included the year and underneath that would have been a last name."

Savannah sat down at one of the chairs. "You mean either 2004 or 2005"

"Yes, that means that there had to be a common solution of 200 in the answers. So, I was looking for a setting that would produce not only the 200, but also Lansing. That reduced the number of trials. The machine is now set up, so let's type *Lansing* into the machine and that will give you the code for the name on the label."

Jacob sat down at the Enigma machine and firmly pressed the typewriter keys to spell out *LANSING*. He wrote the name on a piece of paper and each

coded letter directly below each letter in the name,
then gently tore the sheet from the pad and handed
it to Savannah. "That's the label to look for."

L A N S I N G
G C H R V Z T

"Fantastic work!" Savannah clapped her hands
and started to hug Jacob. She quickly dropped her
hands onto the surface of the table. "You are awesome. I'm curious. What is the setting for the three
rotary dials?"

Jacob pointed to the digits he used for the dials.
He had written 7 1 9 = G A I.

"Seven one nine equals G A I? It's a simple substitution."

Jacob spoke quickly. "Yes, I should have guessed
that earlier. He used your birthday. July 19th."

"But my birthday would be six or even eight
digits."

"Not if you used only the month and the day.
Seven one nine for July 19 and then he used the
numbers to generate the letters. So, the rotaries
were set to G, A, and I."

"Not the kind of obvious guess that would have
led me to solve the cipher. I'll get Amanda to check
the file cabinet."

She dialed Webb's Glass Shop and told Amanda
to search for the label that matched the code and
said she would hang on the line.

After a long five minutes, Amanda came back on
the line. "I found it! It was down in the third
drawer." Amanda sneezed right into the handset.
"Oh, excuse me. Those files are dusty."

"Can you bring it over? I think we need a quick meeting so we can look through the file and determine what our next steps should be. Don't you dare peek inside. I want us all to examine it together. Oh, could you also call Edward?"

"What?"

"Never mind. I'll do that."

"Is something wrong between you two?"

"We're fine. Just a few little . . . don't worry. I'll text him. See you in a bit."

Savannah ended the call, then punched in a text to Edward. Jacob has solved code and Amanda has the file. Meet at the studio ASAP?

In an instant, he replied, Yes.

Savannah frowned. Edward was usually chatty with his texts. *Rats! He's still annoyed. He has a right to be annoyed with me. I need to fix that.* She looked up at Jacob. "I'm going to make us all some coffee and get you a root beer. The others will be here in a few minutes."

When she returned to the conference room, Jacob had tidied all the papers into one neat stack and had a blank sheet of paper next to the Enigma machine. Setting the cups in everyone's usual place, Savannah felt excited about what they might find in the file.

Amanda bustled through the door followed by Edward, who carried a file that was at least an inch thick. He plopped the file in the center of the conference room table, which caused a puff of dust to rise.

"Oh yuk, Edward," said Amanda. "What a dusty mess. Now I'm going to—" She sneezed so loud that Suzy whimpered.

Jacob quickly scooped her into his lap.

"Sorry," said Edward and he sat in his usual seat. He smiled at Jacob. "Well done, Jacob." He offered a high five and Jacob complied with a small grin.

Savannah looked at Edward and mouthed *sorry* before she sat down. He returned her look with a small smile, but didn't say anything.

"I'll get this cleaned off before we torment Amanda further. Jacob, you can move the machine into your workroom. That will clear things off for us to look at the file and I need that space for my class tomorrow." He moved everything while Savannah took the file over to the rinsing sink, wiped the front and back of the file with a slightly damp paper towel, then ran the towel along all the exposed edges. When she placed it back on the table, she said, "I'm going to glance at each paper and then pass it around. Hopefully, this is full of good information."

She opened the file and held up the first sheet. It was coded. "Jacob, this one is yours. I'll bet it's a summary of the rest of the file, but you'll have to translate it for us."

Next were several stapled bundles of applications for jobs—again with the applicant's name and address encoded. "It looks like Dennis applied for quite a few jobs." She passed them to Amanda. Then there were various employment records that documented the terminations from companies whose names had been blacked out. The next set of discipline reports was from various teachers at St. Petersburg High School followed by at least twenty photocopies of newspaper clippings relating to gang violence and purse-snatching incidents.

There was a letter from the social services manager, who handled all the referrals. It described an action plan that was agreed to by the manager, John Webb, and the applicant's name in code, which by now Savannah recognized.

The last thing in the file was a copy of an arrest record with all the names redacted in bold black marks. The charge was petty larceny and underage drinking. She passed that one over to Amanda, who passed it to Jacob, who passed it to Edward.

"This is what probably got him enrolled in the program," said Edward. "It looks like he was struggling to keep a leg in both camps—the apprentice program and the gang as well."

Amanda raised her hand. "Before we get too far along, can you explain how the apprentice program worked?"

"Sure," said Savannah. "In a nutshell, the students were matched to a job in the community that had art connections. After they were hired, their school classes were rescheduled for the morning, and then they would work all afternoon. It was pretty challenging for the students because they had to keep their grades up."

"Did they get paid?" said Jacob.

"Yes, it was important to Dad that artists were paid for their work. It appears that the gang should be a key point in our investigation, but I'm going to need to get that information from Officer Williams."

Amanda pulled one of the employment reports

over to her place at the table. "There might be some hints in these employment reports. I could do some researching on the Internet for companies that participated."

"Oh, thanks. That reminds me. Officer Williams and I interviewed Dennis's wife Harriet. Could you also make a trawl through the social media sites to see what her situation is? I'd like to look over your shoulder if it wouldn't bother you. Harriet doesn't seem all that disturbed by the loss of her husband. During her interview, she made a bad-mannered remark about wanting Dennis's body quickly so she could dump him in the bay. I don't understand their relationship."

Amanda motioned for Jacob to give her the pad of paper in front of him. He looked down and carefully tore out a sheet from the back of the pad and scooted it over to her. She took a pen out of her huge patchwork handbag and made some notes. "If I make duplicate copies of these sheets, I can take them with me."

"Brilliant, go ahead. Even better, use our artwork scanner to make extra copies," said Savannah. "Edward, do you mind meeting with Officer Williams about the city's gang history? She knows that I work with all of you, but if she objects, I'll do it."

"Happy to do that. I'll call her right now and set up a time. Can you text me her number?" Savannah pulled out her cell and texted him.

Edward nodded when his phone pinged the message. He pulled his phone out of his pocket and left the room to call Officer Williams.

Savannah cleared her throat. "Another thing we

haven't investigated yet is how Dennis's past might be the motive for his murder."

Edward returned, "Appointment made."

Savannah nodded. "We found the name of the social worker that coordinated the apprentice program with Dad. His name is James Armstrong. I think we need to talk to him and see what isn't in the reports."

"He could also still have current contact with Lansing," said Edward. "I know I still send Christmas cards to my sixth form tutor." He looked around the table and saw confusion. "Oh, right. Here in the States, that would be about the same as twelfth grade."

"That's good. Let's try to speak to him today. In fact, hang on, let me give him a call." Savannah opened the folder and flipped through a few pages. "Let me get that number." She punched it into her cell and put it on speaker. "Mr. James Armstrong?"

"Yes, this is he."

"Hello Mr. Armstrong, my name is Savannah Webb. I'm John Webb's daughter and I'm working with the police department to investigate the death of Dennis Lansing."

"Yes, I saw that on the news this week. In fact, I'm disappointed that my health won't permit me to attend the candlelight ceremony at the Dali Museum tonight. His death is such a shame. Dennis overcame so many challenges."

"Is it possible to talk to you about the apprentice program and anything about Dennis's past? I would be grateful."

"I don't see why not. I'm pretty much housebound now and mostly spend the day reading and bird watching. My wife died two years ago, so a little company would be welcome."

"That's very accommodating. I really appreciation your cooperation," said Savannah. "What about this afternoon before the ceremony?"

"No problem. One moment." There was a bit of a pause while he coughed. "Don't you need my address?"

Savannah palmed her forehead. "Sorry, of course I do."

Mr. Armstrong rattled off an address in the Gulfport area and Savannah copied it down. "I've got that. I'll see you then. Just so you know, I'm bringing our current apprentice."

"It will be a pleasure to see you both." She heard the start of another coughing fit before he hung up.

"Okay, that's settled." Savannah looked around the table. Amanda was looking up and away at the corner of the room. Jacob was looking down at the surface of the table. "Fine, but thinking about the timing, Jacob and I need to get the next kiln load ready before I have time to talk to Mr. Armstrong. I'm sorry, Jacob, you'll have to go with me. I'm not sure if I'll have time between everything. It will be simpler for me if you ride along."

Jacob paused for a long moment. "I'm good with that. I can use more customer interaction practice."

Savannah nodded her head and smiled. Jacob was growing into this job.

Amanda leaned over to Savannah. "What's up with you two? Did you have a fight? What gives?"

"Not a fight really. We just have a different view of how fast things should progress. Later," said Savannah, clipping the word short.

Edward returned. "I'm all set up with Officer Williams for lunch at Ferg's Sports Bar. I'll need the folder."

Savannah handed the folder over to Edward.

"Jacob, we'll have to go to Frank Lattimer's shop right after this and pick up the fused plates. He'll be antsy until I'm out of his hair . . . well, if he had hair."

"So, I can load them?"

She nodded. "You can load them in the Mini. Are you okay to do that?"

Jacob turned to look at her and smiled. "I'm good."

Everyone stood to go. Savannah grabbed Edward's arm and whispered, "Stay a second."

He turned to her with a calm but wary look.

She reached for both his hands and pulled them up to her lips, kissed them both, and placed them around her back. "I'm sorry. I'm sorry. I'm sorry. I have been behaving like a petulant brat and you've been behaving like a perfect gentleman."

He smiled at her and folded her into a warm hug. "I'm trying to take into account just how much change you've endured over the past year. There are bound to be rough patches. I need to be a patient man. You're worth waiting for."

He kissed her like he would wait forever and a day.

Chapter 20

Thursday noon

Edward parked his motorcycle in front of Ferg's Sports Bar right across the street from the St. Petersburg Police Department's dated headquarters. Ferg's was one of the first eateries that had opened in the district. The owner had quickly staked out his location when the whispers of a baseball stadium began floating around town. His gamble had been successful and he enjoyed the patronage of many loyal customers during the off-season months.

Edward pulled off his helmet, fastened it to the Indian, and pulled the file folder from the left side leather bag. He spotted Officer Williams at one of the rustic wooden tables near the sidewalk. She had a large glass of iced tea in front of her and another one setting across the table.

"Thanks." Edward sat and drank deeply from the glass. "How did you know I liked this?"

"Savannah, of course. She thinks it's funny."

"Iced tea in Florida is bliss. Have you ordered?"

"Not yet, although they already have me down for my regular burger." She glanced up at the server who had magically appeared at her elbow.

"Your usual, Officer Williams?"

Joy smiled and nodded.

"What will you have, sir?"

Edward smirked. "I'll have the same."

Officer Williams frowned. "Hey. You don't know what it is. That's dangerous."

"Since moving to St. Petersburg, I've come to appreciate the fact that without fail the typical fare here is tasty, served with a smile, and the portions are generous."

"Well, I hope you're pleased with an old-fashioned medium rare hamburger with fries and coleslaw. That's my usual. The trick is that I get mine wrapped in lettuce instead of a bun"

"In that case, I'll have her regular the regular way, with a real bun."

The server smiled and left.

"Savannah said to tell you that Jacob was remarkably inventive in his choice of key codes. If he hadn't tried a few typical guesses, it could have taken months. Anyway, it turns out that the key was her birthday."

Officer Williams had taken a sip of her iced tea and nearly choked. "Oh, that's priceless. His daughter's birthday. That's so ridiculously typical that no one would have thought of it."

"Sometimes the easiest thing is best. Anyway, here's the file." He gave the dusty package to Officer Williams.

Before she could open the file, the server plopped down two large hamburgers. The plates were heaping with hot French fries and a huge mound of coleslaw.

Officer Williams waved at Edward to start eating while she immediately opened the folder and looked at the number of encrypted words in the documents. "I can't read this! Are you sure this is the right file?"

Edward put down his burger, wiped his mouth from the juicy bite he had just taken, and spoke indistinctly. "Jacob is translating everything for you." He chewed and swallowed quickly. "It shouldn't take too long now that the machine is set, but Savannah thought you could get a general idea of the contents. She wanted you to have as much as possible as early as possible. Right?"

"Of course, she's right." Officer Williams carefully gathered up her juicy burger. "That's what makes her irritating sometimes, don't you think?"

Edward nodded. "Oh, yes."

Chapter 21

Detective Parker stood in front of the whiteboard with his hands folded across his chest. The newest picture on the board was of Lucas Brown. It had been placed there by Officer Williams.

"Let me hear your reasoning for selecting him as a suspect," said Detective Parker. "Merely being overly helpful is insufficient justification."

"Actually, I have a solid foundation for suspecting our helpful, so very helpful, security manager. Savannah called in to report that Jacob had detected a pattern of overnight vagrants sleeping in the museum garden. She doesn't think that could be happening without the knowledge of the security manager."

Parker rolled his hand in a *tell me more* gesture.

"Maybe Dennis somehow became aware of that and challenged Lucas with exposing him to the director. She would fire him on the spot." Officer Williams chewed on the corner of her lip, caught herself, pressed her lips together, then smiled. "Do you want me to interview him down at the museum or should I bring him here?"

"Let's see what he has to say first before we bring him in here. Make your own assessment, but keep me up to date."

Joy felt a little flutter in her chest. Detective Parker was beginning to use her more and more in the course of casework. The feeling lasted for about two seconds until she realized that added opportunity also meant added responsibility. The familiar thoughts about distrusting her own success began to rise. She took a deep breath and pushed those thoughts down deep.

She drove to the Dali Museum, parked her cruiser at the visitor drop off lane, and had barely walked fifteen steps toward the entrance to the museum before the doors opened and Lucas rushed out to meet her. He wheezed from the effort and a sheen of sweat appeared on his forehead.

"Good afternoon, Officer Williams. What brings you back here? Do you have more questions?" He wiped his face with a handkerchief and waited for her to speak. His eyes shined with excitement.

"Yes, there are a few details to verify. Is there somewhere we can talk? Hopefully in the air-conditioning inside. Maybe a conference or community room?"

"Of course. The community room is vacant. I've got the key."

Lucas walked her into the museum and gave a dismissive wave to the cashier as they walked through the gift shop, passed the café, and stood before two white doors with gold lettering overhead indicating that the community room was sponsored by a local bank. He unlocked the door and held it while Officer Williams entered.

The room was large and felt open and airy due to the floor-to-ceiling windows along the entire wall facing the garden. There was a speaker's podium in front of the central window and white garden style chairs arranged in a semicircle around the podium. Lucas led her to the first row of chairs. "Is this good?"

"This is fine. It's at least cool." Joy sat down and pulled out her officer's notebook and a pen. She looked at Lucas who was sitting precariously on the edge of his seat. Sweat was again glistening on his forehead. "We have evidence that there have been some late-night visitors to the garden who are actually spending their nights there. When did you start allowing the homeless to use the garden as a haven?"

Lucas leaned back so quickly he nearly turned over the chair. "Who says that?"

"So you're not denying it. Merely curious as to who figured it out?"

"No. That's not what I mean." He swiped his forehead in a smooth automatic movement. "I mean, yes, I'm not denying it."

"Why did you lie to Detective Parker?"

"I don't know." Lucas took out his handkerchief and held it with both hands twisting it into tortured knots. "There's no harm in letting those guys bed down in the maze. I make sure that only the quiet ones get a place."

"So, you only allow certain ones?"

"Yes, I look for the ones that are getting bullied and end up walking the streets all night to stay out of the way." He looked down at his handkerchief, shook it out, wiped his face, then returned it to his back pocket. "Look, no one is being harmed or inconvenienced in any way at all. It's just that . . . well you've met the director. She doesn't understand or even care what happens to those guys. I would probably get fired and then I can't help them. Are you going to tell the director?"

Officer Williams said nothing. Then she continued to say nothing. She was learning that some people can't stand a silence.

Lucas dropped his voice to a raspy whisper. "Please, please don't tell her. I'll help you anyway I can. Please."

"Then you must tell me the absolute, bald-faced truth. If you don't, I'll charge right up there to her office and tell her myself." She pointed in the direction of the second floor.

Lucas released a long-held breath. "Thank you. Thank you. Thank you. I promise."

"Tell me about the normal routine each evening," Joy said with a pen poised above her notebook. "I need every detail."

"It started about two years ago when I got here early to open up the building for one of our landscapers. He needed to adjust the water pressure or something on the sprinkling system and needed access to the utility room. Anyway, as he checked out a broken sprinkler head, he came upon a homeless veteran." Lucas leaned back in the chair and chuckled. "I don't know who was more startled, but I ran out and calmed both. The vet wouldn't tell me his real name. He said he was known as Pappy. He had been in the Navy during the Korean War."

Joy looked up from her scribbling. "He was pretty old then."

"Yeah. Ancient. He must have been at least eighty. He looked clean though. And he only had a small bag with him, so I asked him where he was staying. He didn't want to tell me, but I promised I wouldn't tell anyone. He told me that he was in a halfway house and appreciated that, but sometimes he needed to be out, and spending a night in the garden now and then helped him cope with such crowded conditions."

"Then what did you do?"

"I didn't see any harm in giving the old man a little peace and quiet now and then."

"But it's more than that now?"

"Yeah," said Lucas. He pulled out his handkerchief for an automatic face wipe. "There are currently about twenty vets who use the garden at night."

Joy's eyes widened. "Twenty? That's so many. And only veterans?"

"He insisted on only vets. Oh, not all twenty at once. They sort themselves out and only let three or four stay each night. The thing about staying the night in the garden is that it helps them cope with their problems better. They stay on their meds. They don't run away from their residence. I know I'm doing some good."

Joy put down her pen. "But you know this can't last. Someone in management is going to hit the roof and you'll be out of a job. You can't help anyone then."

"I know, I know, I know." He covered his face with both hands. "I've been working on a better solution, but it isn't quite ready yet. Soon, though."

Officer Williams picked up her pen. "First things first. Who was here that night?"

"It was a typical night. Only three vets were bunked in the maze and one guy had the privilege of camping out on the green bench. That was the prized site. Everyone wanted to sleep there."

"Who was it?"

"He's called Ol' Cap. He lives in the Lighthouse group home. He's the informal leader of the vets that stay here."

Joy finished writing in her notebook, then stood. "I'm going to check this out. The problem with lying to the police is that now we don't trust anything you say. So, I'm going to have to confirm everything ."

Lucas stood and looked down at his feet. "I didn't want to make things worse for those guys."

Officer Williams nodded. "Try not to worry." She smiled. "I don't want to make things harder for those guys, either. I'll get back to you. I'm sure we'll have more questions." She walked out to the car and looked back at Lucas standing in front of the entrance watching her.

Could one of them have killed Dennis to keep him from ending the sleeping arrangements? Would that be a motive to a desperate vet?

Chapter 22

Thursday afternoon

Savannah drove downtown to Frank Lattimer's glass shop with a sour feeling of indigestion in her stomach. Although he had been cooperative in the use of his kiln for her emergency firing, his moods were unpredictable. She looked in her rearview mirror at Jacob calmly petting Suzy in the backseat. *He had better not upset Jacob.*

The parking slots were all taken when she drove by, but they managed to find a two-hour time limited spot a block away.

They went into the shop and Frank waved them over from the doorway to the fusing room. "You're early. I thought I said not to come by until six. Class will be over by then and you can unload."

He hadn't said anything about after six.

Savannah pressed her lips together. "Oh, I misunderstood. That's why there's no parking, then."

"Of course. Come back then. After six." He looked at her as if she were a simpleton.

Savannah, Jacob, and Suzy returned to the car.
"I'm going to go talk to Mr. James Armstrong. Are
you good with coming along? Do we need to make
a pit stop for Suzy? Or yourself?"

Jacob looked down at Suzy and then at his shoes.
"There's the comfort station downtown. That would
be good for both of us."

Savannah smiled. Jacob was getting more and
more independent over time. A couple months
ago, he would have suffered in silence and then
possibly had an anxiety attack, rather than simply
say that he needed a restroom.

The comfort station at the corner of Bayshore
Drive and Second Avenue NE was one of the first
public restroom buildings in St. Petersburg and it
still served beautifully. Built in 1927, it featured an
octagonal shape capped with a red tile roof and a
copper cupola and finial.

It was a pleasant fifteen-minute drive to the waterfront community of Gulfport. Savannah loved the
quirkiness of the community. The City of Gulfport
sponsored a First Friday and Third Saturday Art
Walk all year. The slogan was "Keep Gulfport
Weird," accompanied by a stylized lizard. That
pretty much covered it.

Mr. Armstrong's condo was on the third floor of
one of the gated mid-century condominiums facing
the Gulf of Mexico. A short, wizened man with
skin that looked like blotted tissue paper opened
the aluminum screen door while holding on to a
wheeled oxygen tank that provided air through
a cannula. He waved them past his galley kitchen
and through his sparsely furnished living-dining
room to the screened-in balcony that had a ceiling

fan cooling at top speed. It barely made a dent in the heat of the afternoon. He settled himself into a well-worn chair and offered them tall glasses of freshly brewed iced tea. He shakily poured the tea from a tray that held a pitcher, ice bucket, and glasses. "What can I do for you?"

"I have some questions about my dad's apprenticeship program. I understand that you worked with him to establish the program."

"Yes, that was about three years before I retired. He took over completely after that for a couple years. Then, I think it got too much for him and most of the value of the pilot program had been incorporated into all the high schools so he didn't need to worry about the day to day anymore."

"As I said on the phone, I'm interested in a student named Dennis Lansing. He was part of the program in 2004 or 2005. I think that was early in the program."

"Dennis." Mr. Armstrong smiled. "He was a character, all right." The former social worker was silent for a bit. "He was the one they found dead, wasn't he?"

"Yes."

"Why are you asking?"

Jacob spoke quickly. "She's investigating his murder. We need to know more about him so that we can find out who killed him. You would have known him well since he was one of the first apprentices in the program. Correct?"

"Yes, young man. That's right. John and I worked closely with Dennis and his friend Chuck. The program got a rough start. Those two could start trouble just standing next to each other. We finally figured out we had to separate them completely."

"By Chuck, do you mean Charles King, the politician?"

Mr. Armstrong nodded. "Yes, he started to build his public service career at the local level not long after graduation."

"Did you have them share a job with Dennis working in the mornings and Chuck working in the afternoons?"

"That's exactly what we had to do and that worked. Dennis helped out with the classroom instruction and Chuck helped with the business and administrative job at the Art Center downtown. They weren't together either at work or at school. Separately, they each found their own footing and made great progress. How did you guess?"

"I've been analyzing the files for codes and some of the shifts were identified with a.m. and p.m. It was simple. How did the school accommodate for the afternoon shifts?"

Mr. Armstrong offered Jacob and Savannah more iced tea, which she gratefully accepted. She was sweltering. Old people seemed to tolerate the heat.

"We had to arrange for one of the teachers to shift their hours by one class period so that the afternoon apprentices could get enough hours in to qualify as full-time high school students. I remember that one of the teachers volunteered so that she could leave for school a little later in the morning. She didn't mind the shift in her hours. The school was open for extracurricular clubs and sports practice so it worked out."

"Did you keep in touch with Dennis after he left the program?"

"I heard about him in the art world from time to time. You know, press releases and publicity events and such."

"What about his wife? Did you know her?"

Mr. Armstrong frowned for an instant and reached over to check a setting on his oxygen tank. "No, I didn't know her."

"May I have some water for Suzy?" said Jacob. "It's warm today and she wears a fur coat all the time."

"Of course. I should have thought of that." Mr. Armstrong rose slowly from his seat and went into the kitchen, pulling his oxygen trolley after him.

As soon as the screen door snapped shut, Jacob turned to Savannah. "Suzy is fine. I made that up because I wanted to talk to you."

Savannah smiled. "Clever. What is it?"

"If Mr. Armstrong knew Dennis as well as your dad, why didn't he get invited to the reception, too? You were there. You should ask him."

"Great idea. I didn't think of that."

Mr. Armstrong brought back a stainless-steel mixing bowl sloshing with water. "Watch out. I'm not as steady as I used to be." He placed the bowl on the concrete patio in front of Jacob's chair.

"Thank you." Jacob placed Suzy on the floor and she lapped delicately.

Savannah leaned forward. "Mr. Armstrong, did Dennis invite you to his Dali Museum reception? I don't remember seeing you, but it was a large crowd."

He chuckled. "No, the truth is that John and I

disagreed over Dennis. I thought he should have been removed from the program." His voice weakened to a raspy whisper.

"I'm sorry, Mr. Armstrong," said Savannah. "I didn't catch that."

He gulped in some air. "I'm sorry. I get out of breath easily." He swallowed and started again. "John and I disagreed over Dennis. I complained to him rather strongly more than once about Dennis's connections with drugs. In my opinion, he gave Dennis too much attention. He had him apprentice with the glassblowing shop downtown at the Arts Center. I wanted to give that job to Chuck. Instead John gave Chuck an administrative assistant role."

"And Dennis knew about your opinion?" asked Savannah.

Mr. Armstrong nodded. "It wasn't a secret."

Jacob lifted Suzy back onto his lap and stared at the top of her head. "Mr. Armstrong, did you keep records of the students?"

"No, I let John take care of that. He was obsessively careful with their personal information. I was happy to receive his reports. They were full of graphs and pie charts along with a lengthy analysis of progress in improving the high school dropout rate in the city."

"Did you know of any other members of the gang that Dennis ran around with?" Savannah asked.

"There was one other boy. I can't remember his name, but I think John placed him in a restaurant. I think he was the only other member of that same gang. We didn't take them on after that."

"Why?" said Jacob.

Mr. Armstrong chuckled. "That was where John

and I finally found common ground. Since we had struggled so much over those young men, we felt it was better to concentrate on more students with family issues, discrimination problems, or financial hardships. Those students were easier to support and we could make a bigger difference to the community. Those gang members nearly sank the entire program before it had a chance to prove itself."

"What happened to Chuck?" Jacob asked.

"Chuck is now known as Charles King, our state representative in Tallahassee."

Jacob and Savannah returned to Lattimer's shop. They easily backed into one of the vacant parking spots. Obviously, the shop was empty of students.

They opened the door and Frank was standing in the doorway to the kiln room in Superman pose. "What took so long? I've got to get the kiln loaded so that the class projects will be ready for tomorrow's class."

"Sorry, Frank. We're only a few minutes late. We'll get unloaded and out of your way in a jiffy."

Without a word, Jacob handed Suzy to Frank. "Hold her while I work." He turned to Savannah. "I can load the car fast. Just bring me the plates."

Frank stood statue still with his eyes wide in abject fear. He whispered, "Dogs don't like me. Take her back."

Jacob raised the lid to the kiln, lifted the first layer of plates out, and took off for the car. Passing Frank, he said, "She's a service dog, not a pet. She's fine. We'll wash these at our shop."

Savannah followed Jacob's lead, grabbed the

next layer of plates, and hustled to her car. She waited while Jacob packed the car, then returned for the last layer and finally all the support blocks. In less than ten minutes, the kiln was empty and the car was packed. She and Jacob cleaned the kiln for the upcoming load and washed their hands in the rinsing sink.

"We're done," said Savannah to a still frozen, shocked Frank.

Jacob lifted Suzy and smiled. "Thanks for watching Suzy. She likes you."

Chapter 23

Officer Joy Williams parked her police cruiser in front of the Lighthouse Free Clinic on Central Avenue. She knew that the building was part of a free clinic, but she hadn't yet met the organizers. She pulled on the entry door and found it locked.

"They don't open up the door until four," said a slurred voice from the vacant lot next door. A disheveled black man with white buzz-cut hair stood nearby, leaning heavily on a four-pronged cane. "If you want the boss lady, you need to go around to the back. She'll be in the kitchen putting our supper out on the line."

"You may know what I need. Do you know a man called Cap?"

"Ol' Cap?" He lowered himself back onto a bench built out of two-by-fours and a plank. It didn't look sturdy enough to support a child, but held the old man's weight without a flinch. "Everybody knows Ol' Cap. He's not too keen to talk to any kind of authority. I don't know why, but I didn't ask either. We don't ask each other many questions here, ma'am."

"Can you describe him for me?"

"Ma'am, he pretty much looks like the rest of us. Rode hard and put away wet."

"Do you think they might know about him inside?"

"Not sure, ma'am. I haven't told them anything about me. They don't ask."

Joy smiled. "Thank you, sir. I appreciate your frankness." She headed toward the back of the building, walking carefully through the dirt lot that doubled as a waiting area, and stepping carefully between upside down buckets, wooden chairs, and tree stumps. It was haphazard, but neat. No trash and no litter.

She pulled the back door open quietly and Officer Williams stepped inside a bustling commercial kitchen with boiling pots of soup, large trays of roasted chicken quarters, and serving pans filled with mashed potatoes, gravy, and a pastry-covered dessert. The delicious aroma caused Joy's stomach to growl. It had been a long time since lunch.

"Go around to the front! We're not ready," shouted a tiny woman standing on a step stool stirring the large pot of soup and adding salt from an industrial sized container. "You know that's the rule. It's on the front door, for pity's sake."

"I beg your pardon, ma'am. I'm not a patron."

The tiny woman turned her head like a startled bird and looked at Joy from top to toe. "I'm sorry, Officer. You have no idea how many times a day I have to chase folks away. Rules are to be followed exactly . . . to get a meal, a shower, and a bed." She stepped down from the stool. "Johnny, take over seasoning the soup for me. It's too bland. I'm going to talk to this lovely woman police officer."

A thin quiet man, whose leathered skin had seen too many days outdoors, scooted the step stool aside with his foot and took over.

"We can talk in my little office. My name is Wanda." She raised her eyebrows and led the way to a tidy eight-by-eight office crammed with a desk, a PC, an office chair, a side chair, and two filing cabinets. She sat in the office chair and motioned for Joy to take the side chair. "I'm assuming you want to ask me about one of our clients."

"Yes. I need to know about—"

Wanda raised her hand in a stop motion when Joy started to speak. "Before we start, let me tell you that we don't keep records or statistics or ask for any identification from our clients." She plucked a brochure from the upper left drawer of the desk and handed it to Joy. "This fully explains our mission. In brief, we provide safe, transitional shelter to single, homeless men. We serve up to twenty-five men at any one time. Residents work with staff to set goals, save money, and work toward independent living." Wanda folded her small hands in front of her on the desk. "Now, with that out of the way, how can I help you?"

Joy cleared her throat and straightened up to sit tall. "I am Officer Joy Williams, reporting to Detective David Parker of the Major Crimes Division." She made a little production out of taking her pen and notebook from her pocket, opening the notebook and clicking the pen to write. "First, what is your full name and legal designation of this facility?"

Wanda nodded approval. "My name is Wanda Hunt Seine and the full name of this organization is Free Clinic Lighthouse. Yearly financial records are posted on our website and we are managed by a local board of directors."

After scribbling that information in her notebook, Joy asked, "In particular, I'm trying to determine the whereabouts of a homeless vet called Cap. He may have witnessed an incident at the Dali Museum in the early hours of Monday this week. We need to talk to him urgently."

"Do you have a description?"

Joy flipped back a few pages of her notebook. "It's not very specific. Cap is of average height, thin frame, wears ragged camo gear—typical veteran description."

"That describes more than half our clients."

Joy sighed deeply and put away her pen and notebook. "Well, that's a dead end then."

"Now, now. Don't give up so easily. Most social workers have been burned by answering seemingly straightforward questions from the police, only to be betrayed. I lost more than one veteran that way." Wanda reached over and patted Joy on the knee. "I know Ol' Cap reasonably well. He is an institution here at the Lighthouse. What are the times you need to verify?"

"From about four in the morning to no later than seven. Why?"

Wanda held her head in her hands for a moment as if wrestling with conflicting ethics. "He wouldn't mind, but I won't reveal his name. I *can* confirm to you that during that time he was talking to his sobriety sponsor. The rescue conversation lasted from about three in the morning until nearly eight."

"How on earth can you confirm that?"

"Their conversation kept me up most of the night. His sobriety sponsor is my husband."

Chapter 24

Thursday afternoon

On the way back to Webb's Glass Shop, Savannah called Edward to meet her and Jacob for a meeting to discuss progress with the investigation. When she parked in the back of the shop, Amanda and Edward helped them unload the plates.

"I'll wash the charger plates after the meeting, Jacob. You've more than done your share today. You can go home right after our little meeting."

"What about decoding the summary sheet of Dennis Lansing's file?"

"I don't mind if you work on it for a little while after our meeting, but I think you'll be better for taking time to rest. Suzy also needs some down time. She is on duty all the time you're away from home. This has been a stressful week for us all."

"I didn't think about Suzy. Thanks. She needs some rest."

They gathered in the small office in the far back of Webb's Glass Shop. Savannah sat in the old oak chair in front of the rolltop desk while Jacob and Amanda dragged in stools from the classroom. The side chair was Edward's spot by habit.

Amanda pursed her lips. "What's up with you and Edward?"

The bell over the front door of the shop rang and Savannah shushed her. "Not now. We have investigation matters to discuss."

Edward carried in a tray with a pitcher of iced tea, four glasses filled with ice, and a plate of cookies that smelled of ginger. "It's still hot out there. Remind me again, when does autumn actually arrive? In England, we can get snow in September."

Amanda grabbed one of the cookies and laughed. "For you, our whole winter is probably warmer than a British summer."

"Okay, okay." Savannah fidgeted in the oak chair so that it squeaked. "I want to go over what we've learned and figure out what to do next. But first, I got my weekly e-mail newsletter from the Dali Museum this morning. They're sponsoring a candlelight memorial ceremony on Friday night. It will start at seven-thirty p.m. I would appreciate it if we could all attend."

"So we can talk to our suspects without being obvious?" asked Amanda.

"That's the plan," said Savannah. "Now, on to what we know. What still hasn't turned up is a guest list from the reception. Officer Williams may have forgotten to tell me about it but that seems unlikely. They certainly don't have to share that with me. I'm only supposed to be looking into my dad's records. Anyway, Amanda, what have you found out about the director of the Dali Museum?"

"Well." Amanda stopped abruptly as some crumbs escaped her mouth. She put a hand to her mouth and mumbled, "'Scuse me." She gulped some iced tea and began to choke.

Edward leaped up and gave her a quick slap on her back.

She coughed and then blushed nearly purple. "I'm so sorry," she said when she recovered herself. "The ginger is a little strong and for me that translates as hot pepper spicy. Sorry."

"So . . ." Savannah waved *come on* to her.

"Okay, I made a preliminary troll through the cyber footprints of Lucas, Gina, and Harriet. First, our exceedingly friendly security guard, Lucas Brown, doesn't appear to have ever owned a computer and I'll bet his phone is a basic flip phone with no features at all except maybe text messages using the phone keys—painful. He's a pure Luddite."

Jacob reached for a cookie and looked at it closely. "It's okay not to like fancy phones." He took a tiny bite. "My phone is basic. I am not a Luddite."

Savannah looked over to Amanda with raised eyebrows.

"Right, that was rude," Amanda said slowly, then gathered speed. "We all know you hate using the phone, but—"

"You have so many strengths in other areas," finished Savannah. "He's fine. Go on, Amanda, my hacker maven."

"I had some trouble with the information I found

about Harriet. She acts as Dennis's business manager and publicist. Her online presence is massive. She posts to Facebook, Twitter, Instagram, and Pinterest. She has a Pinterest page for every exhibition that Dennis has put on. It's a wonderful record of his progression as an artist. It will be easy to create a catalog of his entire body of work from her pinned images."

"Did she use any social media for personal communications?" asked Savannah.

Amanda nodded. "She apparently used her cell phone to text personal conversations. I found a couple requests for Facebook contacts to message her a phone number so that they could continue their conversation more privately. It's not unreasonable for a public person to do that. I can't get into phone records."

Savannah drew a hand through her curls. "So, if we want more information about her, we'll have to ask. First, I'll talk to Joy and see if she's willing to share at least something. I know the department is overloaded right now with the St. Petersburg Arts and Culture Festival and the tragedy in Orlando."

The month-long celebration of St. Petersburg's artistic creators and creations is often referred to as the SPF or SPFestival. It consists of fifty-seven events at 149 venues by 102 organizations and/or performers during the thirty days of September. It focused on events and activities produced by local and national artists, arts organizations, and arts-related businesses in and around the city's unique arts districts including the Grand Central District, where Webb's Glass Shop was located.

Amanda spoke. "The last person I chased is Gina, the moody and erratic museum director. She's a powerhouse on social media. She is active on Facebook, Twitter, YouTube, Tumblr, Snapchat, GooglePlus, Pinterest, Instagram, and Reddit. I don't see how she can keep up with the noise. She must have an assistant. Anyway, the one she uses the most is Twitter. There's a tweet every ten minutes on her feed. They're all public posts using the museum accounts. She uses them exclusively."

"Okay, but I want—," said Savannah.

Amanda held up a hand. "Let me finish. Because her feed is so active, it's obvious when she's off-line. She normally stops at about ten o'clock in the evening and then starts up again at about five a.m. That's a regular pattern. What's not so regular is that there are some unusual periods of no activity at all."

Edward frowned. "What does that tell us?"

"One of those times was during and immediately after the reception at the museum. On that evening, all social media stopped after about ten o'clock. She was off-line until midnight when she posted a few pictures. All social activity normally ended at ten o'clock in the evening, so I noticed it. She resumed at four a.m., which is earlier than her normal time of five a.m."

"That's something to consider. That means she was offline during the reception. But during the interval when Dennis was murdered," Savannah paused, "she was working away." She quickly pulled a tissue from her pocket and stemmed her running nose with a quick wipe. "Excuse me."

"Yes, I was disappointed about that, too." Amanda looked at Savannah in concern, then reached for another cookie but pulled her hand back. "So, I looked back into her history and found a couple other three- or four-hour blocks of time in the preceding month where she was completely off-line."

"So, if we extrapolate a bit," said Edward, "we can assume that she was spending that time with someone who was more interesting to her than Facebook. I wonder who?"

Amanda shrugged her shoulders. "I haven't checked out Dennis yet. I'll be able to do that this evening." She grabbed another cookie. "You said you wanted to learn a bit about social media. Tonight, after this meeting, would be a great time."

"I did say that." Savannah rolled her eyes. "I'll look over your shoulder this evening. I'm good with searching for information, but social media? Yuk!"

Amanda rubbed her hands together. "Yay! Teaching the teacher. Oh, what did you find out from Dennis's social worker?"

"One thing I found out is that having Jacob along means that the questioning will take a couple drastic twists. Do you want to tell them about our discussion with him?" She nodded toward Jacob.

He ducked his head and shook it. "No, you tell."

"Sure." She sipped her iced tea. "Our social worker was helpful, but he wasn't in the best of health. He uses an oxygen tank all the time. He certainly enjoyed talking about the program and his memory was clear. He confirmed that my dad kept all the records and that Dennis's partner in the apprentice program was nicknamed Chuck."

"Chuck? You mean, short for Charles?" said Edward.

"Yes, our very own state representative. Dennis and Chuck were members in the same gang that caused a lot of trouble around town. His records have got to be in the file cabinet somewhere. So Jacob, if you can work out which one it is . . . that would be helpful. Maybe there's more information about their activities that we can investigate.

"Sorry, Amanda, there's another name to add to your list of social media investigations—Florida State Representative Charles King."

"You mean *our* list of social media investigations." Amanda rolled her hands over each other. "Mwu ha ha ha. This is going to be fun."

"Okay, I walked into that one. That's all for now, guys. Jacob, you and Suzy need to get going." She turned to help Edward gather the glasses on his tray. "I'll meet you next door for dinner. That is, if our Thursday dinner is still on."

Edward smiled. "Brilliant."

After they left, Amanda put the work stools back in the classroom and pulled up the guest chair close behind Savannah. "Now, the first thing we need to do is create accounts for you. You need to do that anyway for Webb's Glass Shop."

Savannah faced the PC display screen that sat on the oak desk surface. It had been her father's and his PC system was a powerful hand-built tower with custom boards that provided extra processing power and additional security checks.

ETCHED IN TEARS 199

"Okay, which social media sites will be most useful? You know I don't have a lot of spare time, so I want to get the most bang for my buck."

"That's easy. Facebook and Twitter are the largest and most popular, but because your clients are interested in crafting, Pinterest should also be one of your sites." Amanda pointed to the mouse. "Click on that little icon in the corner."

"The blue one with the f?"

"Yes, now press the ENTER key and the Facebook application opens. Now, let's sign you up for a profile page so we can visit Gina's site."

After more than an hour, Savannah finally had a page with a profile picture, a cover picture, and she had filled out most of the information needed to put up a bare account.

"While we're here, let's set up a fan page for Webb's Glass Shop. We can actually start doing some real promotion after this." Amanda quickly filled out the information needed and inserted a cover photo and profile picture.

Setting up that page didn't take as long. The next social media site they tackled was Twitter.

"You might actually like this one better than Facebook. Tweets are limited to a hundred and forty characters. So, it's short and sweet for interacting quickly and there are already a jillion people on it. After you get used to using the hashtags you can interact real time with people who are interested in the same things you like. I think the best path is just to set one up for Webb's Glass Shop and you can use that for everything." Amanda took a few minutes to walk Savannah through creating a Twitter account called @WebbsGlassShop and they pulled in the same profile picture they had used for Savannah's Facebook page.

"Now let me show you around a little bit. Do you mind if I type? Your two-finger hunt-and-peck is driving me crazy."

Savannah stood up. "Well, excuse me. I grew up in a glass shop, not a tech lab, so I never learned to touch type . . . but I am pretty quick with those two fingers."

"Come on. Don't get huffy. I don't want to be here all night. Tomorrow's a busy day for both of us. It's the last day of class. I not only look forward to the last day, but I also dread it. Busy, busy, busy."

Savannah moved to the guest chair while Amanda took over the typing. "You're right. I'll watch.

"I want to show you what Gina's normal Facebook posting patterns look like and when she was silent a couple weeks ago." Amanda's rapid-fire typing brought up Gina's Dali Museum Facebook page and they scrolled through both the normal activity and the silence.

"What does it look like on Twitter?"

Amanda unloosed her flying fingers on the keyboard and Gina's twitter feed was displayed on the PC screen. She scrolled down the multiple-times-per-hour Twitter messages, called tweets, to a gap one evening. "That's the only one I found and that wasn't repeated except for the evening of the exhibit reception. Let me show you that section." Amanda scrolled the display. "Then Gina started up again in her normal pattern at five a.m."

Savannah squinted at the screen. "These messages, I mean tweets, is there a way to get more information about how they were broadcast? I know you can use a Twitter app on your smartphone. Is that different?"

"We can look closer into her account by clicking on her Twitter handle, then we can click on the clock symbol. It tells what posting mechanism she used."

Savannah got up and leaned over Amanda's shoulder. "These here look different from the rest of them. See, this bit of wording here says they were scheduled via Hootsuite. What does that mean?"

Amanda put both hands over her mouth. "Oh my goodness. I hadn't noticed that. She doesn't do that, ever. I mean I checked over the last month and all her tweets were written either from a PC or from her phone app. This means that she planned ahead of time to make sure that block of time was covered."

Savannah sat back in the chair. "That means she has no alibi for the time that Dennis was killed. I'll call Officer Williams."

Chapter 25

"Why did you choose this place for dinner? I love the meals at Queen's Head Pub." Savannah and Edward stood on the sidewalk in front of Ricky P's Orleans Bistro about ten blocks east of Webb's Glass Shop on Central Avenue.

"I thought we should meet on neutral ground." Edward opened the door to the spicy smell of simmering Jambalaya, sugary sweet beignets, and sizzling Andouille sausage. "We have some serious issues that need discussion."

Savannah frowned a bit, but said nothing. She hated difficult discussions. She was an expert in avoiding difficult discussions. She inherited that from her dad and it didn't look like a trait that would be easily overcome, certainly not in the next few minutes.

The inside décor of Ricky P's Orleans Bistro was an homage to the French Quarter in New Orleans. It was decorated with beads in Mardi Gras colors of gold, green, and purple dripping from every available surface and scattered hooks. The walls were hung with fantastical masks from the various costumes that the owner had collected when he lived in NOLA.

Edward spoke before their server had even handed them the menus. "We'll start with a tower of onion rings to go along with a pint of Beach Blonde Ale for her and a pint of Summer Storm Stout for me."

"Yes, sir. I put that in right now."

Savannah glanced around. The restaurant was busy since Thursday night during the late autumn was the new Friday as many companies had offered employees a four-day week. "What is the bad news?"

"How did you know?" Edward tilted his head. "I haven't said anything."

"Exactly." She tilted her head in the same direction. "You usually have critiqued a restaurant nine ways from sunshine before we even get a menu. What's the trouble?"

Edward cleared his throat. "I have been looking through the accounts and I think you might be in trouble with the State of Florida."

"What? How could that be? I had everything arranged with Burkart in setting up Webb's Studio. Are you sure?"

The server placed their beers on coasters. "Would you like to hear our specials?"

Edward looked up. "No, thank you. I'll have an order of the shrimp étouffée with a side order of creole slaw and Savannah will have the combo platter with fresh tomato salad."

"Thank you, sir."

Savannah's face was pale. "I'm not sure I can eat. My stomach just hit the floor."

"I found a letter from the State of Florida which indicated that you are more than thirty days past due in submitting your quarterly sales taxes for Webb's Studio."

Savannah shook her head violently. "I don't sell products out of the Studio. I sell services and Florida doesn't have a sales tax on services. At least not yet. All my supply sales are run through Webb's Glass Shop. This is insane."

"Insane or not, it only takes one slip of the cash register to alert the powers that be for tax collection. Your dad was my hero when I was setting up Queen's Head Pub's accounts. I would have stumbled into serious trouble if he hadn't been there to explain what I needed to do to resolve my tax issues."

"How much money are we talking about?"

"Six thousand two hundred and forty-three dollars."

Savannah dropped her head. "That's a lot of money." She slowly looked up. "Perfect timing."

Edward reached across the table and placed his warm hand over Savannah's. "Don't look so worried. I think I figured out what happened."

"What do I have to do?" Savannah asked.

"I have a plan to fix this."

The server placed a golden pile of crispy onion rings on the table. Edward grabbed one. "These are brilliant. It's every man for himself. I'm not going to be polite until they're gone."

Savannah laughed and grabbed two.

"Savannah, I'm running into you every time I

turn around." Charles King stood over their table rocking slightly on his heels. He was wearing his signature casual look of white dress shirt buttoned to the top, navy trousers, and a colorful vest. "I hear that you're working as a subject matter expert with the St. Petersburg Police Department. Is that true?"

Savannah craned her neck to look up at him. "Yes, I've been lucky to be able to help them in a small way."

King grabbed an unused chair from the next table, turned the back to face the table, and straddled it. "Good to see you again, Edward. How's Queen's Head Pub faring?" He extended a hand.

Edward wiped his mouth and hands on his bright purple napkin and shook hands. "Very well, indeed. We have a large local following . . . not only tourists for my place."

King smiled and turned to Savannah. "I have inside information that you've been more than a little helpful. You've solved a couple murders. Who would have thought that you, me, and Dennis would have come so far from our underprivileged beginnings?"

"Pardon me. I-I—" Savannah stuttered.

"Don't get me wrong. I meant that as a compliment. You were a motherless girl being raised by a more than slightly paranoid father who was an ex-government agent not only running a stained-glass business, but spearheading a revolutionary program to salvage gang members from certain doom."

Savannah narrowed her eyes. "It was an effective program. You've done particularly well, haven't you?"

"Dennis and I were so much alike, I'm not sure

why my assigned apprenticeship at the Art Center was in the administrative office and Dennis went directly to teaching. It could easily have been the reverse. How are you helping the police with Dennis's death?"

"That's confidential."

"Of course." He stood. "I'll let you get back to your dinner. If there's any way that I can help, give me a call. I would like to be as informed of what happened as soon as possible, since Dennis was an old friend and I am the state representative for this district." He gave her a business card and left the restaurant.

Edward stood and replaced the chair back at the adjoining table. "I think you should take him up on that offer. He knew Dennis."

"Yes, but he's a politician."

"Yes, but he's a successful politician." Edward returned to his seat and grabbed another onion ring.

Savannah snagged the last one. "The only time a politician lies is when his lips are moving."

Chapter 26

"With a dose of good luck today, you should be going home with your final project in your hands." Savannah walked around the large table in the conference room. All four students had a piece of artwork taped to a small oval piece of glass with a hole in the top to make a key chain.

They went outside to do the etching for their projects.

Faith tapped Savannah on the arm. "We saw in the paper this morning that there's going to be a candlelight celebration for Dennis Lansing."

Rachel frowned and elbowed Faith. "She already knows about that, silly goose. Tell her what we talked about this morning."

"Hold your horses. I was just about to do that." Faith pursed her lips and put one hand on her hip. "We would like to go to the ceremony, but we don't drive at night anymore. Could you take us?"

The twins simultaneously planted an artificial smile on their faces and begged. "Please?"

Savannah ran down her mental list of everything that needed to happen before the ceremony. Check on the last loading of the kiln that would make up the order for the Vinoy Hotel. Feed and exercise Rooney. Edward was coming to the house. Amanda was picking up Jacob. She could feel herself getting tense and exhaled a breath she didn't know she was holding. *I need to relax and spend time with my family. These ladies are my family. Tomorrow isn't guaranteed.*

"I'd be delighted. Write down your address before class ends."

Jacob arrived with Suzy and walked straight into his workroom.

Savannah ran her hand through her curls. "Hi Jacob. You're in early."

He reappeared in his doorway. "Good morning, Miss Savannah. I'm early because I want to finish the decoding of Dennis Lansing's file. You were right. A good night's rest was helpful." He turned and disappeared into his workroom.

After cleaning up their key chains following the sand etching of their monograms, the four students completed their final project by chemically etching a border design. Even the Rosenberg twins were attentive and the class finished a little early. As farewells were passed around, it was the only time Edith Maloney smiled at her.

Chapter 27

Detective Parker leaned back in the conference chair with his hands behind his head. "I'm leaning toward the wife. Statistics support my choice. Harriet has a powerful motive and no confirmed alibi. That trust fund of hers is worth over five million dollars."

Officer Joy Williams stood in front of the white board in the Murder Room and pointed to a picture of Harriet Lansing. "Okay. Let me be devil's advocate. How did she get him to the green bench sculpture? She's not a big person. There are no drag marks at the scene, so presumably, he was carried and carefully arranged."

Detective Parker lifted his eyebrows. "The gravel area around the green bench sculpture could easily have been raked or swept clear of marks."

"What if that assumption is wrong? What if he was only injured somewhere else? Let's say he was rendered unconscious. Then, after using his inhaler, he recovered enough to make it over to the bench. This could still be an accident."

"But the autopsy report is clear about the body being moved shortly after death. Dr. Gray noted signs of lividity in two separate areas. One was for a short time and one was more long-term."

"It still could have been an accident and then he was moved. Why do so many people have a motive to kill him?" asked Officer Williams.

Detective Parker lowered his arms and leaned forward so the front legs of his chair returned to the floor. "That's a good question. His reputation as an emerging artist was rising. His work was beginning to get global recognition. The exhibition at the Dali was a smart move. The art pieces that were sold at the reception are worth many times their purchase price. Would someone have killed him to increase their value? You can ask about the sold pieces and who bought them."

Officer Williams made a note on the white board and turned to face Detective Parker. "That's reaching a little far, don't you think?"

"Maybe." He smiled. "So you can tell when I'm grasping at straws, can you? That's good. Another question is would Dennis have threatened Lucas Brown with telling the director that he was using the gardens to help out the homeless vets?" He paused. "Also, what kind of information have you received from Savannah about Dennis's time as an apprentice?"

"She discovered a connection to other members of his gang, but she didn't yet know how many are still in the area or, for that matter, how many are even still alive. She found the name of the social worker. His name is James Armstrong. She went to see him. She thinks he might know more about Dennis and the other apprentices than he told her. She's still making more connections with the files that her dad encrypted."

"You need to follow up with Mr. James Armstrong and see if your badge will extract more names. Those encrypted files are a pain."

"Certainly, sir."

"Our problem director, Gina, has been continuing to avoid an interview. She needs to be questioned again, but I think you should give it another try before I resort to more formal demands on her."

"What line should I take?" Joy pulled out her notebook and poised her pen to take notes.

"We need to catch her in a lie. Any lie. It can be about the delay of the guest list. It certainly makes no sense that it would take this long to get the list to us even with computer problems. It can be about any errors you might find on the list of employees that were present for the reception. Use your intuition to see if you can find a discrepancy. That will give us a strong reason to bring her in for formal questioning with a lawyer present."

"When did you ask her about the guest list?"

"At our first meeting on Monday morning. It's now Friday morning. You can tell her that I'm in a blind fury and have started the process of serving her with a warrant." Detective Parker stood up. "In truth, I'm slammed right now, so I want you to temporarily—notice that I said *temporarily*—take the lead on this. Follow up with Gina and talk to the social worker."

"Are you going to the candlelight memorial service tonight?"

"No, I'll be stuck here wrapping up paperwork on my last two cases. I think it would be helpful if you went. Take note of who attends and what their reactions are. It might be a complete waste of time, but emotions run high at these events and something may come up that will narrow our investigation."

Officer Williams nodded. "I'll stop by here on my way back and type up a report."

"I'm confident that you will have something new to tell me about tonight."

Chapter 28

Friday morning

Savannah felt a huge sense of relief that the etching class had finally ended. After Jacob completed the translation of Dennis Lansing's file, they drove over to Webb's Glass Shop, unloaded the kiln, and reloaded it for the last time to complete the big Vinoy Hotel dining room order. The last load would come out of the kiln early Saturday morning. They were going to finish in the nick of time.

"Good morning, Amanda. Happy last day of class to you," said Savannah as they passed through the office into the classroom.

It was empty and Amanda was flipping through her planning book on the lectern. She looked up. "Hi guys. Hey, before I forget, I've got an idea. I want to open up Webb's for some open instruction hours. It occurred to me that some of our students are not quite ready for a permanent workspace at Webb's Studio, but could use help with projects after they've had a beginning class."

"That's a wonderful idea," said Savannah.

"Sure is." Amanda stood tall at the compliment. "When a class is held from ten to one o'clock, that still leaves, say, from two to five that could be scheduled that way. We could offer some introductory prices to start."

Savannah looked up to the ceiling. "If we charge about a third of the class fee, that should reduce the expectation of instruction, but give folks a place to work. Brilliant idea!" She raised her hand and they high-fived.

"I'll make up some flyers and hand them out to my students. I think the invitation should be personal, don't you?"

"Absolutely. That way you can play up the individual instruction aspect. You know, only a select few of my students are invited. That will keep it exclusive."

Jacob followed Savannah into the supply room and they checked the kiln. She bent down and read the temperature on the control panel. "It's still too hot inside to open the lid. We've got to wait until it gets down to at least under two hundred degrees or the quick change in temperature might crack the plates. That would be a big disaster. Patience is good."

She turned to Jacob. "Sorry, I miscalculated the cool-down time. But then sometimes in this heat and humidity, the kiln holds the heat longer." She reached over to scratch Suzy who never seemed to tire of being carried everywhere.

The front door bell jangled. Edward pushed in the door with his shoulder and made his way into the shop carrying a tray with three iced coffees, a root beer, and a plate of scones. "Good morning, all. I've got a new scone recipe I want you to test before I inflict it on my customers." He rested the corner of the tray on the edge of the cash register counter. "Are we meeting in the back?" He bobbed his head toward the office.

"What kind of scone?" Jacob asked as they made their way to the back of the shop.

As soon as she entered the office, Amanda pulled out one of the shelves in the oak rolltop desk.

Edward placed the tray down and handed Jacob his root beer. "The scones are a new recipe of ginger cinnamon with golden raisins. It's a new flavor for you, so you get to try a miniature version." Edward sat, then pointed to a scone that was literally bite sized.

Jacob grinned and took the scone. "I'll try this later."

"Well, I love ginger." Savannah grabbed one and sat, which prompted a squeak from the old oak chair. "We need to talk about Dennis's investigation. Jacob, did you bring the slip of paper with the encrypted gang member names?"

"No, but I remember them."

"Great, before we leave, get them from the file cabinet. I want to study them before I hand them over to Detective Parker."

Jacob smiled. "Yes, ma'am."

"Ma'am? Ma'am?" Savannah could feel a flush in her cheeks. "I despise—wait, you know I don't like that."

Amanda giggled. "Looks to me like someone's developing a sense of humor."

Savannah scratched the back of her neck. "Well played. Anyway, let's recap. I'll update Parker on Dennis's past after we get the kiln loaded for the last run of the Vinoy Hotel charger plates."

Edward spoke around the half-scone that he had in his mouth. "That's cutting it pretty fine, isn't it? They're due tomorrow?"

"Yes, you have a responsibility as my new paper-work drudge, to remind me to build twice as much slack time as I think I need into any large order. On a bright note, they're going to pay me the balance on delivery."

"That should be enough to get you out of sales tax trouble."

Jacob looked directly at Savannah. "What do you mean by tax trouble? Is this bad? Are you going out of business?"

Savannah reached out to pat Jacob, but pulled her hand back just in time. "No, this is a misunderstanding with the State of Florida that Edward has untangled for me. I owe a fine, which Edward is still negotiating with the Florida Department of Revenue. Even at its current value—which is in error—I can easily pay as soon as the charger plates are delivered." She calmed her voice. "There's absolutely no chance of closing Webb's over this. It's an administration error."

Amanda reached for the last scone. "As far as Savannah and I've been able to figure out regarding the instances of Gina's blackout times in social media, the first one corresponds to the times that

Dennis was off-line as well. That was a couple weeks ago and then he was off-line at the exhibit reception and never posted again. I think we should talk to Gina about that coincidence."

"Officer Williams said that Gina hasn't been cooperating with her and Detective Parker," said Savannah. "But we can talk to her at tonight's candlelight memorial ceremony."

"We also need to confront her about her prescheduled posts," said Amanda.

"I'll leave that to the police." Savannah drank the last of her iced coffee and put the glass back on Edward's tray. "Is everyone available to attend the candlelight memorial ceremony? It's tonight at seven in the Dali Museum gardens."

Jacob nodded.

"Sorry," said Edward. "I've got a new sales representative from an Atlanta brewery, called Sweetwater, coming to Queen's Head tonight. Their IPA 420 is a fast seller around town and I want to offer it to our customers. If I miss this appointment, I'll lose at least a month's worth of sales."

"I'd love to come," Amanda said. "Jacob has been telling me about Dennis's exhibit and I want to see it before it moves on."

"Actually, it's attracting record crowds and each of the exhibit pieces have sold at triple their original prices. I think it will extend by a few weeks at least." Savannah stood and ran a hand through her hair. "Hang on a second. That's something that the police need to know." She reached for her phone and texted Officer Williams. She nodded to Jacob.

"Let's check the kiln again. I'm getting restless for some reason."

Jacob drained the last of his root beer. "Maybe it has something to do with the exhibit. Did you know that there's a handwritten love letter etched into one of the pieces? It is signed from Savannah. Is that you?"

Edward frowned. "A what?" He bolted straight out of his chair. "A love letter?"

Savannah put her head in her hands. "Yes, Jacob. That would be me. I saw that some of his etched pieces had personal mementoes etched into the works, and I did spot that one."

"Of course there would be love notes!" Amanda got up to stand in front of Edward. "She was fourteen. That's what girls do. How many girls sent you love notes when you were in high school?"

Edward reacted with a crooked little smile. "Fair point." He walked over to Savannah and stroked her arm. "Sorry, luv. I'm a bit twitchy." He bent down to kiss her on the cheek.

"I hate for anyone to see which one it was." Savannah sighed in a puff. "I saw it at the exhibit reception. It was one of the sickeningly sweet ones. I was too embarrassed to point it out."

Amanda sat back down. "No complaining. Embarrassing or not, you are commemorated in an artwork. How cool is that?"

"Way cool," said Savannah and she smiled wide then her brow wrinkled. "Wait a minute. If there is one of my love notes in the exhibit, what about other mementoes?"

"Has anyone examined the pieces?" Edward placed his empty glass on the tray.

"No, but Jacob could spot something. We need to get over there and look at each piece closely," said Savannah. "Maybe we can squeeze in a trip right before lunch?"

Jacob nodded. "Is the kiln ready?"

Savannah jumped up from the desk. "Right." She checked her watch. "It should be ready to unload. Okay, guys. I'll see you all at the ceremony. Let's meet at Webb's Studio after. Four sets of eyes should be able to pick up some indications of suspicious behavior. All four of our current suspects will be there." She ticked them off on her fingers. "The widow, the museum director, the security guard, and the politician."

Amanda laughed. "It sounds like the tagline of a new blockbuster movie."

At the Dali, Jacob held Suzy in his arms while he examined each piece in Dennis Lansing's exhibit. Savannah followed him with a notebook copying down a list of each piece and the documents that were forever immortalized in his works.

The exhibit was crowded. The sensation of Dennis's murder had been artfully reimagined as a "young artist's last dreams" and only available as a complete collection for a few weeks. It was an effective campaign by the museum, but felt tacky commercial. There was barely enough room to move and it slowed their progress through the exhibit.

The etching elements were in varying levels of precision. Some were distorted images that had been unevenly sand etched to create a carefree tone. Other pieces were etched to almost a scientific precision so that you felt the actual document was embedded in the optical quality glass. One of those pieces was the image of Savannah's love letter.

"Rats!" Savannah said when she saw which one of her girlish love notes Dennis had chosen to etch into a large red swirl of glass. *Did he mean to embarrass me? It would be one of the gushy ones with a heart and initials at the bottom.*

She felt her cheeks turn red as Jacob examined the piece with a serious amount of attention. But it only appeared that way to her because of the note. He gave that no extra attention. He studied them all equally.

She turned around suddenly as she felt the tears slide down her cheeks. She wiped them away quickly and lifted her eyes to stop the flow. *Buck up. This is not helpful to Jacob.*

He moved to the next piece and began the same type of studied examination.

Savannah felt the tension slip from the back of her neck. *Of course he doesn't get the connection. He thinks of these as art objects, not emotional icons in a young man's life. I feel so sad that Dennis is gone. He was kinder to me than I knew. So much of what I am today is tied to his actions so long ago. Stop thinking that you were rejected. You were saved.*

They continued to examine the exhibits until all were listed in Savannah's notebook with the etched documents described and copied word-for-word. "Does anything strike you as odd or unusual?"

Jacob nodded yes.

"Really? Which one?" Savannah could hear the high pitch in her voice.

Jacob picked up Suzy.

This place is not good for Jacob. She calmed herself by taking a slow breath. "Had enough of the crowd?"

He nodded yes.

"Let's find a quiet place to talk about the exhibit. Okay?"

He nodded yes. She led him downstairs and out into the back garden. He was still holding Suzy when they sat on a small stone bench beside the wishing tree. It was a Florida ficus, over two-stories tall, that carried thousands of plastic streamers created from the admission wristbands. On the back of them were the written wishes of museum visitors from around the world.

"Is this better?" Savannah asked.

Jacob put Suzy down on the ground and she settled into her Sphinx pose looking up at him in concern. "Yes, that's better. I found a note in one of the artworks that could have been a dangerous choice. It was a note from someone named Chase. It was telling Dennis to meet him at the regular drop site in order to get his normal order. It also urged him to be on time so that his brother wouldn't be left to go cold turkey."

"That's the name that was mentioned in my dad's letter." Her forehead wrinkled; then she turned back to Jacob. "Which artwork is it?"

"It's the one right next to your love note."

Savannah looked down. Suzy was at ease and rested her head on her paws. *Jacob is fine now.*

"Sorry about the crowds. I should have considered that. Let's get you back to Webb's Studio."

Savannah stood to go and nearly bumped into Lucas Brown. She looked down at him with a stern frown. "How long have you been listening?"

Lucas took a step back. "Not more than a minute. I wanted to know if Suzy needed a drink. It can get hot out here and I saw that you didn't have a bowl of water for her." His handkerchief appeared to swiftly wipe his forehead. "I didn't mean to over-hear."

Jacob looked down at Suzy. "That's very kind. Suzy would like some water."

Lucas merely nodded and escaped into the museum.

"Jacob? Suzy doesn't appear thirsty. What did you want to tell me without Lucas overhearing?"

"I want you to ask Lucas if he has read those notes. It could make a difference in our investigation."

Savannah smiled. "Good thinking. I'll be pro-moting you soon if you continue to show this much initiative."

Jacob's eyes lit up like beacons.

Lucas returned from the museum with a stainless-steel dog bowl filled to the brim with water. Savannah and Jacob watched him walk as smoothly as he was able. It wasn't good enough to avoid water splashes down the entire front of his uniform. He placed the water bowl on the ground next to Suzy. She looked up at him, then looked at Jacob, then looked at Savannah. She tentatively drank a few laps, then lay back down with her head on her paws.

Jacob said, "Thank you Mr. Brown."

"By the way, Lucas"—Savannah cleared her throat—"have you examined Dennis's exhibit pieces closely?"

Lucas hitched his water streaked pants up. "No, I haven't." He glanced in the direction of the third-floor exhibit. "I didn't think of that. Have you discovered something? Is there a clue?"

Savannah turned to give Jacob a look. "We're not sure, but wanted to know if you had noticed anyone behaving strangely after viewing the exhibit."

"No, but that's a great idea. I'll ask the other guards and then I'll see if I can find a clue. Thanks for letting me help." He rushed into the museum with a bounce in his step.

"Thanks, Jacob. That was helpful, but I'm not sure we're going to get anything useful."

"Maybe not," said Jacob. "More eyes on a problem is always good."

Chapter 29

"This is a surprise. After months of trying to get our schedules aligned, we have two lunches in the same week." Savannah smiled at Officer Williams who had texted her to meet at Pom Pom's on Central Avenue for a quick bite. Savannah ordered the turkey with ginger cranberry chutney sandwich along with the specialty iced milk tea, with a splash of half-and-half. Joy ordered a gluten-free version of the same sandwich and a cold pressed coffee with almond milk.

"I'm gluten intolerant. It's been a distressing discovery and is a royal pain. When my doctor suggested it, I thought he was reaching for straws."

"That makes eating out a little tough, doesn't it?" Savannah smiled as the server brought their drinks.

Joy half smiled. "You bet it does. However, I've been restricting all gluten for about a month now and damned if I don't feel fantastic. I have a few local choices, but I've noticed that more and more eateries are offering gluten-free."

"So, why the quick lunch?"

Joy leaned over the table and lowered her voice. "Detective Parker has given me the lead in the Dennis Lansing case."

"Really? He did? That's amazing and a visible vote of confidence."

"I'm thrilled and nervous. Temporarily, he says. It's mostly because there was something that took priority. You heard about the terrible shooting at the nightclub in Orlando? He's gone over there to lend a hand."

"That's been all over the news," said Savannah. "What a heartbreaking tragedy. He's working on that?"

"Yes. He was instantly pulled off Dennis's case—all his cases in fact—to assist the lead investigator. They're sending the best officers from all over Florida. Good choice by the Orlando chief of police, wouldn't you say?"

"Absolutely. She's not only incredibly smart but not afraid to ask for help. No stinting on giving the victims' families justice."

"Coroner Gray also left to help with the identifications and autopsies," said Joy.

"It's horrible that an area known for its fairy-tale magic now feels unsafe and intolerant." Savannah let a silence settle between them. "You know working the massacre will change them both."

"True," said Joy. "I hope it finally drives them together. They've been dancing around each other too long."

"They have?"

"Oh yes. The best kept secret romance that everybody knows about. Except you, of course. Speaking of romance, when are you going to let that handsome Brit move in with you? You love him, don't you?"

Savannah felt a rush of warmth creep up over her ears. "Not shy, are you? Yes, I do, but I seem to be nervous about sharing my dad's home with him." She folded her hands and propped her chin on them. "Hearing about the tragedy, hearing how young most of the victims were . . . makes one think." She stared in silence.

They sat without moving for what seemed like a long time.

Joy broke the silence. "It's a reminder to get on with it." She picked up her sandwich and took a huge bite. "You know," she mumbled, "if Detective Parker solves the case quickly—he will if it is at all possible—I think the Orlando chief will petition our chief to promote him outside the normal cycle."

"Wow, no pressure for either of you, huh?" Savannah smiled.

"Since we're short staffed, I was the only one available to handle the Lansing case. It also means that I won't have access to anyone else. They will all be working on the big investigation."

"So, you have to do this by yourself? That's not fair."

"Opportunities don't come with a guarantee of fairness. I'm grabbing this with both hands." Joy took a huge mouthful of the sandwich and followed it with a sip of tea. "Detective Parker's vision has always been about serving justice, but he will be the youngest major ever."

Savannah tilted her head. "So, if Detective Parker gets promoted, what about you?"

"It does leave a vacancy. I could not be promoted to his level of course, but I would be delighted to step up a rank." A smile lit up Joy's face.

Savannah finished her sandwich and folded her hands in front of her. "Okay, what do you want me to do? How can I help?"

"I'm on my way over to see Mr. Armstrong. Tell me what you asked and what you said. I want to be sure to get as much as I can from him."

Savannah related the conversation that she and Jacob had with Mr. Armstrong.

"Were there any unusual reactions to your questions?"

"It's hard to say. His breathing was labored and it was difficult to understand him most of the time. His voice was thin and tended to drop away at the end of sentences." Savannah propped her chin on top of her overlapped hands. "But now that I'm talking about it, he reacted in an odd way to one name. He looked annoyed and uncomfortable at the mention of Dennis's wife. He frowned and then quickly recovered. Honestly, though, it could have been his irritation at not being able to speak properly."

"He seemed to know Harriet? Did you follow up?"

"No, I was interested in his participation in the apprenticeship program. But now that I think about it, Harriet is the same age as Dennis was. I didn't know her very well in high school. We didn't meet much at all. I vaguely remember her as a confident and focused student in a popular group of girls. I was never one of the cool kids."

Officer Williams took out her notebook and made a few notes and returned it to her back pocket. "What about Dennis's friends? Did he give you any names?"

"No, we asked, but again he seemed very uncomfortable. By that time, I thought we were exhausting him. His health appears quite fragile."

"Thanks, that will give me a chance to not only cover the same ground that you did to see if his story matches yours, but I'll also have a chance to find out more about Harriet." Joy leaned forward again. "In Detective Parker's opinion, she's the most likely one to have killed Dennis."

"I can certainly agree with her having the most motive. Apparently, she'll soon have control of her trust fund and she hasn't bothered to hide her irritation at Dennis's ability to spend large amounts of money arranging for these exhibits. Just think about shipping all those pieces." Savannah shuddered. "It gives me the sweats. Each piece would have to have a custom box created for it. All the insurance required for a specialized shipper would be pricey. I wonder how they managed?"

"So you think Detective Parker is right about Harriet? He's quite good."

Savannah downed the last of her iced tea. "He's usually right. However, I have to tell you that I have had several experiences with him being completely wrong."

Chapter 30

Friday evening

"I wonder why Gina wanted a candlelight memorial?" Savannah asked Amanda as she parked her Mini in the member parking lot.

"You didn't really have to pick us up. We could have taken one of those share-ride cars . . . or even a taxi." Rachel pushed open her door and stepped out in head to toe white except for bright teal eye shadow that covered her entire lid, meeting up with her penciled eyebrow.

"That's nonsense." Faith stepped out of the car from the passenger side of the backseat. She was also in white except for a pale purple slash of eye shadow. "You're too cheap to call a cab."

"I prefer *frugal*," said Rachel.

"It looks like it's going to be well attended. The lot is nearly full and we're almost half an hour early." Savannah looked around. She saw that the public parking garage also received a steady stream of cars.

"That would be something to find out tonight," said Amanda. "The invitation was from the Dali Museum using their normal member newsletter. Harriet could have asked Gina or Gina could have done this on her own." Amanda was also dressed in head to toe white including white sandals and white fingernail polish.

Savannah had chosen a white button-down blouse over a light tan pencil skirt. She wore a pair of tan kitten heels. The instructions in the newsletter had been explicit. She wondered if the dress code had a deep philosophical meaning or was it petty to think that Gina was looking for an artistic image that would align with the Dali esthetic. Savannah preferred to think the former.

They entered the museum and followed the quiet, slow moving crowd out to the garden area. A museum employee stood beside a table outside the double doors. He handed them a small white candle slipped through a white paper circle and motioned for them to join the crowd that was slowly filling up the entire garden area.

"There's those brothers who have an antique shop." Faith grabbed her sister's arm and spoke back over her shoulder. "They know lots of gossip. We'll find you after the service." They swooshed away.

Savannah walked toward the green bench sculpture. There was a bouquet of white lilies loosely tied with a white satin ribbon around the green stalks that had been placed on the seat. She felt a heaviness slip into her chest and quickly grabbed Amanda's hand. "I'm glad that you're here. It didn't feel right to ask Edward to change his plans to attend. I could be wrong, of course. We haven't been seeing eye to eye lately."

Amanda squeezed her hand. "Even when things don't work out, a first boyfriend is a special, special person."

They stood in front of the bench until Savannah felt the sadness lift and a renewed sense of resolve replaced it as she regained her composure. "Let's move closer to the speaker's podium. I want to hear what Gina and Harriet have to say."

The crowd began growing larger as more and more participants dressed in white arrived. It was taking on the look of a Victorian garden party. Conversation was hushed. Even so, the noise level was beginning to rise. Savannah recognized quite a few of the faces she saw at the exhibit opening reception. She caught a glimpse of Dennis's mother, Betty, and Chuck was looking uncomfortable in just a white sport jacket, white shirt with no tie, over khaki trousers. Lucas was there and had found an all-white uniform.

A few minutes after seven o'clock, Gina and Harriet approached the podium.

Gina's face was flushed dark and she pulled at the Dali red lips on a black background scarf that was the blatant bit of color in her all-white blouse and her white pencil skirt. Except for her bloodred stiletto heels, of course. Following aggressively closely was Harriet and the reason for Gina's ire became obvious. Contrary to the instructions in the newsletter invitation, Harriet wore unrelieved black from head to toe. A jaunty black fascinator perched just over her right eye.

Gina placed a sheet of paper on the podium,

then tapped the microphone twice politely to not only get everyone's attention, but also to make sure that it was on. She looked behind her and nodded to Lucas Brown. He stood at a military parade rest position, but his eyes were scanning the crowd. Gina also threw a tiny glance at Harriet.

Gina cleared her throat and stared at the memorial celebration participants. "Thank you." She paused a moment. "Thank you." She waited until the crowd fell into silence. "My dear friends, thank you for attending this candlelight memorial for Dennis Lansing. He was a local boy who overcame a troubled misspent youth to rise to the top tier of an elite group of artists. His vision, energy, and creativity never failed to please his benefactors and clients. We have lost a brilliant star. Our memorial tonight pays homage to his enormous talent. I believe we have the peak expression of his talent in our gallery. As a special tribute to his memory, this exhibit has extended its run to the end of next month."

There was a murmuring rustle through the crowd forcing Gina to tap the microphone again to gain the attention of the crowd. "Please, please." She paused until there was silence. "Our memorial program tonight is as follows. We'll have a few words from Dennis's widow and business partner, Harriet Lansing, followed by the lighting of our candles, during which Kate Finburg, star soprano with the St. Petersburg Opera Company, will perform. At the end, we'll say our farewells to Dennis by leaving our candles by the green bench sculpture and quietly exiting the garden." She waved her hand toward Harriet and stepped back to stand by

Lucas. Her hands were clenched and her posture stiff.

Harriet spread a small crumpled piece of paper flat onto the podium, then she took a deep breath and exhaled slowly. Her voice was high and thin as she read her testimonial directly from the paper without looking up. "Dennis was the guiding light of my life. He calmed my nerves as the world turned and now here we are at the edge of night trying to understand that it will be another world without him here."

Amanda leaned over and whispered softly into Savannah's ear, which surprised Savannah so much that she jumped. "She must have written that. It's horrible. Did she think we wouldn't recognize the names of those daytime TV soap operas? She could have paid someone to write a beautiful testimonial. That's unbelievably crass and petty. Do you think this is an act of some sort?"

"If she's hoping for a distraction from being investigated, this is an epic fail." Savannah shook her head slowly.

Harriet grabbed the crumpled speech and crushed it into a ball. She looked around for somewhere to dispose of it, but ended up just holding it. She stepped back an awkward distance away from Gina.

After Harriet left the podium, Lucas walked over to Gina and lit her candle with a white butane lighter. She allowed the flame to strengthen and walked out into the crowd and lit several of the candles near her. "Please share the light of his spirit." The visitors began lighting each other's candles and soon the garden was dotted with the flickering of several hundred candles.

Gina returned to the podium. "Next, we have Kate Finburg, from the St. Petersburg Opera Company. She grew up here and will sing an aria from Puccini's *Gianni Schicchi*. It's about deep love and tragic loss." She nodded to a tall, thin, young black woman with wild curly hair and bold pink lips who was dressed in long white robes.

The opera singer stepped in front of the podium and solemnly scanned the guests until absolute silence fell, then rested her sad gaze on the green bench. She leaned down to the microphone and announced, "I am singing the aria 'O Mio Babbino Caro.'" She lifted her head to look at the sky and began to sing in a lilt that portrayed the tragedy of a life lost before it began.

Savannah thought the selection was perfect and looked at Amanda to see her reaction. Amanda was in thrall with her eyes wide and her mouth slightly open.

Bending down to Amanda's ear, Savannah whispered, "Is this your first live opera?"

Amanda nodded as tears slipped down her cheeks.

Savannah gave her a side hug. "You'll never be able to live without it again."

The clear notes of the diva rose sweetly to a full and rich finale that left a haunting echo hanging large in the warm air.

A resounding slap broke the spiritual silence and everyone turned around and saw Gina holding the side of her face. "You can't do that!" She stepped back from Harriet and her eyes flashed murder. Harriet screamed, "I'll have you fired. I can do that now that I'm rich."

"Rich isn't going to help you in jail, you killer,"

shrieked Gina as she lunged toward Harriet with clutching hands and grabbed her by the throat.

Lucas Brown pulled Gina away from Harriet. "Stop that! Are you two crazy?"

Several members of the crowd began to move toward the disruption. Before anyone got close, Officer Joy Williams suddenly appeared at Lucas's shoulder. "Thank you. I'll take it from here. Ladies, this is disruptive behavior. We're going to have a serious discussion. Is there somewhere inside where we can talk?"

Gina adjusted her skirt and glared daggers at Harriet. "There's the Community Room just inside."

"Let's go." Officer Williams held both women by their elbows and then looked into the crowd. "Savannah," she called.

"Yes, Officer Williams, I'm right here." Savannah moved out of the crowd, closely followed by Amanda.

"Come along, then." Officer Williams tossed her head toward the entrance to the museum. "We're going to have a little cooling-off conversation." She proceeded to propel the two furious women with her firm grip on their upper arms.

Gina's assistant promptly stepped up to the microphone with a soothing voice and calmly directed the participants to the next part of the ceremony.

The group arrived at the double doors of the Community Room. "I'll get that." Lucas Brown unlocked the doors and opened them both wide to let the five women enter with as little crowding as possible.

"You may as well join us." Officer Williams nodded to Lucas. "The more the merrier . . . except that this isn't supposed to be a merry occasion." She released her grip on both Gina and Harriet.

They grabbed their arms in a mirrored action.

Savannah observed that the furnishings were arranged similarly to the café with four chairs at each table. None of the tables were configured for a large group.

Gina rubbed her arm as if it had been mauled by a bear. "We had a luncheon social here, today. The staff should have removed everything and stowed them away. Why does no one ever follow my orders?"

Savannah motioned to Lucas. "Let's push a couple tables together so we can at least sit down."

He hopped to it and in a flash they were sitting with Officer Williams at the head of the table and Lucas at the foot. Gina and Harriet sat across from each other closest to Officer Williams, and Savannah and Amanda took the remaining chairs with Savannah between Gina and Lucas.

"I simply cannot believe the behavior you two displayed here tonight." Officer Williams looked sternly at Gina and then at Harriet. "You are this close to being charged." Her fingers indicated an inch. "I haven't decided what the charge might be, but I'm sure I could figure something out. Maybe inciting a riot would work." She looked back at Gina. "You're a different case. I don't think the museum board of directors would be willing to continue your employment if you were arrested and charged with assault."

Savannah leaned into the table. "Why did you do it?"

Harriet made a choking noise in her throat. "She was Dennis's lover." She covered her face with both hands and propped her elbows on the table. "I found a note in one of Dennis's pockets as I was getting them ready for donation."

"Well, it certainly didn't take much encouragement on my part," Gina said. "He was starved for affection. You were so focused on taking possession of your big trust fund that he was desperate for someone to help him recapture his creative energy."

"Wait!" piped in Amanda. "Are you saying that Dennis was blocked? He couldn't create?"

No," said Harriet. "That is an absolute lie. He was full of new ideas. He said that his life would never be long enough to create everything that he wanted. That's not true."

Gina stood up. "And how would you know? When was the last time you even shared a room, much less a bed?"

"This is ridiculous. I don't have to listen to this." Harriet looked at Officer Williams. "Do I have to stay here and be ridiculed and insulted while my murdered husband is in the morgue?"

"It depends." Officer Williams turned to Gina. "Are you going to press charges?"

The room quickly filled with silence. Gina narrowed her eyes and you could see the wheels spinning through her choices. She looked down at the table. "No. It wouldn't be good for the Dali or for Dennis's legacy."

Officer Williams turned to Harriet. "Are you going to press charges?"

"No, I'm just fine." Harriet flounced out of the room and tried to slam the door, but the door closer piston wouldn't allow her to do anything but push it slowly. She huffed in frustration, then left the room.

Gina stood but nearly fell backwards. She recovered. "If you have nothing else"—she looked at Officer Williams—"I have guests to attend to."

Savannah pointed a finger in the air. "Speaking of guests, has the guest list shown up?"

Officer Williams rolled her eyes at Savannah in an *I should have asked that* look. "Right, you were requested to turn that over to us on Monday, along with the names of the employees who were working that night. Where is it?"

"Oh," said Gina in a quiet voice. "I was hoping I wouldn't have to admit that our server went down that night."

"That's quite a coincidence, don't you think?" Savannah asked.

Officer Williams gave Savannah a quick hand signal to be quiet. "Why have you waited this long to reveal that? We are, in fact, now in the process of serving the museum with a search warrant for your employee records and all paperwork that is associated with Dennis's exhibit. You could avoid more bad publicity if you would voluntarily turn over everything you have. The *Tampa Bay Times* is a fair newspaper, but this will make excellent copy."

"I know, I know. The press coverage has been distressing to the members of the board. I've been able to trace a preliminary guest list that was generated prior to mailing the invitations. We have an off-site records facility and our IT manager was able to extract it. Our employee records were not affected by the server crash. I will turn those both over to you tomorrow. Can I go now?"

"No problem. This was a cooling-off intervention. You're free to go."

"Lucas, let's get back to work."

Lucas nodded, then stood and followed Gina out of the community room. As he was closing the door, he said, "You can stay as long as you wish. I'll come back later and lock this up." He smiled at the three of them.

"We suspected that there was an affair," said Officer Williams. "Did you?"

Savannah nodded to Amanda. "Yes, I've been looking into their social media activity and it looks like their absences are at the same times. I haven't been able to find out where they were meeting, but I still might be able to track that down."

Officer Williams turned to Savannah. "You're going to continue your investigation, aren't you?

"Yes. This is more to me than investigating encrypted records. One of those women is responsible for the death of my first boyfriend. I'll keep combing through the past for more clues about Dennis's gang activities, but I think it was one of those two."

Chapter 31

Savannah stopped by Webb's Glass Shop to pick up the encrypted records that Amanda had extracted from the file cabinet. There were six that had been associated with Dennis in some way. She scooped them up and drove home.

Rooney wriggled a suppressed greeting until she unlocked the door, dropped her keys in the ceramic bowl on her mother's antique Spanish chest, and put the files onto the dining room table. Then she turned to Rooney and gave him tons of hugs and scratching behind his ears and along his back. "We've got to find a way for little Snowy to like you." She sat on the floor and held his gray head with both hands. "You know you're adorable. I know you're adorable. We have to convince Snowy of that or . . . well, I don't even want to think about that." She got up and looked down at the beautifully muscled blue-gray dog that had wrapped himself around her heart. "We're going to solve this so Edward and Snowy can come live with us.

"Okay, boy. Give me a minute to change and let's do our run."

They were out the door in five minutes on their normal route around the neighborhood. Then they took a longer loop because Rooney didn't seem at all winded and Savannah also still felt the edge of tension and restlessness that she was trying to relieve.

They returned to the house tired but calm. After she fed Rooney, she opened a pack of peanut butter crackers and poured a glass of milk. She started examining the records as she ate, eliminating one of the students right away as he had moved to California with his parents after only a few months in the program. A second folder was eliminated because the student had been killed in a drive-by shooting only days after signing up for the program. That made two in the eliminated pile.

Could that have been a warning to other students not to participate in Dad's program? No, that's overreacting.

She opened the next folder and this one appeared to have been successful in the program. He had gone on to help with some of the outreach excursions to community businesses to find more apprentice positions for students. Savannah put that one into a separate pile for further investigation.

The fourth file was interesting in that it seemed to be apprenticing the student to a foster care home to assist the house mother. Savannah didn't quite understand how that could be helpful, then looked at the applicant's name. Jeri was a female student and was escaping a violent home life. She was keen to learn more about foster care homes and apparently went on to create an agency in Indiana. She was married with four children and worked in Indianapolis with social services to place at-risk children in good homes. She put it in the elimination pile.

That is so typically Dad. He saved this young woman from a bad situation and she went on to have a good life. I'm so proud to be his daughter.

Savannah opened the fifth file. It documented the many times the young man had entered the program—quit the program—then entered again. A total of five times. What kind of patience did that require?

I have my moments, but this is completely out of my league. Dad had it covered.

She looked at his final apprenticeship job—for a cook's assistant at one of the oldest hamburger joints in St. Petersburg, El Cap's on 4th Street North. It was the last job listed in the folder. It must have done the trick because there were several letters from the owners about how much they appreciated his work. She put the folder in the further investigation pile.

"Hey, Rooney. We need to go down to El Cap's tonight. Doesn't that sound good?"

Rooney tilted his head and looked up at her with patient eyes. After she turned back to the folders, he put his head back down on his front paws.

She picked up the last folder. According to her father's notes, it also contained the records of a boy who was difficult to place. He was the same age as Dennis, but for some reason, in this record, the name was never revealed. Her dad just avoided it.

Savannah ran a hand through her curls. How was she going to figure out who the guy was? Maybe Jacob would be able to figure it out from clues that she couldn't put together.

She put the three folders that needed further investigation in her backpack and left the other three on the dining room table.

Savannah called Edward. "Has your new brewery rep been there?"

"Yes, he just left. He's going to give me a great price break for the first month."

"Perfect. Can you leave Queen's Head Pub for about an hour? I have a lead I want to chase at El Cap's. We could grab a hamburger."

"Hmm. Hang on a second. Let me check with Nicole."

Savannah heard him ask Nicole if she was good with him leaving for a quick visit to El Cap's and overheard Nichol's reply.

"No worries. If you get delayed, just give me a call and I'll call in one of the part-time servers."

"No, no. It's going to get busy later. I'll be back in an hour, tops." He talked into the phone. "I'm good. Do you want to ride the Indian?"

"No, stop by my house. I want to take Rooney. They have outside seating and he can just lay down underneath the table while we eat and do our research."

"Even better. I'll just meet you there. Nicole is being nice. It's the busiest night of the week and we're trying to cover for some servers that are on vacation."

"No problem. See you there." She ended the call and loaded Rooney into the Mini Cooper.

* * *

Rooney walked right up to the outside table that was closest to the parking lot and slipped underneath. Edward stood up from the next table.

Savannah raised her eyebrows. "Rooney's been here before." She sat on one of the three concrete benches that surrounded the worn concrete table furnished with a much-needed shade-producing umbrella. "Did Dad eat here often? He didn't mention it to me."

"I think so. He would tell me stories about the owner from the early days of the Florida tourist boom." Edward sat at their table. "Who are you trying to find?"

"I need to ask about one of Dennis's friends from the records. Dennis must have taken out some time to meet up with his buddies from the past."

A stout white-haired server kicked open the door with her black running shoe and approached their table. She wore black polyester pants with an elastic waist and a white short-sleeved, button-up camp shirt. She held a classic green order book in one hand with a Bic pen ready to write in the other. "Have you two been here before?"

Savannah said, "A long time ago."

Edward said, "No."

She pursed her lips. "Well then, you need to understand that the drinks don't come with refills. The tap water is twenty-five cents and the hamburger comes with mustard, onions, and mayonnaise. Everything else is extra. The menus are right there on your table. What would you like to drink?"

"I'll have a Blue Moon," said Savannah.

"Me, too," said Edward as he grabbed one of the small, plastic-coated menu cards.

The server frowned. "Is this on one check?"

They both replied, "Yes."

She made a note on her order pad and went inside.

Edward scanned the menu. "I've never seen anything like this before. How do they stay in business?"

Savannah chuckled. "This place is a St. Petersburg institution. They have customers that have eaten here every week for decades. It's not for everyone and definitely not for the hipster set." She glanced at the menu and smiled. "This hasn't changed much since I was a girl. I'm having their hamburger and the fries with a side of coleslaw."

"I'll follow you. You're the local."

They ordered the same meal when the server returned and she noted that on her order pad.

As she turned to leave, Savannah asked, "How long have you worked here?"

For the first time, a smile spread on the server's face and softened its edges into a surprisingly gentle look. "Oh, sweetie, I've been here since the beginning, more than fifty years ago. I've never worked anywhere else. Why mess with a good thing?"

"Great. Do you remember a young man that worked here named Alex Wilson? He was an apprentice student from St. Petersburg High School."

Her face brightened into a full smile. "Well, of course I remember Alex! We taught him everything about being a short order cook and he's now a famous chef. He started out as a waiter. That just didn't work for him, but the moment he stepped to the grill, he found his calling. I still miss his grilled onions."

"That's wonderful. I'm Savannah Webb. My father John helped establish the apprenticeship program. When you have a break, can you come back and talk to us for a little while?"

She patted the top of Savannah's hand. "Why sure, sweetie. I'll have a chance right after I deliver your food. It's a slow time right now." She left, leaving a faint scent of rose-scented talcum powder behind.

"I'm gobsmacked," said Edward. "That was a complete turnabout."

"I think the sweetie persona is the one that the old-timers get to see."

"That explains a lot."

Savannah straightened up and looked Edward square in the eyes. "We need to discuss the kitten." She reached over and placed her hand on his.

"Too right." Edward turned his hand and grasped Savannah's hand and placed his other hand on top. "I was afraid that Snowy would be the end of us."

Savannah placed her remaining hand on top of Edward's. "I definitely don't want that to happen to us. We need to work together to get this right."

"Agreed. When shall we try again?"

Savannah puffed out a long sigh. "You are pressuring me. You might not realize it . . . although, I have to acknowledge that I'm not good about saying what's going on with me."

"Really?" Edward raised his eyebrows. "Ya think?"

Savannah laughed and took his hands, kissed each, and placed them on her face. "You mean so much to me." She paused. "It's time that I showed you how happy you make me."

"I'm waiting."

"Now, about Snowy. I think the next thing we need to—"

At that point, the server returned with a cheery, "Hi, little lovebirds. Here are your burgers with a little extra onion thrown in as a bonus." She sat across from them and waved them to start eating their hamburgers.

Edward started to take a huge bite, but Savannah stopped him. "Wait, let me show you how my dad used to fix these up for me." She picked up the top bun and forked in a generous plop of the coleslaw and pressed the bun back on top. "Try that."

He took a large bite, shook his head up and down, and said, "That's great," through his full mouth.

The server watched them with a beneficent smile. "That boy you want to know about was here last week. He stops by the kitchen every time he visits from Chicago."

Savannah and Edward exchanged a glance.

"He's living in Chicago?" Savannah lowered her sandwich back to the plate. "When did he move there?"

"A while ago. Sweetie, at the time he left, there really wasn't much to keep him here in St. Petersburg. The current fancy dining craze didn't start here until right after he left, but he found his calling in Chicago and he owns a restaurant right on the lake."

"When was his last visit?"

"Just this past weekend. I was on shift when he stopped by. He was full of chatter about one of his apprentice buddies. Apparently, not from the same high school, but in the same rescue program. He said it was a mixed-up mess."

"Mixed-up?"

"That's what he said . . . mixed-up. Good news and bad news. The good news was that art exhibit down at the Dali. The artist was one of the apprentices. He was happy for another success from the group."

Edward leaned toward the server. "What was the bad news?"

"He wouldn't say at first. Usually, he's open as a book to us here at El Cap's, but not this time. He only hinted at a problem with another apprentice that was a lot of trouble to everyone."

"Do you know when he went back to Chicago?" asked Savannah.

"Sure I do. He stopped in here on Saturday on his way to the airport at about six o-clock. So, he left well before the Sunday event."

Chapter 32

Friday night

"Thanks for driving downtown," said Savannah as she held open the gate for Amanda, who was followed by Jacob. "I think it will save us all time if we consolidate everything we know before I report our findings to Officer Williams this evening."

"How long do you think this will take?" asked Edward who was standing behind her.

"Not long." She walked over to the green bench sculpture where Lucas was standing in military at ease stance. "Lucas has been kind enough to let us into the garden for one more chance to look around."

He nodded solemnly.

Amanda turned to look at the bench. "Oh, look at the memorial they've created for Dennis. All the candles, cards, and flowers are around the bench. It reminds me of the pictures of Princess Diana's flowers outside Kensington Palace." She sniffed and pulled a tissue out of her bag and blew her nose. "Isn't that right, Edward?"

"I'm not surprised to see this. It seems that the US is adopting the European practice of pop-up memorials."

Jacob picked up Suzy. "What are we doing?"

"Oh, sorry. I'm a bit distracted by the display. What we want to do is review the information that we've found before Officer Williams gets here in"—Savannah looked at her watch—"about ten minutes. She wants to interview us thoroughly so she can turn in her first report as the lead investigator this evening."

Jacob spoke. "I have decoded all the files of the gang members associated with Dennis."

Edward folded his arms across his chest. "Just how much information have we told Officer Williams?"

"It's easier to list the four things I haven't told her yet. First"—Savannah raised her left hand and ticked off the fingers as she spoke—"what you and I discovered tonight about Dennis's conversation with his Chicago chef friend, which was related to another of the apprentices. Second, that Jacob discovered a document buried in one of the art pieces that implicated Charles King in drug activities while he was still in high school. Third, that Dennis's wife was trying to quickly divorce him before the trust fund transferred to her control." She paused and left her finger pressed onto her ring finger.

"That's only three," said Jacob. "The last one is that letter that was found in Dennis's pocket. He was using it to get a chance to talk to you again."

Amanda frowned. "What? How do you know that? Why haven't you told us?"

"I found the love note. It's in the only red piece of glass in the collection." He picked up Suzy and rubbed her belly. "It might not have anything to do with the murder."

Savannah looked over to Edward. "It might not be connected to his murder, but it does indicate that our past meant something to him. I'm sorry that we didn't get to discuss that." She smiled. "If he asked, I would have told him that I was taken."

She looked at Edward's serious face and waited. The silence stretched until Edward cracked a tiny frown. "I trust you completely, Savannah. I'm sorry you didn't get to resolve that with Dennis."

"Me too."

"By the way, I called my mum about the flowers that were etched in your love note piece," said Edward.

"You did what?"

"Mum says that daffodils mean regard, unrequited love, sunshine, and respect. Basically, the sun shines when I'm with you. The lilacs stand for the first emotions of love."

Savannah rubbed the corner of her eye and nodded. "I think that's an accurate description of how Dennis felt. Thank your mother the next time you speak to her. I think that helps."

"Sure, luv."

"Another thing Jacob uncovered in the exhibit was a document scrap from the days when Dennis was involved in the gang. The piece clearly implicates one of the gang members in drug dealing."

Amanda spoke. "Can we see it?"

Savannah looked at Lucas. "Could we?"

Lucas shrugged his shoulders. "I don't see why not? It would be great to get this business over and done with." Hitching up his trousers, he took a little skip step and led them into the museum via the garden door into the café. They took the spiral staircase, which opened up onto the second floor special exhibit area. The large exhibit sign outside the gallery space was wrapped in black fabric with a small table beside it filled with floral arrangements. Lucas led them into the exhibit hall.

Savannah tapped on Jacob's shoulder and caught Amanda's eyes. She whispered, "We don't need to hide our talk about our investigation from Lucas anymore. I know we haven't actually cleared anyone in this investigation, but my gut says Lucas is not involved with Dennis's death."

Jacob nodded. "He is very helpful."

"Yes, I think he had a very good reason for pointing us in other directions."

Lucas turned back to see if they were following him. "Do you need—"

"I know where it is," Jacob said. He and Suzy moved into the exhibit hall and stood in front of the largest piece in Dennis's exhibit.

Amanda leaned down to look into the large green and metallic laced oblong. The surface had some etched figures located near the back of the piece. "I don't see what you're talking about. I can't make out anything."

Savannah pointed to the last line of the etched words. "This is what Jacob found. It's a crumpled note signed from someone with initials CK that clearly lists a date, time, and meeting place for a pickup of twenty kilos of heroin on Central Avenue."

Edward squinted at the etched letters. "That looks like it was behind Webb's Glass Shop. What a cheeky choice." He turned to Savannah. "Do you think your dad caught them and that's how CK was brought into the apprentice program?"

Savannah bit her lip. "I think that's how Dad kept control of CK over the years. He had proof that he could hold over him. In the records that I found, it explained who CK grew up to be." She stood in front of the sculptured glass.

Amanda blurted out, "Don't keep us waiting! Tell!"

"I think it's obvious, but apparently not. The apprentice was Charles King."

"Charles King!" Lucas took off his hat and wiped his face free of sweat with his handkerchief. "Are you saying that our sponsor, Charles King, was involved in drugs when he was a teen? That's a powerful bit of knowledge."

"That's way too powerful," said Amanda, "if it could be proved."

"It can with this." Savannah started toward the door, pulling out her phone as she walked. "Officer Williams needs to know about this. I'll have her meet us by the bench. This is too important to wait for a report."

By the time they reached the bottom of the stairs, Officer Williams had answered Savannah's call. "What have you got?"

"We've found an etched note in one of the exhibit pieces that implicates State Representative Charles King in Dennis's murder. Can you meet us here at the Dali?" Savannah ended the call and stowed the phone in her backpack. "She'll be here in a few minutes. We need to meet her by the bench." She looked at Lucas who was slowly descending. "That's all right, isn't it?"

He reached the bottom and pulled out his handkerchief, but stopped midway to his forehead. A loud crash came from inside the glass exhibit gallery.

"Someone's here!" Savannah sprinted past Lucas and launched up the stairs without a thought. "They're destroying Dennis's pieces!"

She bolted into the gallery and saw Charles King lift one of the artworks and smash it to the floor. He moved to the next one and lifted it over his head. It was the piece that had the incriminating evidence etched into the surface.

"Stop!" Savannah shrieked.

Charles lowered the artwork and stared at Savannah with red-rimmed eyes and a dazed look. "I can't stop. This has destroyed me. I must destroy it." He turned and bolted through the emergency exit. He punched the glass square in the security alarm box with the heel of his hand, setting off a screaming alarm.

Savannah followed him out the door only vaguely aware of the sound of doors clicking locked throughout the museum. They were in what appeared to be a maintenance corridor that led to a staircase. Savannah saw Charles at the top of the stairs.

"Stop following me! You don't want to see this."

"Come back." Savannah shivered a cold streak

down her back. His grip on the artwork was loose and careless. "Put down that piece of glass, Charles. Put it down."

He opened the door labeled ROOF and Savannah followed behind him before the door could shut. "Charles, please stop." She stopped cold in front of the door and heard it click behind her. The view was magnificent. The vista of the waterfront park, the Albert Whitted Airport runway, and the newly constructed pier were stretched out before her. They taunted her. Her fear of heights glued her feet to the rooftop. *I need to move, now.*

She saw Charles standing at the edge of the rooftop holding the green and metallic oblong in front of him. "Charles," she screamed again. "Stop!"

He turned a tortured face toward her. "It's too late now. You guys know. You know all about me. It's too late." He lifted the glass oblong over his head.

"I didn't know until now," said Savannah. "Chase is your nickname, isn't it? That's the connection I couldn't make with my dad's letter. Don't destroy the glass. It won't help, now."

"But you're the only one who knows, right?"

"No!" shouted Savannah. "I've told everyone."

He lightly tossed it down in a gentle arc. They both startled when the shattering sound reached them. "No, you haven't. You're lying."

Savannah took a step toward Charles. He was standing at the edge of the roof looking down at the green shards of Dennis's globe.

"Charles," said Savannah in as soft a voice as she could manage. "Charles, please step back from the edge. I can't come out there. Please, Charles."

He turned his red eyes toward her. His gaze seemed distant and he didn't look into her eyes . . . just somewhere around the top of her head. "I'm lost. So lost."

"Charles, explain to me, please." She stepped forward two steps. "What do you mean?"

He looked at her then. Right into her eyes. "I had it all planned out. Each political step—one by one. It's all a ruin now." He turned and placed a foot at the edge of the roof. "I didn't mean to kill Dennis. He was upset that my cash payment needed to stop. He was going to be fine with his wife's money. I didn't know he was sick. He wouldn't have ever told anyone that I was responsible for the death of his brother. We were cursed by our shared past. I should have trusted him, but there's no way to recover from this."

Savannah swallowed her fear and forced herself to move forward reaching to grab him tightly by the arm. "You can't mean this. Think for just a moment."

He turned cold eyes back to her. "I have." He grabbed her hand from his sleeve and pulled her toward the edge. "If you don't tell anyone, I can continue with my political campaign. You're going to jump off this building in despair over your lost love."

Savannah heard herself scream. She didn't recognize the sound. She dropped her full weight straight down as she pulled on her hand with all her strength.

Charles lost his grip on her hand and overbalanced over the edge of the roof.

After an eternity, she heard the terrible sound of his body hitting the ground.

She stood still for what seemed hours but was likely only a few seconds, then backed away from the edge to sit near the roof door, bent her head down, and sobbed.

Chapter 33

Savannah handed the last box of commissioned charger plates to Jacob, who wedged it into the last open space in the back of her Mini Cooper. She carefully closed the hatch.

"Detective Parker has given Officer Williams a recommendation that she be promoted to sergeant."

Jacob said, "That's good for her. She's not that old."

Savannah chuckled. "No, she's not that old. She called me late last night after all the activity at the Dali died down."

Jacob hopped into the passenger side with Suzy on his lap then they drove downtown to the Vinoy Hotel.

As she pulled up to the delivery entrance in the back of the hotel, the catering manager called for several porters in their 1920s-newsboy livery to begin taking the boxes straight into the ballroom.

"Can I see how the chargers look in their final place settings?" Savannah asked the catering manager.

"Don't see why not. The effect of your custom glass chargers is a game changer. We're very pleased that you finished them in time." He gave her a quick wink. "Even with the added quantities. A bit unfair if you ask me, but no one did." He waved a hand to the door and Savannah scurried into the large room followed closely by Jacob holding Suzy.

"Oh." She just stood while the servers quickly slipped one of her chargers under each dinner plate. She soaked in the magnificent table setting for over three hundred places. The glass chargers tied together the colors of the centerpiece flowers and the ribbons that tied the backs of the fabric-covered chairs. The catering manager was right. It was a game changer.

She jumped as he spoke. "You should be incredibly proud. I think this marks the moment when Webb's Glass Shop is not your late father's anymore. I think Webb's Glass Shop now fully belongs to Savannah Webb."

She smiled wide and turned around. "Thanks. I believe you worked with him, didn't you?"

"Yes, I knew John well."

Jacob turned to him and held out his hand. "Hi, I'm Jacob. I work at Webb's Glass Shop and I invented a new loading system for fusing more plates in the kiln. That's why we could make so many."

Savannah smiled. *That was a deliberate overture to a customer. Jacob can do this.*

After a long look and a quick cell phone photo

for Amanda to post on the website, they got in the Mini and headed back toward Webb's Glass Shop.

"It's time for our celebration. Is your mother dropping you off at Edward's condo?"

"Yes." Jacob nodded. "Soon, she won't have to do that."

Savannah turned to him sharply. "Why? Are you going to leave Webb's?"

"No, I would never leave Webb's. I am going to learn to drive." He kissed Suzy on the top of the head and stared straight out the front window.

"That's wonderful. Your mother will be so pleased."

She dropped Jacob and Suzy off at his house and drove home. After a quick shower and a change into her little black dress, she called for Rooney to get into the travel crate she had placed in the back of the Mini. He hopped right in and she drove to Edward's condo. She snapped a lead onto Rooney's collar and entered the elevator. He was behaving perfectly.

The elevator doors opened and she could hear the murmur of happy voices from Edward's open door at the end of the hall.

"Hey, Savannah," said Amanda. She was standing in the hallway decked out in festive green with three red loops of tree lights draped around her neck. "Oh, you've brought Rooney. I thought Snowy and Rooney didn't get along."

"I'm trying out a new approach," said Savannah. "If we can get Snowy to like or at least tolerate Rooney in her own territory, it will be much easier to introduce her to my house." She raised her eyebrows. "Good, don't you think?"

Amanda lifted both hands and shrugged her shoulders. "I don't know. I've never had a pet."

Savannah led Rooney into the condo. Officer Williams was just inside the open living-dining room dressed as a civilian in jeans and a crisp white button-down shirt. She held a fizzing flute of champagne and lifted her glass. "Good, you're the last one. You're here to help me propose a toast." She looked over her shoulder at Edward who was carrying a tray of flutes. "Edward, quick! Give Savannah a glass."

Edward's eyebrows raised at Rooney, but he offered the tray so that Savannah could take one.

Savannah looked over the little group that included Jacob, his mother, Edward, Amanda, bartender Nicole, the twins Rachel and Faith, Officer Joy Williams, Detective Parker, Coroner Gray, Arthur and his wife Nancy, and now Savannah. Savannah cleared her throat. "Thank you, Edward, for hosting this little celebration. Before I propose a toast, can we hear a few words from the lady of the day?"

Officer Joy Williams smiled. "Yes ma'am. I've worked hard from my first day as a cadet. However, it takes more than just hard work to get ahead in the police business. It takes a lot of good luck"—she pointed her glass toward Savannah—"and a lot of support."

Savannah turned and raised her glass to Officer Williams, then to Detective Parker. "To our continuing success as a team that brings justice to this city. Cheers!"

Detective Parker lifted his glass high with one

hand and gathered Coroner Gray into a side hug with the other. "Cheers!"

Savannah sipped deeply and clinked her glass with Joy's. "You so deserve this promotion. No amount of support can substitute for your tremendous dedication and intuition. What a great combination."

"Okay you two," said Rachel. "Fess up. Why did Charles—"

"Smash all the glass and then leap off the Dali?" finished Faith.

Savannah and Joy looked at each other.

"Go ahead," said Joy. "You worked it out."

"It started with my dad. He didn't turn Chuck into the police for dealing drugs while he was in the apprenticeship program. He should have, but that would have probably meant shutting down the program and ruining the chances of everyone who had made a clean start . . . Dennis included."

"Mr. Webb broke the law?" Jacob said in a high-pitched voice. "He wouldn't do that."

"In this case, he did. I think that's one reason he decided to encrypt all the records. He didn't want anyone to know who was involved. What Dad didn't know was that Chuck was the one who gave Dennis's brother the drugs that caused his death."

"But how did Dennis find out?" Amanda asked.

"I think he found that note in his high school papers when he was looking for documents to etch into his collection pieces. I don't think he understood the danger of making that public. Because Charles King was a respected Florida State congressman now, I don't think Dennis realized what a risk he was taking. It angered Chuck enough to stop acting as one of Dennis's patrons. It's all sad."

The party succeeded in that warm pleasant way that required no effort. Everyone seemed happy to nibble and chat about perfectly ordinary normal activities. Savannah blessed her lucky stars for finding this group as her family.

Edward motioned for Savannah to follow him down the tiny hallway to the bedroom suite. He kissed her quickly. "What's the idea behind bringing Rooney? He's going to scare Snowy out of her skin again. I thought we wanted them to get along, don't we?"

Savannah smiled. "I have a clever plan. Where is she?"

"She's under the bed, of course. She'll stay there until everyone leaves."

"Good. I'll take charge when everyone is gone." Savannah gave him a warm kiss and went back into the living room.

The party worked itself out in a couple hours and soon they were the only ones left on the balcony.

"Go on then," said Edward. "Tell me about this clever plan to introduce Snowy to Rooney."

"Go ahead and get her food ready and I'll make sure that Rooney stays calm. It would be best if it's a special treat for her—wet food, if you have it. I'm going to stay with Rooney over here on the far end of the couch."

Edward went into the galley kitchen that had a large pass-through window into the dining-living room. He opened a can of cat food and spooned it into Snowy's aluminum food dish. As soon as he set it on the floor, a white streak dashed from the bedroom into the kitchen. She scarfed up the meal, then began a loud purr as she licked her paws.

"Now that she's really, really full"—Savannah motioned for Rooney to lay down at her feet in front of the couch—"bring her over to me."

Edward scooped up the tiny white bundle and gave her to Savannah.

"Rooney, stay down," she said when he lifted his head.

He lowered his head onto his feet, but his eyes were straining to look at Snowy. Savannah took the little bundle, snuggled her, scratched behind her ears and under her chin, and rubbed down her belly. Snowy responded with a loud purr and tried to catch Savannah's fingers.

"Edward, come and sit next to me and pet Snowy, too."

He snuggled next to Savannah and they held Snowy together.

"Okay, Rooney. You can smell—gently!"

Rooney sniffed the white fur and laid his head on Savannah's knee.

"Stay there, Rooney."

Snowy opened her eyes wide and looked deep into Rooney's. She reached over with a kitten paw and tapped him on the nose. He blinked but stayed still. She tapped him again, then turned herself over and stretched out her paws upside-down to touch his nose. He sniffed. Without warning, Snowy jumped up and tucked herself under Rooney's chin and began kneading bread on his chest. Rooney moved back to the floor and Snowy tumbled down, too.

Edward reached to snatch Snowy, but Savannah's arm blocked the move. "This is just what we want. Let them make friends their own way."

Rooney moved to the center of the living room and stretched out flat. Snowy followed him with her bouncy pouncing and attacked his large paws in play fighting. After a minute with Rooney staying still, Snowy decided it was time to nap and curled up between Rooney's front legs. Rooney followed suit and laid his head back on the floor. The only sound from the two of them was Snowy's purring.

"Houston, I think we've solved the problem." Savannah put Edward's arm around her shoulder, tucked her feet underneath her, and snuggled into his chest. "A few more introductions like this and"—she poked him in the chest with her finger—"you can move into my place."

He sealed that deal with a kiss.

GLOSSARY

Etching Adding designs to glass by applying hydrofluoric acid or a similar product.

Fused Glass Glass that has been fired in a kiln at a temperature high enough to melt different pieces together.

Kiln Insulated chamber for heating and cooling glass or ceramics.

Kiln-formed Glass that is altered, fused, shaped, slumped, or textured by the heat of a kiln.

Sandblasting Creating designs by using high-pressure air mixed with sand to carve texture on the surface of glass.

Slump A technique used to form glass using a mold, heat, and gravity.

INFORMATION ABOUT
ETCHED GLASS
INSTRUCTION

Making gifts of glass is my favorite hobby. My husband and I have a large kiln in the small studio behind our house that we use to fuse glass. In addition, we have been creating a series of etched glass books with the cover of each book in the Webb's Glass Shop mystery series.

Although it looks and sounds intimidating, etching glass is straightforward. Most stained-glass shops offer workshops on how to make sand or chemical etched plates, platters, jewelry, and my personal favorite—Christmas ornaments.

Webb's Glass Shop is inspired by the real-life Grand Central Stained Glass & Graphics business owned by our good friends Bradley and Eloyne Erickson. Their website is http://www.grandcentral-stainedglass.com.

You can find a class in your area by searching the Web for fused, etched, or stained-glass classes in your city.

My husband and I have scaled back our glass work to making gifts for friends, family, and book promotion. Our current interest is making vases using a draping technique over a cylinder mold. They are gorgeous and I usually have one with me when I have an event at a library or festival. To see the process we use in making these vases, go to the website sponsored by Kensington Books. https://www.hobbyreads.com.

Don't miss the first book
in the Webb's Glass Shop Mystery series,

Pane and Suffering

On sale now
wherever books and ebooks are sold!

Chapter 1

Monday Morning

Savannah fingered the key ring her late father had used only a week ago. She knew each key by memory, having used them from babyhood up through borrowing his car with her newly issued driver's license. She clenched them in her fist and took a deep shaky breath. *Dad will never twirl them barely out of my reach again.*

Paint flaked off the heavy, fireproofed and double-bolted back door. *It's like Dad,* she thought, *well-worn, but strong and solid.*

How could her smart, funny, marathon running dad die of a heart attack?

Savannah unlocked the shop, stepped into his office, and keyed the alarm code. With walls built of salvaged barn wood, the tiny space awakened a vision of his shoulders hunched over a mountain of paperwork. The sharp smoky scent of his aftershave clutched her heart.

Stop thinking about him. The students will be here soon.

Forcing a slow breath, she dropped the keys onto the rolltop desk that had once been her grandfather's. Small pilings of papers, files, bills, and Post-it notes covered every available flat surface and all the pigeon holes were stuffed like magpie nests. Grandpa Roy had used the sturdy desk for the motorcycle business he'd started after World War I. In continuous use by her family since the 1920s, it looked at her with serious expectations.

I guess you're mine now. I'll do my best.

She ran her hand over the top and smiled when her fingers reached the dent caused by a wildly thrown toy rocket when she was five. Her dad had yelled at her.

He seldom yelled.

Startled by the ringing of the black wall-mounted phone, she cleared her throat and picked up the receiver. "Webb's Glass Shop. May I help you?"

"Oh my. I wasn't expecting a real person. I meant to leave a message."

Good guess. I don't feel like a real person today. "It's okay. I'm opening up. May I help you?"

"I wanted to know if class has been cancelled. I would completely understand, you know, because the funeral was on Saturday. It was so awesome—all those young men in military uniforms."

Savannah flinched, recalling the haunting echo of *Taps* floating behind the gravestone that marked the final rejoining of her parents. She swallowed quickly. "Classes are being held as scheduled beginning today. Which one are you taking?"

"I'm in Beginning Stained Glass."

"It starts in half an hour. What's your name?"

"Amanda Blake. I signed up for more classes with John, I mean with Mr. Webb, last month, but I thought the shop might close."

"Hugh Trevor is taking over the classes for Dad. I mean Mr. Webb. I'll see you in—"

"Oh my goodness. Are you Savannah?"

"Yes, I'm—"

"I am so, so sorry. I saw you at the funeral. You must be devastated. Mr. Webb was so proud of you. He talked about you all the time."

"Thank you. I have to—"

"He was so proud that you were studying at Pilchuck Glass School on a special scholarship. He told every class about how you won the Spinnaker Art Festival on your first entry when you were only seventeen."

"How embarrassing. Every class?"

"Yes, it was always in his first lecture."

Savannah struggled to keep her voice from breaking. "It's going to be difficult to—"

"Your dad looked so strong, so healthy, and so positively vital . . . if you know what I mean."

"Yes, it was a shock."

"He was such an excellent teacher and mentor. How are you going to manage everything?"

"I'm not sure yet." Savannah's stomach fluttered. "Sorry, but I've got to go. I'll see you in class." Savannah clicked the receiver down before Amanda could continue.

You're not the only one who is confused about why he died.

Savannah finger combed her short black hair, tugged up the waistband of her skinny jeans, and rolled up the cuffs of her classic white shirt. It was her basic teaching uniform. Calm, she focused on getting the shop ready for the day's business.

Shoving the key ring into her back pocket and picking up the waiting stack of student handouts, she walked into the classroom. Situated between the office and the retail area, the large classroom contained six sturdy worktables for students, each with a tall wooden stool. As she placed a large brown manila envelope on each of the worktables, she remembered how her dad had experimented with various table sizes, table heights, stool types, and the number of students per table.

He'd tried to rope in Hugh to help, but his long-time assistant had no empathy for a student's environment. However, the crusty Hugh could teach a mule about the beauty, art, and mystic nature of always-liquid glass. Her dad's meticulous research had resulted in the current configuration of three rows of two worktables facing a whiteboard on the front wall and an instructor worktable facing the class. He'd practically wiggled with joy after he'd found the perfect environment for his students to create great glass art.

She switched on the overhead natural lighting that illuminated the projects of former students displayed around the walls. Her heart wrenched when she noticed her dad had placed her first piece, the traditional green turtle sun catcher panel, on the narrow shelf of the whiteboard. He had been planning to use it for the first demonstration project. Tears immediately formed and she pulled a tissue from her back pocket to press them away.

In her mind's eye, she saw her nail-bitten child's fingers struggling with the pieces of green glass.

She had desperately willed them to be nimble and sure as she assembled the little turtle under her dad's watchful guidance. It must have pleased him to no end to use it as an example for the class.

After switching on the task lighting lamp for each worktable, she walked to the room at the front of the shop facing the street. It served as the student display gallery and retail section. It was neat and orderly as he'd always kept it.

Off to her right, she looked at the closed door of her dad's custom workshop. They had spent many, many hours working on delicate restorations, complicated repairs, and amazing consignments from almost every church in the city.

Deliberately delaying opening up the workspace that held her oldest and strongest memories, she found the right key and unlocked the front door. *If I don't open the workshop door, I can imagine that he's still in there working on his latest project. I know it's childish, but I don't have to be a grown up all the time.*

At twenty minutes before ten, it was a little early to open the shop, but some students preferred to arrive early so they could lay claim to their work area. She looked out the floor-to-ceiling windows that ran the length of the storefront to see a short man with an elaborate comb-over getting out of a red BMW, then striding up to the door.

"Rats," she muttered. It was the owner of Lattimer's Glass Shop, her dad's competitor. She pushed down a rush of panic and put on her face reserved for welcoming customers. Savannah opened the door. "Hi Frank. What brings you down here to the Grand Central District? Your shop is still downtown, right?"

Frank pursed his soft lips into a thin line. "Good morning, Savannah. I see you're opening up. I thought we could talk about my offer to buy Webb's Glass Shop." He stepped closer, but she blocked him from entering.

"I'm not ready."

"What's to get ready? Why are you torturing yourself when you could accept my offer and be on your way back to Seattle?"

Not slamming the door in his face took willpower. "I'm on bereavement leave. My scholarship will still be there when I get back. Besides, I haven't worked out all the finances yet."

"You can trust me on this. It's a generous offer."

Savannah started closing the door, "Yours is not the only offer, you know."

"Oh sure, that land shark Smythe can mention a tempting figure," he said, putting a name to the corporate real estate tycoon who wanted to buy the block to build a Big Value Store. "But he has to work through his corporate office *and* get the other stores to sell along with you. I'm only trying to save you time and trouble. Come on, Vanna. Your dad would have signed in a heartbeat."

Savannah snapped, "That's a bald-faced lie. The two of you hadn't spoken in ten years."

"You know he was a good businessman. That doesn't necessarily mean he wouldn't approve."

"Approve? You didn't even come to the funeral. He would expect me to have thrown you out on your ear."

Frank was quiet and the silence between them grew large and heavy. He looked down. "I'm sorry. I was busy. We did have some pretty wide differences. But that's only natural between teacher and student. He really was a wonderful teacher. I never thanked him for all he taught me. Now it's too late."

Savannah looked at the floor and took a calming breath. "Look. I need to check the books. I'm not turning it down. Quite the opposite. I need to make sure everything is ready and that there are no financial surprises."

"No one was a better businessman. John would have approved."

"He sounded stressed the last few . . . Never mind. Let's meet downtown for lunch, say Wednesday at the Casita Taqueria just down the street. I promise I'll give you either an answer or a counter-offer."

"Fair enough." Frank nodded his head. "I'll see you then. Vanna, trust me. John would have approved."

She leaned out the door. "Don't call me Vanna," she yelled as an afterthought, watching him scrunch back into his sleek status symbol, screeching tires as he drove away.

She had been lying. She had no intention of selling to Frank. If all went well, she would leave for Seattle the next day and let Hugh handle everything else. *I should have told Frank,* she mused. *A little suffering would do him good.*

Closing the door gently enough not to jangle the bell at the top, Savannah slipped behind the retail counter facing the entry door and tentatively pushed the power ON button to the point-of-sale PC. She watched it nervously, her fingers crossed that it would start up. Pushing the button was all she knew how to do.

I hope Hugh is on his way. It's more than strange for him not to be here already. I better call again. We need to finalize the transition plan of ownership of Webb's. I also need him to teach this class.

Savannah picked up the phone beside the screen and ran her finger down the tattered list of contacts taped to the counter top, stopping at *Hugh Trevor*. She dialed the number and heard his answering machine message. "I'm out. You know the drill." *Beep.*

"Hugh, are you there? It's Savannah. I need your help to open the shop. I hope you're on the way. Please be on the way. Please. See you soon."

As she spoke, the doorbell jangled fiercely and a tall man dressed in black western boots, black jeans, and a French blue oxford shirt topped with a black string tie bolted through. "Don't touch it," he cautioned in a BBC-newscaster accent. "If the cash register starts up wonky, it'll be ages before it sorts itself out."

Savannah looked into his seriously green eyes and caught a faint whiff of Polo Black. He crowded her to the side and peered at the PC screen. As she was six feet in stocking feet, not many men looked down on her.

She stretched around his back to hang up the phone. "I didn't want to start it, but I couldn't wait for Hugh any longer. Who are you?"

He peered into the monitor. "Good. Coming online and"—he looked for a certain sign from the monitor—"brilliant. It's happy." He pulled back, then turned to her. "I have the same system next door and I had a meltdown with mine this morning."

"Right, but who—"

The tinkle of the door opening interrupted Savannah's question. A plump young woman with wildly spiked pink and yellow hair entered the shop. Wearing a white peasant blouse and patch-work midi skirt, she shouldered through the door balancing a huge purse, a canvas bag of tools, a briefcase overfilled with glass remnants, and a large plywood square for mounting stained-glass work.

A green-eyed man lunged to hold open the door. "Amanda, you shouldn't try to carry everything at once."

Savannah's eyebrows lifted.

Puffing like an espresso machine, Amanda said, "It's all right. Two trips would take too much energy. My aura has been weak since I heard the terrible news about Mr. Webb." She made a beeline for the classroom.

Savannah scurried over to push the classroom door out of the way. She nudged a doorstop in place to keep it open.

Amanda grunted and plopped her bundles on the worktable in the first row. "I want to sit where I can see." She nudged her bold orange glasses back onto her nose. "Savannah! Oh my goodness. You're just as beautiful as John said." She clamped Savannah in a round tight tug, stepped back, and looked into her face. "And you have his cobalt blue eyes. I'm so happy to meet you."

"Thank you, Amanda. Welcome to class."

Savannah turned to stare pointedly at the green-eyed man.

Again, the doorbell jangled and two slender elderly women entered, wearing matching gray ruffled blouses with gray polyester pants over gray ballet flat shoes. They carried large gray tote bags. One carried hers over the left shoulder. The other twin carried hers over the right shoulder. Even their round black glasses were identical.

Savannah gulped. *I'll never be able to tell these two apart.*

"Let's sit in the back. I don't like others to over-look my work," said one twin.

"Silly. Everyone walks around and looks at each other's projects. It's how we learn. Let's go for the front so we can hear properly," said the other twin.

The first twin put her materials on the far back worktable. "It's my turn to pick the seats. You chose for the pottery class."

"Very well. But don't whine if you can't hear the instructions."

"It's my turn."

Savannah turned to Green Eyes and whispered, "Have they been here before?"

His eyes crinkled, and he leaned closer and whispered, "The Rosenberg twins, Rachel and Faith, are addicted to craft classes."

"So, they're good?"

"Let's just say they make everyone else feel above average. They take classes for the sheer joy of criticizing each other. And they lie. About the quality of each other's work, about who made what mistake. They lie when there's no need to lie. They're the biggest liars in the district."

The bell announced the arrival of a deeply tanned couple. He was brown-haired with brown eyes, wearing khaki cargo shorts, a closely tailored navy golf shirt, and Topsiders without socks. She was blonde with sky blue eyes, wearing a perfectly tailored khaki skirt with a teal sweater set accented by a single strand of pearls. They were perfectly on trend and looked more like they should be boarding a cruise ship rather than attending an art class. They slipped into the remaining open row of worktables.

The early-forties trying to look late-twenties woman looked around as though welcoming them into her living room. She smiled at each person until she caught their eye, and when she had everyone's attention, she said, "Good morning, y'all. We're Mr. and Mrs. Young. I'm Nancy and this is my groom, Arthur. I've called him my groom since the day Daddy announced our engagement. I'm the Director of Programs at the Museum of Fine Arts and my groom plays third chair cello for the Florida Orchestra. We're so happy to be here taking this wonderful class with y'all."

Green Eyes grinned a wide smile and turned to Savannah. He caught himself and the smirk disappeared behind an uncomfortable cough. He shifted his weight slightly foot to foot. "Look. I wanted to offer my sincere condolences. I think the loss of your father is one of life's most devastating events."

"That's very kind, but who—"

"Most of us along this street were at his funeral. I stayed behind to run the pub so most of my staff could attend. John made such a difference in standing up for the small businesses on this block. We'll miss his advice and experience in negotiating with the mayor and city council."

"Thank you so much. I appreciate it."

"I've got to get back to the pub." He walked out, then turned to lean back through the front door.

"If you need anything, I'm right next door or you can call. My number is on the list under Edward, Edward Morris. I own the Queen's Head Pub. Welcome to the Grand Central District." He quietly closed the door with a small click.

Savannah smiled and let out a sigh of relief. She was glad he was right next door. It looked like she might have more on her plate than she originally expected, especially if Hugh made a habit of running late. She checked the list of contact numbers and there was Edward's number standing out clearly on the smudged list. She plugged it into her cell.

Checking her dad's roster, the five registered class members had all arrived. She frowned. Where was the sixth and even more worrying, where was Hugh? She glanced at the large plain clock on the wall. It said 10:00 sharp as did her watch.

I'm going to have to start teaching his class until he gets here. I haven't taught beginning stained glass since I left for Seattle. Yikes, that's over five years ago. I hope it's like riding a bicycle.

She softly stepped behind the instructor's workstation and cleared her throat. "Good morning. I'm Savannah, Mr. Webb's daughter." Her voice shook at the mention of her dad. Ducking her head, she covered her mouth with her fist to clear her voice and stabilize it to a lower tone. "Welcome to Beginning Stained Glass. Each class will be structured roughly the same. First, a short lecture followed by a skill demonstration. Then you'll practice on a small piece to reinforce the skill. Hugh Trevor will be your instructor. He's a master glass craftsman who—"

Amanda's hand shot up into the air. "What's the project?"

"A small sun catcher panel." Savannah picked up her little green turtle sun catcher and held it high. "It's a simple design, but looks complicated. You will learn the skills of cutting glass, applying copper foil, soldering, and bending zinc came."

"What's that zinc cane stuff? I thought we were learning to make proper leaded stained glass," said Nancy.

"Good question." Savannah turned and wrote *C A M E* on the whiteboard. "Lead is a heavy metal that can, over time, leach into your skin. The new came is a preformed miniature U-shaped channel of zinc that can be bent to follow the edges of the panel. Modern knowledge sometimes overtakes tradition."

She looked at the door once again. *Hugh better have a damn good excuse for not coming in today.*

"Now, for a quick history lesson. Honest, I do mean quick. As a material, stained glass is colored by adding metallic salts during its manufacture. In ancient time, the colored glass was crafted into windows held together by strips of lead and supported by a rigid frame. The oldest known—"

A scraping shuffle and the jangle of the doorbell turned all heads to the front of the shop.

Thank goodness. That must be Hugh.

A gangly blue-jeaned young man with a black backpack over his shoulder rushed through the display room and into the classroom. He stopped cold in front of Savannah. "Sorry, I signed up for this class," blurted the pale-faced teen. He looked down at the floor. "Mr. Webb told me I could attend this class. He promised me his apprentices don't have to pay."

Okay, here's the last student. How on earth could I forget about the apprentice? This must be Jacob. Dad was wildly enthusiastic about his talent, raving in fact. He said Jacob reminded him of me at eighteen. But, really, where is Hugh?

Savannah pointed to the remaining vacant work space. "It's no problem. You see we have plenty of room."

"I've been working with Mr. Webb and Mr. Trevor." The young man's eyes widened to owl-sized intensity.

"You must be Jacob. Mr. Webb told me so much about you, I feel like we're already friends." She pressed her hand over her heart. It was so like her dad to take this awkward fledgling under his wing as an apprentice. "My name is Savannah Webb. I'm Mr. Webb's daughter."

He gulped and nodded vigorously, then stepped forward to solemnly shake her hand. "My name is Jacob Underwood. Pleased to meet you."

She smiled. "Dad's apprentices are always invited to classes. Go ahead and get yourself settled." Savannah guided him to the remaining worktable.

"Where's Mr. Trevor?" Jacob perched on the work stool with his feet resting on the bottom rung and placed his backpack on his lap without letting go of the straps.

She moved back to the instructor station. "Mr. Trevor is delayed and I'm filling in until he arrives. Now, where was I?"

Amanda launched her plump hand into the air

like a rocket. "You were telling us about the origins of stained glass."

"Yes. As I said, they crafted the colored glass into windows or objects held together by strips of lead and then supported by a rigid frame. The oldest known stained glass window was pieced together using ancient glass from an archeological dig."

"What did she say?" One of the twins leaned into the other's ear, whispering loud enough for everyone to look back at them.

Faith flushed from her throat to the roots of her white hair and whispered even louder, "Turn on your hearing aid, Rachel. You've forgotten again."

"Oops," muttered Rachel, turning the tiny volume control up with her polished blood red fingernail until there was a high-pitched squeal.

Gotcha! Rachel wears nail polish. Faith doesn't.

"Now, it's too loud!" Faith frowned. "Turn it down and be quiet."

Rachel adjusted the volume and ducked her head in a sheepish grin to everyone. "I'm ready now."

Savannah started again. "First things first. Before we start learning to cut glass, make sure your work surface is clean and clear of debris. If even the smallest glass chip is under your work, it will break in the wrong place and ruin your day. The best thing is to use a very soft brush on the entire work surface before you start anything. A well-worn paint brush works great, but Dad always used an old drafting table brush."

He gave me mine when I took my first class. It's back in Seattle. She swept her worktable clear and spread newspaper on the work surface.

"I want everyone to take out their clear window-pane glass for scoring and breaking practice." She held up a small nine-by-nine-inch square piece for everyone to see. "The green piece of glass is for your project. Just put that aside."

"Ouch!" Arthur dropped his practice pane onto the worktable in a shattering crash. "I cut myself." He squeezed his thumb until a large drop formed, stuck it in his mouth, and began to suck the blood.

"Don't, honey bunny. It'll get infected. You have to be ready for the next concert." Nancy dived a hand into her purse, hopped off her stool, pulled Arthur's thumb out of his mouth with a soft *pop*, and pressed a tissue onto the cut. She looked around and eyed Savannah. "Is there a first aid kit?"

Savannah crossed the room to the large Red Cross first aid kit attached to the wall. A quick rummage produced a square compress pad and some ointment. She handed them to Nancy who was right behind her.

"Let me see," said Amanda, leaning over Arthur's hand. "I'm a trained caregiver, you know. I work in a nursing home."

Ah, she must liven up that atmosphere considerably. Savannah edged in between the women to get to Arthur. "I've got this, ladies. I can't even begin to tell you how many cuts I've dressed here and in Seattle. I've a finely tuned judgment for stitch count." She gently removed the sodden tissue, refolded it to expose a clean section, and then pressed it firmly onto the cut. "Good, it's small. No stitches."

Nancy fanned her face. "Thank our lucky stars, Arthur. You know that second chair cello player is unreliable." She mimed that he was a drinker. "You must be prepared to step into first chair at any performance."

Amanda peered over Savannah's shoulder. "It is quite small, but glass cuts are the evil older brother of paper cuts—so much blood for such a tiny nick."

"Miss Savannah, Miss Savannah." Jacob hugged his arms around his chest and rocked his weight from side to side. "I need to get my tools."

"Of course." She softened her voice and tilted her head. "Where are they?"

"Mr. Webb let me keep 'em in the workshop."

"No problem." Savannah pulled the key ring from her back pocket and handed them over to Jacob. "Go fetch them, please. It's the blue key." She turned back to deal with the Arthur situation.

"No need, Miss Savannah." He returned the key ring. "I have a set of my own."

Nancy wedged her body between Arthur and Savannah. "Excuse me. I can take care of my Arthur, thank you. Just hand over everything I need."

Amanda flushed a bright hot pink and returned to her seat, struggling to control her trembling lip.

Savannah used her teacher voice. "I'm sorry, ma'am. I'm the only one present who is authorized to give first aid in this shop. If you want to treat him yourself, that's fine, but you'll have to leave the class." She looked from Nancy to Arthur's bleeding finger, then back to Nancy. "Both of you."

The woman pressed her lips into a thin scarlet line. "Very well. Of course, I didn't understand that. We have similar rules at the Museum of Fine Arts."

The class watched silently as Savannah removed

the tissue, applied an ointment, and taped the sturdy bandage to Arthur's wound.

As one, the class looked up at Savannah.

"Okay, first blood goes to Arthur. Well done. Amanda is right. Glass cuts bleed like fury, but by their nature, the cuts are clean and normally heal quickly."

"Miss Savannah," shrieked Jacob, his voice breaking. "Miss Savannah, please come quick!"

Savannah nearly jumped out of her skin, then bolted through the door of the classroom, ran through the gallery and into her dad's workshop. Amanda was on her heels.

Jacob was pointing to the far wall of the custom workshop behind a long workbench. "Mr. Trevor won't wake up."

Savannah saw Hugh lying on his side with his face toward the wall. "Uncle Hugh, Uncle Hugh!" She could hear her voice shriek as she struggled to roll him over onto his back. His kind face was ash gray and he had been sick on his clothes. The sour smell was sharp and fresh. His chest was still and he wasn't breathing.

"Amanda, call 911!"

She was aware of Amanda's sharp gasp and heard her feet pound steps toward the phone. Savannah straightened him as much as possible in the tight space. Making a fist with one hand and the other hand wrapped around it, she started chest compressions to the rhythm of "Staying Alive" as her CPR coach had taught her. She didn't know that she was crying until the tears dropped one by one onto her forearms.

No way was she stopping. Uncle Hugh was all the home she had left. He needed to stay alive.

She dimly heard the ambulance arrive and numbly got to her feet when the paramedic gently lifted her up from the floor by her elbow.

Uncle Hugh can't be dead, too.

Catch up with Savannah in

Shards of Murder

On sale now wherever books and ebooks are sold!

Chapter 1

"You're going to love the Beach Blonde." Savannah raised her glistening pint of straw-colored beer to clink her former mentor Keith Irving's glass. "It reminds me of my favorite ale back in Seattle."

"You had a favorite? I seem to recall that you were determined to try a different beer every time we walked into a brewery."

Is he saying that I was flighty? When she had been Keith's student back in Seattle, she *had* been a little prone to fancy. She was always exploring new glass-working techniques before she had completely mastered the old ones. That must have been frustrating for him—he drew on an unlimited reserve of patience with her erratic experimentation.

Keith sipped the ale and his dark bushy eyebrows raised over his iris blue eyes. Putting his pint back on the beer mat, he looked around the 3 Daughters Brewing tasting room. "You have a point, though. This is as good as anything back home."

"Damn straight," Savannah grinned wide. It was a warm reminder of how much she desired his approval. She and Keith were sitting at a high top near the back of the tasting room. The noisy after-work happy hour crowd had gone and the Friday night date crowd hadn't yet arrived. That meant that the modern industrial décor felt cozy and intimate rather than raucous and celebratory.

Keith looked down into his beer. "My condolences on the death of your father. He was a significant loss to the stained glass world. I'm very sorry."

"Thank you, I appreciate that. I didn't realize how well respected he was until after he was gone."

"How are you coping?"

"Not as well as I would like. It was a—" She was startled by the tightening of her throat. It had already been a couple of months. "It was a difficult time. It still is, for that matter. But now, I've got some great help. My office manager, Amanda Blake, is an outrageously cheerful person and I've taken on Dad's apprentice, Jacob Underwood. He's incredibly talented, and the deep concentration required for the craft helps him manage life with Asperger's syndrome. Jacob is flourishing to the real benefit of Webb's."

"Is it true what I heard?" He tilted his head slightly with a gentle smile. "That you were involved in the investigation of your father's death?"

Savannah wiped a hand across her forehead, then cupped her pint. "Yes, it turned out that both Dad and his longtime assistant were murdered. I arrived here planning to sell up and return to Seattle, but I was driven to decode the messages my father left behind. Dad had been a cryptographer for the government. The result of the adventure was that it helped the police catch the murderer. Everyone helped and I felt like I found my forever home."

"So, you not only dealt with the death of your father, but helped catch his murderer—I just can't imagine the emotional toll."

Savannah looked around the brewing house, taking a long moment to clarify her feelings. "It was a horrible experience, but oddly satisfying in the end. I learned some valuable lessons. First, I have some incredible friends who care about me. Second, the local business community has supported Webb's from the time my grandfather had a motor-cycle business here in the twenties until my dad started the glass shop. My family inspired that."

Keith nodded slowly and sat silent for a few moments. "Speaking of Webb's, what's it like to go from student to business owner in a heartbeat?"

Savannah looked up at the ceiling, "Wow, you are literally correct with that one. I'm still struggling with the abrupt change of focus. There are so many things that Dad took care of that I'm discovering surprise by surprise."

"It requires a totally different skill set from a carefree creative artist. The transition from student to master requires tremendous personal growth. Some can't do it. You appear to be doing fine."

Squirming in her seat, Savannah replied, "Carefree artist is a good description of my former self. I'm having difficulty with the role of community leader within the Grand Central District of St. Petersburg, Florida. I don't have a background in politics and it's all about relationships and history and things that I don't know about."

Keith leaned over, a conspiratorial glint in his eyes. "I'll tell you a secret. No one understands small-town politics."

Savannah laughed. "I'm so glad you're here. I've been tossed a huge speed bump. My dad's friends appointed me as the judge in the glass category for the Spinnaker Art Festival this weekend."

Keith was in town for the festival to support one of his current protégés in entering the competition. He already knew all about Savannah's appointment as a judge—and her nerves surrounding the job.

Keith chuckled. "As my former star pupil, I expect it won't take very much advice to bring you up to speed."

"Judging was not a part of your curriculum back at the studio." She sipped her beer. "Seriously, how do I choose?"

"I've never found it difficult to choose a winner. My challenge has always been to keep from alienating the chief judge and the other artists. Innovation in the glass arts is not always of interest to the mainstream art collectors or appreciated by the organizational committee. Did they give you some guidelines to follow?"

"They didn't have time to give me anything. The original judge was going to be my dad. He was famous for his widely popular choices—he wouldn't have needed them. Their first replacement had a family emergency, so they turned on the charm and I accepted. I'm simply a last-minute solution."

"Do you think the reason they called on you as a judge was solely due to your dad's reputation?"

"Frankly, I think it was the safe thing to do. They

could give it to me as a tribute to my dad's memory and give the snub to Frank Lattimer once again."

She named the owner of Webb's rival glass shop. Frank was not well loved in town, and his failed attempt to buy out Webb's during a vulnerable time was well known. Even though she was nervous about judging a competition, she was privately pleased that the festival committee had given their support to her over Frank.

Keith looked surprised. "Oh, come on now, you can't believe that. Surely they wouldn't go that far to insult him. He has a business right downtown with a huge display gallery."

"I don't know who in particular he has annoyed on the committee, but Frank can annoy even the most amiable of supporters." She paused, then admitted, "Honestly, in all practicality, they should have given him the job this year. I don't have very many qualifications other than being John Webb's poor orphan daughter."

"Don't sell yourself short. I can give you enough practical guidance to get you through the Spinnaker Art Festival—I've been judging for more years than I care to admit. But, in reality, all I can do is tell you how I approach judging." He grinned. "Judge for yourself what makes sense to you. Your instincts are good."

"If you say so." Savannah sipped her beer.

"I say so. Remember what I used to say?"

"Oh no, not a test! You were a fountain of inspirational quotes."

Keith chuckled. "Okay, but this one is true. 'Life begins at the end of your comfort zone.'" He paused and poked a finger into her upper arm. "You know that."

Savannah leaned away and nodded. "I remember that one. I've been living it."

"Anyway, first I walk around and get a quick look at each exhibit booth and see if any of them hit me emotionally without analyzing or thinking about it. That gives me a chance to see if there are any works that immediately stand out from the rest, and it has been my experience that the winner is usually among them. Later, I stop in front of each booth and analyze what I see in design, color, and mastery of technique."

"That's easy enough."

"Also, if the technique is traditional, such as a Tiffany-style stained glass lamp, it should be a new approach. I always look for something unique showing me a deep understanding of the underlying principles, or a completely different twist on the ordinary."

"That sounds pretty straightforward."

"It should be—and that's the secret. A truly unique approach to glass should stand out like a flame in the darkness."

"Ugh, I'm terrified that I won't live up to Dad's reputation."

"Understandable, but no one would have more faith in your judgment." Keith covered her hand with his and gave it a light squeeze before letting go. "He was a great judge, but you're his daughter, and I have to tell you, the apple didn't fall far from the tree." He grinned widely, and Savannah smiled as well.

Maybe I have a natural instinct. That would be awesome.

"The timing couldn't be much worse." She ran a hand through her closely cropped curly black hair. "I'm starting a new weeklong workshop on Monday."

"Timing will never be right. What type of class?"

"This one teaches the major aspects of fused glass. I've got a monstrous new kiln installed along with one that Dad already had and we're almost ready to go. I haven't even tested the big one yet, but I'll do that this weekend. It has an electronic control panel to automate the timing and temperature changes for the firings. That makes the process less math intensive. Even better, we can let it run overnight and increase our production.

"That's good for both students and clients. The ones we use for teaching in the studio require hand calculations for glass size and a timer for changing the manual temperature settings. It's tedious, but the real purpose is to teach a thorough understanding of the principles of fusing."

"That's exactly the right approach." He touched her arm softly. "How about dinner?"

"Sorry, I'd like that but I'm totally distracted by everything that's swirling around right now. How about after the festival is over? I'll be in a much better mood."

She sensed a movement behind her.

"So, this is your mentor?" Edward pulled up a bar stool between Savannah and Keith. His posh British accent oozed smoothly from a thin frame in a black shirt over tight jeans tucked into tan rattle-snake Western boots. He extended a hand. "Hi, I'm Edward Morris, owner of the Queen's Head

Pub, right next door to Webb's Glass Shop. I hear that you're the best hot glass teacher in the world."

Savannah widened her eyes. Edward must have stopped by to arrange for more beer for his pub. She didn't specifically invite him to meet Keith here. Edward was not yet a lover—but definitely a strong candidate. Savannah's reticence was mostly because her feelings were still a mess of unresolved ex-boyfriend angst. Plus there was the complication that Edward had been a principal suspect in the murder of her father.

Keith stood and shook hands with the very tall man. "Keith Irving. I've heard about you, too."

They stood looking eye to eye. Savannah felt the tension sizzle while also realizing in a flash that both men were the same height.

Savannah patted Edward's stool. He took the hint and sat.

Keith sat and looked sideways at Edward. "Glad to hear the nice part of my reputation precedes me."

"There's a not nice part?"

Savannah smothered a huge cough with her hand, then rearranged her face to disguise the surprise and slight annoyance at Edward's comment. "Keith has the well-deserved reputation for destroying glasswork that doesn't meet his exacting artistic standards. I've left the studio shattered in every sense of the word more than once."

Keith stiffened his back a bit taller. "In truth, there's no room for the merely ordinary at Pilchuck Glass School. It's not helpful for the growth of a student to condone mediocrity. Remarkably, the threat of immediate destruction brings out their best work. For the naturally gifted"—he eyed

Savannah—"it gives them amazing confidence to start a successful career as a true artisan."

Savannah grimaced over at Edward. "A lecture I've heard more than once."

Keith sipped his beer and looked at Edward over the rim. "I've heard about your escapades with Savannah, as well. Helping her find the man who murdered her father is a task most would not have accepted."

"It was a team effort. We're a very close community here in the Grand Central District. Besides, an actual third-generation St. Petersburg native is as rare as bluebells in July. She deserves to be safe from harm."

Edward waved a hand to the bartender. "Hi, Mike. My regular pint of Brown Pelican, please." He turned to Keith. "So, other than the lovely Savannah, what brings you to town?"

Savannah looked sharply at Edward. *What's wrong with you?*

"Good question," said Keith. "I am a long way from home."

Savannah smiled and propped her chin into both hands.

Keith raised both hands in surrender. "I confess I'm here for more than just a visit to see a former student. Two of our students from Pilchuck have taken jobs with the local Chihuly Museum as interns to learn the business end of art."

"But I thought there was a program for that in Seattle," said Savannah.

"There is, but there aren't enough positions for each student to have an opportunity to rotate through the program. It's not just learning about the various methods and history of the glassworks; they also learn to care for the exhibits and discover the harsh realities of an invisible monster named 'cash flow.'"

Edward squinted. "What do you mean by caring for the exhibits? They're all glass. They don't need to be fed or watered or anything."

Savannah and Keith looked at each other for a second. Keith motioned for Savannah to answer.

"It's extremely important that the glassworks in the museum stay dust free. It's not such an issue in Seattle, but here in hot, sandy Florida, it's quite a challenge. Each visitor brings in a bit of the outside and it's impossible to control that. So someone needs to dust the priceless and very fragile exhibits without breaking them. That's what students learn to do."

"Oh." Edward looked sheepish. "Duh."

"Don't feel bad." Savannah squeezed Edward's arm. "It's not particularly obvious."

"Anyway," said Keith, "I'm here to check up on the program and also to help one of them with setting up an exhibit booth tomorrow at Spinnaker."

"You have a student in the show?"

"Yes, he was admitted in good time so that we could arrange the intern position with the Chihuly Museum. Another of my former students, Megan Loyola, has also been accepted into the festival. She reminds me very much of you." Keith nodded toward Savannah.

"How so?"

"She's wicked smart and has a genius for inventing glass techniques to form something completely different and spectacular. I can't wait for you to see her work."

"Hey, you're not trying to influence a judge, are you?"

Keith shook his head. "No chance. You are your father's daughter; he was unbelievably ethical. The interns are Vincent O'Neil and Leon Price. Vincent is a good craftsman with broad technical and mechanical knowledge. Leon, however, is a bit of an uptight urbanite and that rigidly controlled approach comes out in his work. They're sharing living and travel expenses. Leon is the one who has an exhibit booth at the Spinnaker Art Festival. Vincent applied, but didn't make the cut."

Edward shifted a bit and signaled the bartender for another round. He turned to Savannah. "Have you told Keith about your new project?"

"Not yet." She looked crossly at Edward. "I'm still in the investigation stage."

"What new project?" Keith drained the last of his beer.

"I'm going to open a new glass studio in this area. It will be the largest in the South once I've got it up and running."

"Wow, that's the kind of success we hope our students will achieve after they leave. Will it be in this area of town?"

"Only a few blocks south of here in an up-and-coming new industrial park district. It will be an artist's loft space with reasonable rental rates on a month-by-month plan. As an incentive to the eternally cash-strapped prospective client, I'm offering the space without a long-term lease."

"How much square footage?"

"I'm thinking over ten thousand square feet. Part of that will be an exhibit space. That will give my students a transition phase between student and professional artist. There will also be a media room for presentations and tutorials."

Edward shifted in his seat. "But you're keeping the original Webb's as well?"

"Absolutely." She sipped her beer. "That building has been in the family forever and is the anchor store in that block. It's absolutely perfect for beginners—but not for the intermediate- to advanced-level artists."

"Wow, Savannah," said Keith with emotion cracking his voice. "I predicted great things from your skill and talent, but this fantastic news is beyond my expectations. What are you going to call it? Where is it going to be?"

"Webb's Studio is the working title I'm using until I register it as a business name and have my accountant file the corporation paperwork. He'll organize a name search to make sure it's unique, but I think it is." She smiled. "I've been looking at some available warehouse properties a little south of where we're sitting. I think I've found a candidate location."

Edward lifted his glass. "A toast to the success of Webb's Studio." The three glasses clinked in perfect harmony.